Arm in arm, they staggered along the sand.

Mia could feel the warmth of his body as it brushed against hers and couldn't help but remember the feel of his chest underneath her hands.

'Stop it,' she muttered to herself.

Will stopped suddenly, causing her to career into him. She suspected normally he would be able to withstand the force of a small woman travelling at such a slow speed, but in his weakened state his knees buckled and he fell to the ground. Mia tried to pull her arm from his, but was too slow. She felt her feet stumble, followed by the inevitable fall towards the ground.

She landed squarely on top of him, her nose touching his.

'Ooof...' he said quietly.

Stunned, Mia couldn't move for an instant. She could feel the hard muscles of his chest pushing against her breasts. Their legs were tangled together and their lips so close that just a small twitch and they would be kissing. She tried not to notice how his hips were pushed up against hers, but couldn't deny the heat that rose through her body in response to his closeness.

'Mia,' he murmured. 'My angel.'

AUTHOR NOTE

The Caribbean: over seven thousand islands, with lush interiors, golden sandy beaches and clear blue seas, inhabited by people with an eclectic mix of cultures and backgrounds. When I visited the Caribbean for the first time on my honeymoon in 2013 I, like so many others before me, fell in love immediately. Each and every island I explored had its own unique ambience, traditions and history, but one thing united them all: piracy.

Between the mid-sixteenth and early nineteenth centuries the Caribbean was not a safe place to live—especially if you earned your living at sea. Pirate attacks on merchant ships were common, and devastating town raids were also a constant threat for those living on the Caribbean islands. As the eighteenth century dawned the issue of piracy did not go unnoticed by the European political and military leaders, and there was a push to clean up the Caribbean. The number of Spanish and English Naval ships posted to the area dramatically increased and slowly many of the pirates were hunted down. By the mid-eighteenth century there were only a few pirates left capable of evading the British Navy. This time of change seemed the perfect backdrop for THE PIRATE HUNTER.

In the process of my research I became fascinated by the people who lived in the Caribbean; on the one hand they were surrounded by natural beauty, but on the other they were constantly under threat from piracy. Therefore I think it is important to say that, although the characters and events portrayed in THE PIRATE HUNTER are completely fictional, I have endeavoured to depict the setting and atmosphere as accurately as possible, to give a true sense of the Caribbean at the time.

THE PIRATE HUNTER

Laura Martin

First published in Great Britain 2014
by Mills & Boon, an imprint of Harlequin (UK) Limited,
Large Print edition 2015
Harlequin (UK) Limited, Eton House, 18-24 Paradise Road,
Richmond, Surrey TW9 1SR

© 2014 Laura Martin

ISBN: 978-0-263-25526-3

Harlequin (UK) Limited's policy is to use papers that are natural, renewable and recyclable products and made from wood grown in sustainable forests. The logging and manufacturing processes conform to the legal environmental regulations of the country of origin.

Printed and bound in Great Britain
by CPI Antony Rowe, Chippenham, Wiltshire

Laura Martin was born and bred on the South Coast of England into a family of two loving parents and a spirited older sister. Books were a feature of her life from early on. One of her earliest memories involves sitting with the family on a rainy Sunday afternoon, listening to the exploits of a clumsy but lovable stuffed bear and his assorted cuddly friends.

Laura's first ambition was to be a doctor, and in 2006 she went off to Guy's, King's and St Thomas's Medical School in London to study medicine. It was whilst she was earning her degree that she discovered her love of writing. In between ward rounds and lectures Laura would scribble down ideas to work on later that evening and dream of being an author.

In 2012 Laura married her high school sweetheart, and together they settled down in Cambridgeshire. It was around this time that Laura started focussing on the Romance genre, and found what she had always suspected to be true: she was a romantic at heart. Laura now spends her time writing Historical Romances when not working as a doctor.

In her spare moments Laura loves to lose herself in a book, and has been known to read from cover to cover in a day when the story is particularly gripping. She also loves to travel with her husband, especially enjoying visiting historical sites and far-flung shores.

This is Laura Martin's fabulous,
swashbuckling debut novel
for Mills & Boon® Historical Romance!

For Luke, my spider-catching,
dinner-making, crocodile-fighting,
modern-day hero.

Chapter One

'Secure the rigging.' The Captain's voice was half carried away by the wind, his orders sounding like an exaggerated whisper.

Will slipped across the treacherous deck as the ship rolled from side to side, trying desperately to keep his feet, knowing one mistake would be all it took to plunge him into the stormy sea.

'More hands to the wheel,' the First Mate shouted.

Will was close by. He struggled up the few steps and grabbed hold of an empty spoke, immediately feeling the power of the sea beneath them.

'Hard to starboard.'

He responded immediately, throwing his body weight against the wheel with the two other men. The wheel barely budged. He dug his heels in and pushed against the sturdy spokes until he thought the muscles in his arms would burst.

'Merciful Lord,' the First Mate whispered.

Will looked up and knew he was about to die. They were heading into the biggest wave he'd ever seen and they were side on. There was no way a single man was going to survive this.

'Brace yourselves men,' the Captain shouted. 'Brace for impact.'

Will gripped the wheel tightly and watched as the wave began its descent. Thousands of tons of water against one insignificant little ship.

When the water hit, the force knocked all the breath out of him. His hands slipped from the wheel and he was tossed into the blackness as if he were nothing more than a rag doll. His lungs burned as his body screamed for air, but Will knew one single inhalation would be the death of him. Instead he tried to orientate himself, allowing his body's natural compass to turn him the right way up before swimming for the surface. He broke through and immediately sucked the vital oxygen his body so sorely needed into his lungs before being buffeted by another wave and disappearing once again under the water.

He struggled back to the surface and started kicking off his shoes, knowing the extra weight could be the difference between survival and a watery grave. A good distance away he could see the boat, resting at an unnatural angle and sinking lower into the water every second. Nearby men were screaming in fear and shouting for help— most of the sailors could not swim despite a lifetime spent in such close proximity to the water. One man was only a few feet from him, panicking and thrashing around. Will knew if he got too close the man could take him down with him, but he couldn't leave a fellow human being in such fear. He grabbed a piece of driftwood and swam the few strokes over to the drowning man.

'Take this,' he shouted, thrusting the plank at the sailor.

The sailor grabbed hold of it gratefully and stopped shouting for a few seconds.

'We should strike out for land,' Will said when his new companion was a little calmer.

'It's miles away. We'll never make it.'

'We have to try.'

'The Navy will send a boat. They'll come to rescue us.'

They probably would send a boat, but it would be far too late. Everyone who had survived the initial storm would be dead from exposure by then. The Caribbean waters might be balmy during the day, but at night with stormy skies they didn't make for comfortable swimming.

'Land's only a couple of miles away. We'll make it, I promise. It could be hours before the Navy even knows the ship has sunk.'

'I'm staying here. If you're mad enough to try and swim for it, then good luck to you.'

Will recognised the obstinate look in the sailor's eyes and decided to try to persuade the other men. He swam slowly back towards the boat, carefully dodging the bobbing debris washed from the deck when the wave had hit. He thought there were maybe a few more than a dozen men visible in the water and silently hoped the rest of the crew hadn't suffered before they had died.

'We need to swim for shore,' Will called as he approached a group of four men. They were all clutching on to buoyant pieces of wood, the colour drained from their faces. At first he got no response and wondered if his suggestion had been carried away by the wind.

'We can't stay here.' He tried again, 'We'll die.'

The men all looked at him as though he were mad.

'Shore's miles away,' one sailor said, 'We'll never make it.'

'You're mad,' another shouted, 'We wouldn't be able to cover even half the distance.'

'We can't stay here, I honestly think we can make it. If we don't start moving, the cold will get to us and we'll die of exposure before anyone comes to rescue us.'

Will could see his pleas were not getting through to the group of men, but he didn't want to give up, knowing if he left them behind the sailors would all be dead in a couple of hours.

He swam closer to one of the sailors, a man he'd shared a few conversations with on the voyage, hoping to reason with him individually.

'Jim,' Will said, placing a hand on the man's shoulder.

He wasn't expecting the reaction he got. Jim lashed out, his hand catching Will on the forehead. Luckily it was a glancing blow, but he felt stunned all the same.

'Leave me alone,' Jim yelled, pushing Will even further from him. 'Go off and die if that's what you want, but don't insist on bringing us along to drown with you.'

Making sure he was out of arm's reach from all the men, Will raised his voice and called out, 'I'm going to try to swim for shore, I'm sure we can make it. If anyone would like to come with me, I promise I will do my best to get us to safety.'

There was no response. He could see everyone had heard him, their faces were turned towards him as he spoke, but no one moved.

He was torn. Deep down Will knew if he stayed there with the rest of the survivors they would all die. Soon the cold would seep in and slowly their bodies would start to shut down. One by one they would slip unconscious, then slide under the water. He knew he had a chance of survival if he swam for the shore. Telling himself he'd given the crew the option of joining him, he reluctantly turned away.

Mentally Will steeled himself, trying to put the other survivors from his mind. He pulled his shirt off over his head and started to swim. The island was just visible in the distance, a black shape just a shade darker than the night sky. It was probably four miles, maybe five at the most, further than he had ever swum, but possible. Just.

He set off at a slow pace, all too aware his energy levels were going to dip as he started to cover the distance. With his eyes focused on a spot on the horizon so he didn't go off course, he gradually progressed.

He'd grown up with the sea as his playground so

he was used to the sting of the salty water and the chill bite of the wind against his face. His brother had always challenged him to swimming races, never this sort of distance, of course, but he could happily swim a mile in the inhospitable English Channel. He'd never swum during a storm before, though.

After what seemed like hours later he stopped for a break, slowly treading water with just enough effort to keep afloat. For the first time a small sliver of doubt crept into his mind. What if he couldn't make it? He pushed away the negativity and gave himself a mental slap. That kind of defeatist attitude was what got you killed.

Will ploughed on. Hour after hour, mile after mile. His body went numb and soon after, his mind followed. He swam out of instinct, striving to get to shore, but no other thoughts entered his mind. After a while his legs stopped working, they just refused to kick, and his arms complained under the extra strain.

As the sun started to rise above the horizon Will glanced once again at the shore. He was so close now, close enough to make out the individual trees on the cliffs that towered above the water. For a second his mind didn't register what he had just seen, then it hit him. Cliffs. Not a white sandy beach or a natural harbour, cliffs. He felt like shouting and cursing, but just didn't have the energy. He'd made it all this way only to be defeated by some cliffs, and he would be defeated; he barely had the strength to pull himself on to some sand, let alone climb a jagged rock.

Will wasn't a quitter. He had never left anything unfinished in his life, but he knew this was the end. He didn't have the strength to climb the cliffs and he didn't have the energy to swim the shoreline until he found an easier route to dry land.

He did a few more strokes towards the cliffs just in case there was a handy set of steps carved into the rock face. Nothing. Not even an easy handhold. He didn't dare get any closer, knowing the sea would dash him against the rock without a moment's hesitation.

Will closed his eyes and allowed his body to float, knowing sooner or later the pull of the sea would submerge him and take him to his watery grave.

'That's no place to sleep.' The voice was carried to him on the wind and had a kind of ethereal quality to it. He opened his eyes and with a tremendous effort looked around him.

Finally he glanced at the clifftop and in that instant he knew he was dead. A beautiful woman dressed all in white was standing looking down at him. She must be an angel, Will thought, a beautiful, heavenly angel.

Finally accepting his fate, Will closed his eyes one last time and let the sea envelop him.

He was actually going to sleep. Mia stood frozen for a second, unsure what to do, then instinct took over and she tugged at the laces securing her dress. She threw the billowing white garment over her head and, clad only in her underwear, dived head first into the sea. It only took her a few strokes to reach the bedraggled man and she looped her arms under his to help him keep afloat.

'Heaven,' he murmured, his eyes flickering open for a few seconds.

'No, Barbados,' Mia said, struggling to keep both their heads above the water. 'You're going to have to swim.'

'No more swimming.'

'Well, it's either you swim or I let you sink to the

bottom of the sea. Don't think I'm carrying you to
the beach.'

'Beach?' He perked up slightly.

'Yes, beach; sand, palm trees, lapping waves.'

'What are we waiting for?'

Mia cautiously let go of her new companion and
watched to see if he was going to sink. His kicks
were weak and his eyes barely open, but he put
enough effort in to just about stay afloat.

She grabbed his hand and they awkwardly started
to swim, making slow progress around the bottom
of the cliff. After about ten minutes she allowed
him to stop and pointed to the distance.

'Can you see the beach?' she asked.

His eyes scanned the horizon and as they settled
on the thin strip of sand he grinned.

'Dry land. Race you?'

Mia stared at him—he was beyond exhausted.
His face was completely drained of colour and his
lips were starting to turn an unhealthy blue.

'Maybe another day,' she said.

They set off again, fighting against the tide for
each inch. It seemed like an eternity to Mia and
she had to keep glancing behind her to check her
companion was still afloat and breathing.

Her foot hit sand and she gave a whoop of delight.

'You can stand,' she shouted over her shoulder, 'we're in the shallows.'

She saw him put his feet on the seabed and his knees buckle. In an instant she was beside him again, supporting him under his arms and half dragging him to shore.

They collapsed on the beach, arms and legs entangled, both too exhausted to move. For a minute Mia lay with her eyes closed, allowing her breathing to become steady and regular and her heart to stop pounding. When she felt a little recovered she propped herself up and looked down at the man lying beside her.

His eyes were closed and his chest barely moving. She inched closer, wondering whether the final push to shore had been too much for his heart. Tentatively she laid a hand on his chest and felt the reassuring thud as the blood was pushed around his body.

'Thank you,' he murmured without opening his eyes. 'You saved my life.'

Mia looked down and realised her hand was still lying on his chest. She knew she should move, but found herself captivated by his tanned skin. Lightly she drew her fingers backwards and forwards over his hard muscles, feeling them quiver with exhaustion under her touch.

She glanced at his face and wondered if he was sleeping. He looked so peaceful, so content, not like he'd spent the night battling with the elements. His eyebrows were crusted with salt, as were his lips, and his hair was sticking up in every direction. She ran a few strands through her fingers. It was golden—even soaking wet the colour still shone through. She hadn't seen many people with golden hair. A few of the soldiers at the fort and a few sailors in the distance, but no one like this.

'What's your name?' he murmured.

Mia guiltily drew her hand back from his hair as she realised he was watching her with some amusement.

'Mia.'

'Mia. That's pretty. Like you.'

'Are you always this smooth?'

'I've just been in a shipwreck and swum hundreds of miles to shore. You have to forgive a man for not being quite on top form.'

'You're forgiven.'

'I'm Will,' he said, struggling to sit up. He held out a hand and Mia hesitantly took it in hers. He raised her hand to his lips and gently brushed a kiss on to her skin. 'It really is a pleasure to meet you.'

Mia could feel the blush rising up her cheeks and had to force herself to meet his eyes. Even after a near-death experience this man could turn on the charm; he would be deadly when fully recovered.

'What happened?' she asked softly, trying to distract herself from the intensity burning behind his eyes.

'I was on *The White Rose*. We were only a few miles from shore when the storm hit.'

'Let me guess—the Captain decided to make a dash for the harbour instead of battening down and riding it out.'

He looked at her appraisingly.

'You don't spend a lifetime in the Caribbean without learning a thing or two about the moods of the sea,' she said.

'He did his best, but we didn't stand a chance.'

'Were there any other survivors?'

'I saw a few, tried to convince them to swim with me for shore, but most of the sailors can't do more than a few strokes and wanted to wait for the Navy to mount a rescue.'

Mia saw the pain in his eyes. He was mourning for the dead sailors, probably a whole ship of young men in their prime now dead, swallowed up by the sea.

'I'd just about given up when I saw you on the cliff.'

He turned to look at her again and the intensity in his eyes made her self-conscious. She glanced down and to her horror remembered she'd thrown off her clothes before jumping in to rescue him. Her undergarments were sodden and sticking to her skin, revealing almost everything that lay beneath.

He must have seen her stricken expression and hastily looked away.

'I'd offer you my jacket, but I seem to have mis-placed it.'

Mia forced herself to smile. He was just a man, she repeated in her head. He might be a very hand-some man with an infectious smile, but he was just a man all the same. They were from very different walks of life and after today she would probably never see him again.

'My house is not too far,' Mia said. 'Do you think you will make it if I help you?'

'Lead on.'

Mia stood, forcing herself not to cover certain parts of her anatomy with her arms, and held out a hand to help Will up.

'Thank you, my lady,' he said, struggling to his feet, then offering her his arm.

Arm in arm they staggered along the sand. Mia could feel the warmth of his body as it brushed against hers and couldn't help but remember the feel of his chest underneath her hands.

'Stop it,' she muttered to herself.

Will stopped suddenly, causing her to career into him. She suspected normally he would be able to withstand the force of a small woman travelling at such a slow speed, but in his weakened state his knees buckled and he fell to the ground. Mia tried to pull her arm from his, but was too slow. She felt her feet stumble, followed by the inevitable fall towards the ground.

She landed squarely on top of him, her nose touching his.

'Ooof,' he said quietly.

Stunned, Mia couldn't move for an instant. She could feel the hard muscles of his chest pushing against her breasts, their legs tangled together and lips so close that just a small twitch and they would be kissing. She tried not to notice how his hips were pushed up against hers, but couldn't deny the heat that rose through her body in response to his closeness.

'Mia,' he murmured. 'My angel.'

Before she realised what was happening Will had reached up and pulled her lips on to his, sealing them together with a passionate kiss.

'Mia, Mia, Mia,' he whispered in between frantic kisses.

Her body responded immediately, moulding to his and burning with desire. She knew she shouldn't. They were from different worlds, and he was almost certainly delirious, but what was the harm of one kiss?

'Stop!' The shout came from quite a distance away, but it paralysed Mia.

Slowly she raised her head and groaned. Coming towards her were four men wearing the unmistakable uniforms of the English soldiers garrisoned in Bridgetown.

'No, no, no,' she whispered.

She glanced down at her companion, wondering if he was able to make a dash for it into the trees that lined the beach. He had passed out on the sand with a contented smile on his face. She shook him none too gently and glanced once again at the soldiers. They were much closer now, making good progress over the powdery sand. She contemplated

leaving Will and making a run for it on her own—
he didn't strike her as being a wanted man.

Too late. She'd just staggered to her feet when
the first of the soldiers arrived and threw her back
to the ground.

'Don't move,' he shouted rather unnecessarily.
With the rifle to her back Mia wasn't planning on
moving a single muscle.

Will felt as though he'd slept for a month. He
contemplated rolling over and letting sleep con-
sume him for another few hours, but the unusual
sound of keys jangling was enough to make him
open his eyes.

He was lying on mouldy straw in a fetid cell with
only a sliver of light to illuminate his surroundings.
Probably for the best, he thought.

The jangle of keys came closer and Will pushed
himself up into a sitting position. Every muscle in
his body screamed and begged him not to move
again for another few days at least.

The door to the cell opened and through his half-
open eyes Will could see a large figure standing
in the doorway.

'William Greenacre, what on earth happened
to you?'

Will's eyes opened fully and peered into the gloom. He recognised the voice, but couldn't quite place the owner.

'We thought you were dead.'

'So did I,' Will murmured.

The figure in the doorway strode into the cell and clapped Will on the shoulder.

'Edward Thatcher,' Will said. 'It's been years.'

'Last time I saw you must have been at your old man's funeral. Good fellow, sorely missed. That must have been what, seven years ago?'

'Eight.'

'Let's get you out of this hellhole…' Thatcher held out his hand to pull Will up '…then you can tell me how you managed to survive that awful storm.'

'There was a woman…' Will started.

'Don't you worry about her, old chap, we've got her safe. Let's get you cleaned up and then I'll fill you in on what's been happening. The Governor is expecting you.'

'But Mia…'

'Good work there, Greenacre, we've been after her for months. You survive a shipwreck and apprehend the sister of Barbados's most wanted in the same day.'

Barbados's most wanted? Will screwed his eyes up, trying to concentrate. It had been a long day and he wasn't sure he could recall exactly what had happened. He remembered the storm and the swim and the feeling of dread as he saw the cliffs towering above him. Then the vision of Mia on the clifftop, her saving him and finally the kiss on the beach.

He groaned. He'd kissed her. He owed his life to her and he'd assaulted her when all she'd been trying to do was help. He wasn't sure why he'd done it. He had been pretty delirious, but really that was no excuse.

Will squinted as they emerged from cells into the bright Caribbean light.

'It's only a couple minutes' walk to the Governor's residence. Think you'll make it, old chap?'

The muscles in his legs felt battered and achy, but it did feel good to stretch them out. If it was truly only a couple minutes' walk he was sure his legs would get him there.

'What are you doing out here, Thatcher?' Will asked as they walked.

He'd known Thatcher from school—both boys had been at boarding school together—and whilst not in the same year they'd come across one another plenty of times on the sports field or during illicit night-time missions into the nearby town.

'Advisor to his Majesty's Governor of Barbados.' Thatcher said it without much enthusiasm.

'Can I deduce it's not a post you care for?' Will asked quietly.

'The Governor's a fool. I spend most of my time trying to right the mistakes he's made.'

They'd reached the grand Governor's residence and Thatcher knocked on the door. It was opened immediately and they were shown inside. Thatcher was obviously well known in the residence. The footmen nodded their acknowledgement, but otherwise let him pass unimpeded from the entrance hall to the inner corridor.

'Mr Greenacre, or is it Lord Sedlescombe?'

Will stopped and turned.

'I offer you my sincerest apologies. My men had no idea who you were. I regret you had to spend time in one of our cells—most unfortunate for a man of your standing.'

A man in a pristine white shirt and a decorated red dress coat was coming down the corridor behind them.

'Governor Hall,' Will guessed out loud, 'it is an honour to meet you.'

'Come, come, Thatcher, get the man a drink. He's been through hell and back.'

The Governor led the two men into a cavernous dining hall which had a table laid out with food at one end.

'Sit, eat, drink.'

Will sat and took a long draught from the cup in front of him. He savoured the liquid, allowing the cool wine to soothe his parched throat.

'I want to hear all about what happened,' the Governor said.

Will shrugged, running a hand through his hair, a delaying tactic so he could push the memory of the screams of the sailors from his mind.

'We were only a few miles offshore. The storm hit and the Captain tried to make a dash for it.'

The Governor shook his head. 'Captain Brent was a good friend of mine.'

'The ship went down quickly and the few sailors who did survive the initial shipwreck wanted to wait for the Navy to rescue them.'

'We've sent the boats, but I doubt anyone will be left now.'

'I swam for shore and I'd just about given up when a woman dived in and saved me.'

'Ah, yes, the infamous Mia Del Torres.' The Governor shook his head. 'You're lucky she didn't slit your throat. As you know, her family are notorious throughout the Caribbean.'

Will frowned. That didn't sound right. The woman who'd rescued him was kind and caring and willing to risk her own life for a complete stranger. Not a notorious criminal. And the surname—surely it had to be a coincidence. The woman who'd saved his life couldn't possibly be related to the man he'd come to the Caribbean to hunt.

'What happened next?' the Governor asked.

'I can't really remember any more,' Will said, pushing the very clear memories of kissing Mia's soft lips from his mind.

'It's a tragedy, a real tragedy,' the Governor said, 'but at least you've survived. We've been awaiting your arrival eagerly these past few weeks.'

Will sensed the change of tone of the conversation; they were getting down to business.

'We will give you whatever help you need to succeed,' the Governor promised, and looked enquiringly at Will.

'I'll need a ship, full crew and someone with good local knowledge to assist me, preferably someone with first-hand experience of dealing with these pirates,' he said.

The Governor smiled. 'We can do better than that.' He motioned to Thatcher, who disappeared out of the room. Will wondered what they were going to come up with.

'We've had reasonable success in dealing with most of the privateers and pirates in the waters around the Caribbean,' the Governor explained, 'but there are pockets left. Pockets we can't seem to find.' He tapped his fingers on the table in irritation. 'They seem to go to ground whenever we get close. Someone is sheltering them, must be.'

'Sounds a likely theory,' Will said. 'In my experience a little local support goes a long way.'

'Quite. But it will not be tolerated any longer. I have vowed to clear these waters of pirates and I do not intend to break my vow.'

'Of course not, sir. And whilst the Navy is brilliant in beating the pirates when it comes to an out-and-out fight, often the pirates fight dirty.'

'That's why we brought you in. You come highly recommended.'

Will took another sip of wine and grimaced. 'Sometimes you need someone who doesn't mind getting their hands dirty for the greater good.'

And he didn't. He hated pirates. They were

greedy, cowardly, arrogant fools. Fools who had killed his brother. Governor Hall wasn't the only one who wanted the Caribbean to be free from the plague of pirates. Will had worked for two long years to build his reputation so he would be deemed a suitable man to entrust with hunting Captain Del Torres and his crew.

'Ah, here's the local knowledge,' the Governor said.

Thatcher re-entered the room, pulling a struggling woman behind him. In an instant he saw it was Mia.

'Mia,' he said, standing up.

She glared at him with hatred in her eyes.

'We have been trying to apprehend Miss Del Torres for some months now,' the Governor said. 'Thanks to you we succeeded today.'

'I…' Will started, but realised he didn't know what to say.

'Miss Del Torres's brother is the Captain of *The Flaming Dragon*, the scourge of the Caribbean. In exchange for her life she has agreed to assist you in locating her brother and his crew.'

Will smiled tentatively at Mia, but she just scowled in return.

'Miss Del Torres will be released into your custody for the duration of your expedition and knows she will be killed immediately if she tries to escape or warn her brother you are coming for him. Killed in a most unpleasant fashion.'

'What is her crime?' Will asked.

'Her crime?' the Governor repeated.

'For her to deserve the death sentence.'

'Aiding and sheltering known pirates.'

Slowly Will nodded. He stood and took another sip of wine before walking towards Mia.

'Your brother is a pirate?' he asked.

Mia looked defiantly at him, but nodded after a few seconds.

'And you know where he is?'

'No.'

'But you know where he might be?'

'No.'

He stood directly in front of her and gently lifted her chin so she was forced to look into his eyes.

'I'm not going to hurt you, Mia,' he said quietly, 'You saved my life.'

Her eyes remained stony and no emotion was displayed on her face.

'I have a job to do, a very important job, and I will need your help.'

'What choice do I have?' she said quietly in a voice that betrayed every ounce of contempt she held for him.

Chapter Two

'You'll never catch them in that,' Mia mumbled quietly.

Will turned to look at her with inquisitive eyes. It was the first time she'd spoken since they'd left the fort, despite his valiant efforts to engage her in conversation.

'Well, you won't,' she said after a few seconds.

'I won't be able to outrun them,' Will corrected her. 'I will be able to catch them.'

Mia fell silent again and looked around the dock. She knew some of the sailors judiciously avoiding her eye—she wasn't going to get any help from them. And the shackles that restrained her wrists weren't conducive to escape, either.

'I hope you're not thinking of running away, young lady,' Thatcher said sternly.

She smiled her sweetest smile. 'Why would I want to do that?'

Thatcher grunted.

'I'm being treated so well.'

'Were the shackles really necessary?' Will asked, turning back to look uneasily at the chains on her wrists.

'Can't be too careful, Greenacre. This little lady had evaded us for months.'

'Would have been longer...' Mia muttered, looking pointedly at Will.

Not that she really regretted saving him. If she hadn't jumped into the sea he would have been dead and she would have been free, but her conscience would never allow her to forget she had killed a man. And in her eyes allowing him to drown when she had the capability to save him would have been murder as sure as shooting him in the heart.

'Shall we, my lady?' Will asked, motioning to the ship.

They walked up the gangplank and on to the ship. She saw Will hesitate for just a second before he placed his foot on the wood of the deck, overcoming the memories of what happened the last time he was aboard a vessel like this.

The crew were all lined up along one side, waiting patiently for their orders. One man stepped forward and approached their little party.

'Captain Little. Pleasure to have you aboard, Mr Greenacre.'

The Captain was a lithe man of about fifty. His eyes flitted backwards and forwards all the time as if taking in every detail and his skin had the weather-beaten leathery look all sailors shared in the Caribbean.

'Thank you for your hospitality, Captain.'

'May I introduce my First Mate, Ed Redding.'

A young man stepped forward and shook Will's hand. He glanced at Mia and smiled sadly as if commiserating with her for getting caught.

'And this is Lieutenant Glass.'

Another man stepped up and shook Will's hand.

'A pleasure to serve with you, Mr Greenacre. It will be an honour to assist you in catching these pirates.'

'Lieutenant Glass is here at the Navy's request. He will be representing their interests in our voyage.'

'I am here to give whatever help I can.'

Mia studied him. He looked rather dashing in his pristine white waistcoat and blue coat—each of the buttons shimmered in the sunlight and reflected the mid-afternoon rays. There was not a hair out of place in his ponytail and not a single scuffmark on his shoes. He was most likely a stickler for rules and routine.

She diverted her gaze back to Will and watched as he walked down the line of assembled men, greeting each in turn, asking their names and a little about their lives. He was good at getting people to like him; Mia could see that already. The crewmen were not used to a Commander who took an interest in them as people. In a few days they'd probably lay down their lives for him.

'When do we sail?' Will asked when he was back by the Captain's side.

'The tide is favourable for the next few hours. If we miss that, we shall have to wait until the morning.'

Mia willed them to wait until the morning. That way she might have a chance of escape. Once the ship was out to sea she had no chance.

'No time like the present,' Will said with a smile.

'Where shall I set a course for, sir?'

'Port Royal, Jamaica. I have some information to pick up there.'

Mia allowed herself a small, inconspicuous smile. Port Royal was a notorious haven for pirates even now with their new Governor, but it wasn't where her brother would be hiding out. He'd always said that although you could lose yourself in the crowds in Port Royal and Tortuga, if someone really wanted to find you and had enough gold they would be able to buy information about your whereabouts.

'We will leave within the hour,' the Captain assured him.

'That's my cue to leave,' Thatcher said, clapping Will on the back, 'Best of luck and, whatever you do, don't let those pirates engage you in the open.'

'I'll see you soon, old friend.'

Mia watched as Thatcher walked back to dry land and felt her hope of escape ebbing away.

'Shall we make you more comfortable?' His voice was low and close to her ear and sent shivers down her spine.

'I can't imagine that would be conducive to your plans,' Mia replied.

'I am sorry, you know,' Will said. 'I didn't plan any of this.'

Looking into his eyes, Mia nearly believed him. In fact, she wanted to believe him, but had to keep telling herself to stop being so naive. He was using her. He would extract whatever information he could from her, then deliver her back to the Governor to spend the rest of her days in chains.

'Let me go,' Mia said quietly so only Will would hear.

He shook his head.

'I'm sorry, that just isn't possible.'

'I saved your life.'

'And I'll always be grateful for that.'

'But your gratitude doesn't extend to giving me my freedom.'

Will sighed and turned so he was facing her directly. He placed his hands on her upper arms and looked squarely into her eyes. Mia shivered a little at the contact and the proximity of his body.

'When this is over I will argue your case, that I promise. I will do everything in my power to see you have your freedom back.' His voice hardened. 'But you have to understand, my priority is catching these pirates and I won't let anything stand in my way.'

Mia swallowed hard, but held his gaze. He was a driven man. He reached over and took her hands in one of his, holding them still so he could unlock the shackles on her wrists. His hands were slightly rough against her softer skin, but his touch was gentle.

'Shall I show you your quarters?' Lieutenant Glass offered, breaking the moment.

'Thank you.'

'We can put her in the brig on our way.' He motioned towards Mia, a sneer on his face.

Will turned slowly to face the Navy Officer. 'The brig?' he asked.

'It's a kind of prison cell on the ship, sir.'

'I know what it is.'

Lieutenant Glass stood looking at Will with a perplexed expression. Neither man spoke for twenty seconds.

'It's very secure, sir.'

'I don't doubt the security of the cell.'

'I'm sorry, sir,' Lieutenant Glass said eventually. 'I don't think I understand.'

'Miss Del Torres is helping us with our mission.' Will spoke slowly. 'She has very kindly agreed to impart her valuable knowledge so we may be successful in catching these scoundrels. I don't think we should be locking our guest up in the brig, do you, Lieutenant?'

'Guest, sir?'

'Yes. Guest.'

Mia felt herself scoff. It wasn't a ladylike noise,

but she could see the Captain and the Naval Officer mirrored her disbelief.

'Are you planning on escaping, Miss Del Torres?'
Will said, turning his attention on her.

Yes, yes, yes. Yes a thousand times.

'No.'

'There you have it,' Will said with a smile.

'But…' Glass protested.

'Yes?'

'She's the sister of a pirate.'

'And I once was the neighbour of a man who beat
his wife. Does that make me a violent lowlife?'

Glass looked at him as if he'd grown two heads.

'But what if she tries to escape?' he queried valiantly one more time.

'Then we'll have to catch her.'

The Lieutenant was stunned into silence.

'Lead on,' Will commanded, taking Mia's arm
in his own. 'Take us to our rooms.'

Mia allowed herself to be led forward and down
into the bows of the ship. Men scurried backwards
and forwards, getting everything ready for their
voyage.

'This is your room, sir,' Glass said, opening the
door to a cramped but well-furnished cabin. It had
a large four-poster bed that filled over half the floor

space. Mia felt herself drawn to it and scolded herself immediately; she was there as a prisoner, not to lounge about on the bed of a man she barely knew.

'Nice bed,' Will said.

Mia realised she'd been staring and quickly averted her eyes.

'And for Miss Del Torres?' Will asked.

Ed Redding, the First Mate, came down the stairs behind them.

'Miss Del Torres can have my cabin,' he said. 'Come this way.'

'I don't want to put you out,' Mia said quickly. 'I'll be quite comfortable in the brig.'

Redding turned to her with a laugh. 'No one is comfortable in the brig, miss.'

'But where will you sleep?'

'There are spare bunks with the rest of the men. I'll be fine down there for a couple of weeks.'

'That's very kind of you, Redding,' Will said, 'I appreciate it.'

The First Mate led the way further into the ship and stopped outside a narrow wooden door.

'It's not much,' he said, 'but it's comfy enough.'

'Thank you,' Mia said.

'I'd better get back up on deck. We'll be leaving in a few minutes.'

Redding left and Lieutenant Glass reluctantly followed behind, leaving Will and Mia alone.

'Will you be comfortable here?' Will asked.

Mia realised he was genuinely concerned. He might be her captor and willing to use her to find her brother, but he was considering her comfort at the same time. Things could be worse: she could be in the hands of Lieutenant Glass.

'I will, thank you,' Mia said.

He turned as if to leave, then slowly spun round again to face her.

'Mia,' he said slowly, 'I meant what I said earlier.'

She looked at him. The small frown line in between his eyebrows was back again.

'I might not agree with the Governor's methods and I am sorry you've got caught up in this, but I have made an oath to bring your brother and his associates to justice and I need your help. I know you don't want to be here, but if you help me I promise I will do everything I can to protect you when we get back to Barbados.'

Mia nodded slowly. She felt torn. She believed him, she believed that if she helped him he would try to protect her, but she also knew it would be in vain. She'd watched so many men and boys she'd known from childhood hang and she knew if she set foot on Barbados again as a prisoner she could well be heading for the noose.

'I understand you are going to feel loyalty to your brother, but he has killed hundreds of innocent men and women. I can't let that continue.'

He moved in closer so there was only a sliver of air between their bodies. Mia looked up at him and tried to concentrate—she found it so distracting when he was this close. They stood for a moment just looking at each other, trying to figure out what their next move was. She had to consciously stop herself from reaching up and running her fingers through his golden hair, pulling his head down so his lips met hers.

'Shall we return to the deck?' Will said suddenly, stepping away.

Mia felt as though she had been jolted awake from a trance. She nodded and docilely followed him up the wooden stairs and back into the humid air.

Chapter Three

William cocked his head to one side and listened as the quiet footsteps approached his door. There was a long pause before a soft tap on the wood.

He was on his feet immediately and threw open the door.

'Come in,' he said with a smile.

Mia looked around suspiciously then stepped into the room.

'Afraid of an ambush?' Will asked.

'It's nearly midnight.'

'And?'

'When a man asks you to come to their room at this late hour a girl is allowed to be suspicious.'

Will looked at her closely and realised Mia was joking with him.

'Worried I'm about to ravish you?'

'I'd like to see you try.'

'So you have concerns about my motives, but you still came?'

Mia shrugged, 'It's not as though I had a choice.'

He let it go. It was understandable she felt uncomfortable and didn't want to be there. She'd been dragged in shackles on to the boat and if Lieutenant Glass had his way she'd be shivering in the brig now.

'I thought we could get started.'

Mia looked around for somewhere to sit and finally decided on the bed. She flopped down in an unladylike fashion and Will had to hide a smile.

'Mr Greenacre,' Mia said seriously.

'Will.'

'Will,' Mia refused to let herself be distracted. 'I'm not sure how much the Governor told you about me.'

Hardly anything. In fact, he'd promised 'local knowledge' and then produced Mia. From Thatcher's information, Will had managed to piece together a little more of her background, but she was still in the main a mystery.

'I know your brother is the infamous Captain Del Torres. You've been wanted by the authorities for the past few months and have been in hiding.'

'Anything else?'

'I know you have a kind heart and would risk your life to ensure a stranger doesn't drown.'

Mia turned away from him.

Will leaned forward in his chair. She had a sadness about her this evening.

'Anything else?'

He shook his head.

'When I was captured I was given a choice; help you or be executed the very next day.'

Will felt a knot forming in his stomach. He might have only known her for a short time, but the idea of Mia swinging from a noose was far too disturbing.

'It wasn't a hard decision to make.'

Will sat silently, wondering where she was going with this.

'They didn't ask what I knew or how I could help you, they just told me I would not be killed if I came with you to hunt my brother.'

She paused and closed her eyes.

'I didn't tell them at the time because I didn't want to die, but I've got no idea where he is.'

Will leaned forward in his chair and smiled gently at her.

'Of course you don't.'

'I don't,' Mia said quickly, 'I'm not lying.'

'I know.'

'I'm not lying,' she repeated.

'I believe you.'

She frowned and studied his face.

'Why?' she asked.

'Why do I believe you?'

She nodded.

'Because why would you know where your brother is?'

She looked perplexed.

'When was the last time you saw him?'

'Four or five years ago.'

'And when was the last time you heard from him?'

'I got a letter with some money about eighteen months ago.'

'So why would I think you'd know where he was?'

'But...' Mia started.

Will leaned back in the chair and allowed her a moment of confusion. She looked beautiful in the glow of the candle and he imagined taking her into his arms and laying her down on the bed beneath him. Hurriedly Will pushed the thought from his mind and tried to focus on his mission.

'Why am I here, then?' she asked.

'You might not know where your brother is, but you do know him. I can obtain information easily enough about his whereabouts, but I can't capture him, outthink him, if I don't know how his mind works.'

Mia sat digesting this piece of information for a while. She looked so innocent, sitting on his bed with her legs crossed underneath her. Her hand was moving backwards and forwards across the covers, an unconscious movement whilst she thought about what he was saying. By candlelight she looked young, too young to be embroiled in such dangerous affairs.

Will felt a protectiveness towards her he hadn't felt for anyone in a long time. She was vulnerable and alone and out of her depth. He wanted to shield her from what was to come and guard her from the evils of the world.

His other feelings for her weren't quite so noble. The kiss they'd shared on the beach might have stemmed from delirium on his part, but he couldn't forget the softness of her lips, the sweet taste of her mouth or the way her body had moulded to his. He was trying to keep professional and business-like, but every time he saw her he found it difficult not to take her in his arms and relive that moment when they had collapsed on the sand.

Each time he tried to force his mind back to the business of hunting Del Torres his thoughts seemed to wander instead to Mia. He wondered what it was about her that piqued his interest so much. He'd known beautiful women before, often resisted their advances. Will had always prided himself on being able to control his passions. It was in his nature to be on his own—indeed, as his friends had started to settle down and marry he had always assumed he would not have that domesticated life. Despite all that, he very much wanted to reach out and touch Mia, draw her to him and do wicked things to her.

Suddenly he needed to get out of the cabin. It was far too small and Mia sitting on his bed was far too tempting.

'Shall we get some air?' Will asked. 'It's a little hot in here.'

Mia shrugged, slipped off the bed and followed him to the door.

The sea was so calm it was almost flat. The wind had dropped and the ship was barely moving. It was a complete contrast to two nights previous when the storm had struck *The White Rose*. Had it only been two days? It felt so much longer. No wonder he was so weary, his muscles still protesting every time he moved.

'Tell me about your childhood, Mia,' Will said, trying to distract himself from his inappropriate desires by getting back to work.

'What do you want to know?'

'Everything.'

Mia took a few seconds before she started speaking, looking out to the horizon as if remembering better times. He saw her hesitate and for a moment wondered if she was going to refuse.

'My father was a sailor, or so my mother said. I never knew him. It was always just Jorge and Mama and me.'

Mia pushed a stray strand of hair back behind her ear before continuing.

'Mama was born a slave—her parents were brought here from Africa many years ago. She worked on a sugar plantation on Martinique, but when she was about my age she escaped with my father's help. They came to live in Barbados together to start a new life.'

'So what happened to your father?' Will asked.

'Rum,' she said sadly. 'He was found lying face up on the docks when I was five hours old, choked on his own vomit. Probably died at the same time I came into the world.'

'So your mother raised you and your brother alone?'

It was a very different childhood to Will's. He'd been privileged and pampered and treated to every little luxury. Some elements resonated with him, however; he'd grown up never knowing his mother, the child of a kindly but lonely man. And he'd had his older brother, Richard, to guide him through his early years just like Mia must have had her brother.

'She did what she could. There were always a lot of men around, but what else could a runaway slave do to make money?'

Will couldn't imagine such a childhood.

'Jorge was five years older, so by the time I was walking he was bringing in most of the money.'

'Stealing?'

Mia nodded, 'Pickpocketing mainly, especially when he was young. Jorge was a fantastic thief. He taught me to pick my first pocket when I was five. He was so proud when I got all the way to the end of the street without anyone noticing.'

'So how did he go from picking a few pockets to piracy?'

Again Mia hesitated and Will wondered if he'd

asked one question too many. 'When Jorge was twelve he fell in with the wrong crowd. He'd never hurt anyone before. Sure, he'd stolen things, taken things that hadn't belonged to him, but he'd never harmed anyone in the process.' She stopped and took a deep breath. 'He beat this boy up. The kid was a member of the gang and had been caught taking more than his share. Jorge was the new boy so it was his job to punish him.'

'An initiation?'

'Of sorts. Anyway, he went too far. It was as though he was possessed—a bloodlust came over him and he just wouldn't stop. The boy died.'

Will looked at her carefully. 'You saw it, didn't you? You saw your brother beat this boy to death.'

Mia nodded, the tears coming to her eyes. 'I still remember his pleas and his screams. They were only kids.'

Will moved closer. His instinct was to comfort her, but it would be inappropriate. No matter how much he didn't like it, he was still her captor and she his prisoner. He might want to hold her and stroke her hair and murmur in her ear, but he couldn't.

Mia turned towards him, her face wet with tears. For a long moment their eyes were locked together and Will felt some invisible force pulling him towards her. A few seconds longer and he wouldn't have been able to resist, he would have taken her in his arms and devoured her with his lips, but Mia turned away and broke the spell.

She looked out into the distance and continued. 'The soldiers came looking for him. Normally they wouldn't bother when one pickpocket kills another, but it was an excuse to rid the area of the whole gang.'

The wind whipped another strand of hair loose and this time Mia let it dance in the wind.

'Jorge talked his way aboard a ship and started his career as a pirate.'

'It must have been hard for you to lose your brother.'

'I hated him for a while,' Mia said quietly. 'I hated him for killing that boy and I hated him for leaving us.'

'And now?'

'I don't hate him,' Mia said, 'but I don't think he's the same boy I once knew.'

She shivered a little. Will suspected it was an emotional response as the night was hot and the air humid.

'I hear the stories of the atrocious things he's

meant to have done and I remember the cheeky little boy who would entertain me for hours with his antics.'

'So what happened to you after your brother left?' Will asked, wondering how she'd survived.

'My mother cried for a week when she realised Jorge was gone for good, but then she pulled herself together. She met a carpenter and they fell in love. He was always kind to me. He died six years ago and Mama followed him a few days later.'

'So you've been on your own since?'

Will wondered just how old she was. She only looked twenty-two at the most, but that would mean she'd been on her own since she was sixteen. He didn't want to think of what she'd had to do to survive.

'Not entirely. Until six months ago I worked for Mr Partridge, one of the shipbuilders, in his kitchen. The other girls there were my family.'

'What happened six months ago?'

'They found out who my brother was.'

Will could just imagine Mia's torment of once again having her life ripped out from under her feet.

'I went into hiding. My stepfather had kept a small cabin on the east coast, not far from where

I found you. No one knew about it. It was lonely, but at least I was alive.'

'So have you actually committed any crime?'

He knew the answer before she said it.

'No. But what does that matter?'

'It matters,' he said firmly. 'It matters to me.'

Chapter Four

'Surely you don't mean to take her ashore?' Lieutenant Glass asked disapprovingly.

Will smiled serenely at the Lieutenant and nodded.

'She has invaluable local knowledge.'

Mia suppressed a smile. She'd never been to Jamaica in her life and Will knew it.

'Shall I at least retrieve the shackles for you?' Glass said hopefully. 'Stop her from running away?'

'Are you going to run away, Miss Del Torres?' Will asked.

'No.'

'You believe her?' Glass looked as if he were about to explode.

'I believe her.'

The Lieutenant mumbled a few incomprehensible

words under his breath. As Will turned away Mia had to suppress the childish urge to stick her tongue out at the military man. That certainly wouldn't endear her to him.

'We shouldn't be more than a couple of hours,' Will informed the Captain.

'We need to take on fresh supplies but we should be ready to leave as soon as you return, if necessary.'

Will offered Mia his arm and she placed a hand on the fabric of his jacket.

'Where are we going?' Glass asked as he followed them off the ship.

'Miss Del Torres and I are off to meet a contact of mine in the less salubrious part of Port Royal. You are staying on board the ship.'

Glass actually choked with indignation.

Will let Mia's hand drop and spun to face him.

'I am meeting a secret contact who does not want it to be known he is helping the authorities catch pirates. I can hardly walk in with a Naval Officer at my side.'

Glass looked down at his unmistakable uniform.

'I could change.'

'Even in civilian clothes you have Navy written

all over you. So if you don't want to jeopardise our mission I suggest you stay out of sight.'

The man looked as though he was about to protest, then turned without another word and disappeared below decks.

'I think you've just made an enemy,' Mia said.

Will shrugged.

'You need to be careful. The Lieutenant is a powerful man.'

'He's also rude and so far up his own…' Will trailed off.

Mia giggled, 'You forget I grew up with prostitutes and sailors and gutter rats. A little bit of bad language isn't going to offend me.'

Despite what she said, Mia was quite pleased Will had stopped himself. She might be used to foul language, but she wanted his respect. It wouldn't be a bad thing if he treated her like a lady rather than the commoner she was.

'So where are we going?' Mia asked cheerfully. She was pleased to be back on dry land. It wasn't that she didn't like the sea, but like many who lived in the Caribbean she was wary of the sudden changes in temperament. One minute the sky could be blue and the sea calm, the next the clouds would roll in and the sea would swallow anything and everything.

'I have a source, an acquaintance of a friend of a friend of a friend, who might have some information.'

'What kind of information?' Mia asked.

'He was once a member of your brother's crew, got thrown out a few years ago for some transgression or another.'

'How do you know he'll tell you the truth?'

'I don't. But apparently when they threw him out they were actually trying to kill him, so he has little reason to stay loyal.'

They walked in silence for a minute or two. Mia enjoyed the lively sights and sounds of the port. Women in brightly coloured dresses flirted with the sailors. Voices shouting instructions for the unloading of the ships merged with the shrieks of young children as they ran excitedly from berth to berth. The exotic aroma of spices masked the underlying stench of filth which rose from beneath their feet.

They ambled slowly through the maze of streets that made up Port Royal. Although Mia had never been to Jamaica before, she knew it by reputation. Not long ago Port Royal had been a hotbed of crime and prostitution and pirate activity. The new Governor sent from England had taken a tough stance on piracy and it was rumoured twenty people were hanged a day for piracy-related activities. However, no amount of policy from the Governor could change the people of Port Royal, so the prostitutes and the crime remained and the pirates were just driven a little deeper underground.

A young girl of no more than four sidled up to them as they walked further into the town.

'Spare a coin to feed a hungry child,' she said angelically.

Mia grinned. She had played the same scam numerous times with her brother. Identify the victims, send the sweet girl to entice them to remove their purse from their clothing and distract them whilst the older sibling snatches the purse and runs.

'I wonder who you're working with?' Will said, looking around.

Mia was impressed. There weren't many people who saw the scam for what it was the first time round.

'That little ragamuffin over there,' Mia said with a grin.

The girl froze for a second, then ran off through the crowd.

'So how does a toff from England know how to keep hold of his wallet in the mean streets of Port Royal?' Mia asked, genuinely interested.

Will fascinated her. He was a mass of contradictions. Posh but street smart, a hunter of pirates but compassionate to their sisters. She wondered what had brought him to the Caribbean and what drove him to risk his life hunting some of the most dangerous men on earth.

'Now, that is a long story,' Will said.

They walked on in silence. Mia occasionally glanced at Will, wondering what she could do to make him open up to her. Not that he was obliged to, but she so desperately wanted to know more about him. She knew he found her attractive and not just because of the kiss on the beach. He'd been exhausted and just short of delirious then. But yesterday, outside her cabin, he'd looked into her eyes and edged just so slightly forward. He'd wanted to kiss her, she was sure of it, and she would have let him. She would have felt guilty kissing the man who was hunting her brother, but she wouldn't have wanted to stop him. But something had held him back and this morning he had returned to being friendly but distant, not revealing any more than he had to.

She wondered if she'd gone too far the night before, opening up to him. She had surprised herself in how freely she'd told him of her childhood and her family. Normally she was a private person. When she had worked for Mr Partridge she'd managed to keep her whole life up to the point when he'd employed her a secret. She supposed perversely she felt at ease with Will, the man who was meant to be her captor. He looked at her as though he didn't judge her on the transgressions of her brother as so many others did. When he'd asked her about her childhood it had felt right to open up to him. Mia wondered if a large part of it was also loneliness. For months she'd lived alone, with no one to talk to from one day to the next. When a sympathetic listener came along and seemed genuinely interested in her life she was bound to start talking.

They stopped outside a grubby-looking inn and Mia was forced to put her ruminations aside.

'I won't let anyone harm you,' Will said after seeing the look on her face.

Mia laughed. She'd grown up in places like this, spent hours scuttling under the tables lifting purses and grabbing chunks of bread whilst the patrons rolled about in a drunken stupor.

They entered and found a table in the corner, away from the raucous crowd near the bar.

Will leaned back against the wall and exhaled loudly.

'Tired?' Mia asked.

'I didn't sleep well.'

'The sea has tried to kill you once and you've survived. I wouldn't worry too much if I were you.'

'I wasn't worrying about the sea. I'd have to be very unlucky to get shipwrecked twice in one week.'

Mia refused to let his cheeky grin derail her. She was going to find something out about Will Greenacre if it killed her. He knew so much about her and she so little about him.

'So what did keep you awake?'

Will paused for a long few seconds and Mia wondered if he might just ignore the question completely.

'I was thinking about my brother,' he said eventually.

'Mr Greenacre,' a man said in a low voice.

Mia nearly punched him. Will was just about to tell her something about himself.

'Mr Weston. Please, sit down.'

Will motioned to the barmaid, holding up three fingers.

'I can't stay long,' the mysterious Mr Weston growled, 'might be recognised.'

He glanced at Mia suspiciously.

Will took a cloth purse from the recesses of his jacket and slid it across the table. Mr Weston picked it up, felt the weight with his hand and smiled, treating Mia to a waft of stale breath and the sight of his horrible blackened teeth.

'Who's she?' Mr Weston asked, nodding at Mia.

'A friend.'

He looked her up and down. 'Do I know you?' he asked eventually.

'I don't think we've ever had the pleasure,' Mia replied sweetly.

Mr Weston grunted suspiciously, then turned back to Will.

'So what do you want to know?'

Will leaned forward and lowered his voice, 'I want to know where I can find Captain Del Torres.'

Mr Weston snorted. 'That man's a ghost. The Navy have been after him for years and haven't even got close.'

'You've sailed with him. You must have some

idea where he takes his ship in a storm. Where he goes to take on water and food.'

'He's a very clever man. Difficult to catch.'

A serving boy appeared with three flagons of ale and plonked them down on the table, causing half the liquid to spill out. Weston took a long draught and shamelessly eyed up Mia again.

'Are you sure I don't know you?' he asked. 'You look very familiar.'

Mia hadn't seen her brother for years, but she expected there was still quite a strong family resemblance between them. She didn't think that bit of information would be terribly helpful in this situation.

'Let's get back to Captain Del Torres,' Will prompted. 'Tell me about the ship.'

Weston smiled his blackened grin again. '*The Flaming Dragon* is a beauty. Armed with more cannons than any other ship in these waters and still nimble enough to outrun any Navy ship. She's invincible.'

'No ship is invincible. They all sink eventually.'

Weston took another gulp of ale, nearly finishing the tankard. Will motioned for another to be brought forward. Mia noticed he hadn't touched his own.

'How about the crew? And the Captain himself?'

'The crew are all very loyal,' Weston said, raising a hand to his throat unconsciously.

Mia leaned in closer and realised he had two jagged scars zigzagging across the skin of his neck. They were partially obscured by grime, but they were visible for all to see if you knew to look.

'The Captain only has to give the word and they'll rush to do his bidding.'

'How has he earned their loyalty?'

'Fair division of spoils and fear.' Weston touched his throat again. 'Del Torres isn't afraid to slaughter someone if he disagrees with him.'

Will glanced at Mia. She smiled weakly. She still remembered the little boy who held her hand whilst they sat watching the boats come into port. It was difficult to listen to what a monster he had become.

'And what does Del Torres target?' Will asked.

Mia took a sip of ale to try to fortify herself for the answer that was to come.

'Mainly merchant ships. He has contacts in most of the ports who feed him information about which ships to target. That's one of the differences between *The Dragon* and other pirate ships—when *The Dragon* engages with a merchant ship you know it is going to be a big payload at the end.'

'How about raiding towns?' Mia asked. She didn't want to know the answer, but felt she had to.

Weston shifted his attention back to her. 'Land raids are high risk—you get little return for what can sometimes be a big loss of life or capture of men. Del Torres will raid towns, but not often. He normally focuses on the merchant ships.'

'And on these land raids, does he...?' Mia paused, trying to find the right words without her voice cracking. 'Does he kill civilians? Does he rape innocent women?'

Weston looked at her strangely as if she was asking an obvious question.

'He's a pirate,' he said simply.

Mia felt the blood drain from her head and clutched at the table to steady herself. She had known her brother had been branded a pirate and deep down she knew he must do all the atrocious things pirates did, but a part of her had clung to the hope that he'd been nobler than the rest.

She felt Will move closer and he took her hand in his own under the table. He gave it a reassuring squeeze. Mia wanted to allow her body to sink into his, to feel his protective arms around her, shielding her from the world.

'If you want to see what Del Torres can do, why

don't you take a trip to Savanna-la-Mar?' Weston
suggested. 'Then you can see first-hand what destruction a pirate raid wreaks.'

Mia swallowed convulsively.

'Del Torres and his crew raided the town four
days ago,' Weston explained. 'Think they killed
about twenty people, but there're plenty of survivors to give you the gory details.'

'Tell me about where the ship anchors,' Will
asked quickly, diverting Weston's attention from
Mia and her ashen face.

'Del Torres avoids highly populated areas, especially after an attack. There are some quiet bays on
Tortola and Dominica. When the ship needs more
provisions or repairs he normally takes it to one
of the small harbours on St Vincent or St Lucia.'

'Surely the authorities are on the lookout for *The
Flaming Dragon* even in the small harbours.'

Weston shook his head and smiled ruefully. 'Del
Torres is a clever man. He pays the right people to
look the other way and he never misses a payment.'

He paused and took another gulp of ale, once
again eyeing Mia.

'You look very familiar,' he repeated again.

'Can you tell me anything more about these

bays?' Will asked, determined to get more information from the former pirate.

Weston shrugged, 'I was only a lowly seaman, not privy to any of the plans. They were sheltered, we rode out a few storms in some of the coves. Apart from that I don't know what else I can tell you. I was only on the ship for a couple of months.'

'Why?' Mia asked, trying not to glance at the scars on his neck, 'What happened?'

Weston grimaced, 'I got greedy and I got caught.'

'And they let you live?'

'That was a mistake. Del Torres had one of the crew slit my throat, but they did an awful job. Threw me into the sea bleeding like hell, but in no way dead. I managed to make it back to land and someone patched me up. I was at death's door for a good few weeks.'

Mia didn't feel any sympathy for him. He'd been a pirate, happy to kill innocent people. If he couldn't even stick by the self-imposed rules of piracy, he didn't deserve her pity.

'*Se cosecha lo sembrado,*' Mia murmured.

Weston stood suddenly, the colour draining from his face.

'What did you say?' he asked, his voice choking in his throat.

Mia hesitated, then said again, *'Se cosecha lo sembrado.'*

'Who are you? Are you working for him?'

People were beginning to stare.

'Are you working for Del Torres?'

'Sit down, Weston,' Will commanded. 'You're drawing attention to us.'

Weston ignored him.

'Are you working for Del Torres?' he asked again.

Mia shook her head, but seemingly the reassurance was not enough for the ex-pirate. He backed away from the table, then, when he had reached the door, he turned and ran.

Mia and Will looked at each other in amazement.

'What does it mean?' Will asked her eventually.

'You reap what you sow. My mother used to say it.'

Chapter Five

They began the walk back through Port Royal in silence. Will was trying to process all the information Weston had given them. On the surface it wasn't much. The man had named a few islands with secluded bays and a couple of others with friendly ports. He really needed to sit down with a map and a compass and work out which bays were the most likely.

'I'm sorry,' Mia said quietly after a few minutes.

'What for?'

'I spooked him. I didn't mean to.'

'You weren't to know he connected your mother's proverb with your brother.'

'I'm still sorry. You might have found out more from him.'

'I doubt it. Men like Weston are not privy to the inner workings of a Captain's mind. And he was probably rolling drunk half the time and paralytic the rest.'

'Those scars on his neck were horrible.'

Will looked at Mia's troubled face and realised the meeting had affected her more than he'd anticipated. She'd had to hear first-hand what terrible things her brother had been doing.

They'd reached the harbour, but Will felt Mia wasn't quite ready to set sail just yet. He took her by the arm and steered her in the opposite direction, away from their ship.

'Where are we going?' Mia asked, looking back over her shoulder.

'Just for a walk. We need to talk and I'd rather do it without the whole crew listening.'

They walked in silence for a few more minutes whilst Will tried to find the best way to approach the subject. It didn't help that every time he glanced at her he felt a rush of desire pulse through him.

'That must have been hard for you,' he said eventually.

Mia nodded slowly.

'Hearing all of those things about your brother.'

'I've known he was a pirate for a few years, but I never really understood.'

Will could hear the strain in her voice as she tried to keep it from cracking.

'I thought…' she paused and corrected herself '…I hoped he wasn't like the pirates you hear about. I tried to convince myself he was nobler.'

Will stayed silent, trying to allow her to vent her pain.

'I knew he stole from merchant ships, and I know that's wrong, but it's not as bad as attacking civilians. I can't believe my big brother could give the orders to raid a port, allow his men to slaughter innocent men and rape innocent women. That's not the Jorge I know.'

The tears started streaming down her cheeks and Will gently rested a hand on her arm. He wanted to show her everything was going to be all right.

'Sometimes people change,' Will said slowly. 'Circumstance and the crowd they mix in can change someone beyond recognition.'

'But he's my brother,' Mia said, 'and I feel disgusted by him.'

Will reached up and gently brushed a tear from her cheek as it rolled over the velvety soft skin. He let his hand linger for a second, before dropping it back to his side. Mia turned her face up towards him and looked beseechingly into his eyes.

'I'm scared,' she said. 'If Jorge can turn into that kind of monster, that means I could, too.'

'Never.'

'We have the same blood running through our veins, the same childhood, the same parents.'

'Never,' Will repeated, his voice sharp. 'You are nothing like your brother. You have a good heart, a kind heart.'

He wanted to kiss her, to bend his head and devour her lips with his own. He wanted to feel her body mould to his and writhe beneath him. He wanted to touch every inch of her body, then kiss every place his fingers brushed.

Mia dropped her chin to her chest and broke the moment.

Will stopped himself from reaching out and tilting her lips back towards him. No matter how much he wanted her it would be inappropriate. She was a prisoner under his care. He would be taking advantage of her situation and of her pain. He knew that, but it didn't make it any easier to resist.

He'd been drawn to her from that first moment on the beach when they'd lain there exhausted, legs intertwined. He'd been unable to move and barely able to think, but his awareness of the woman beside him had been heightened. It had been an unfamiliar sensation for Will. Of course he'd been involved with women in the past, normally satisfying himself with short dalliances, but at heart he was a loner, a man who had never wanted to rely on anybody but himself. Now he seemed to be thinking of Mia every waking minute, wondering what it would be like to pull her into his arms and lose himself in her embrace.

Will was a focused man. He always gave everything he had to the mission in front of him, but Mia was making him lose that focus. He found himself thinking about her when he should be concentrating on catching her brother.

Kissing her wouldn't be right or fair to her and it most certainly wouldn't be right for him.

But he wanted to so badly.

'I'll help you,' Mia said quietly.

Will looked at her quizzically.

'I'll help you to catch my brother and his men. I have to or I'm as bad as them. My mother used to say those who knew of bad deeds but did nothing were as bad as the perpetrators themselves'

'Thank you. She sounds like a sensible woman'

Mia nodded and turned away from him. She took a few steps along the path and turned to look out at the sea. Will stayed where he was, sensing she was going to need a few minutes to herself.

He watched her as the wind whipped at her hair, pulling strands loose from the pins at the back of her head. The first time he'd seen her standing up on the cliff her hair had been loose, flying in the wind. He liked it. It seemed to suit her personality more than the demure bun she'd worn the past couple of days. He wanted to reach out and pull at the pins, allowing the dark locks to cascade over her shoulders.

Maybe it's best if she keeps it up, he thought as once again he felt a rush of attraction. In fact, maybe it would be a good idea to buy her a hat.

'What now?' Mia asked, turning back to face him.

'We get to work.'

'That old crook Weston barely told us anything.'

On one level Will had to agree. He'd given them a few vague descriptions and the names of a couple of islands. Del Torres and his crew could be hiding in any one of the thousands of secluded bays dotted around the Caribbean. Equally they might be anchored in plain sight, having paid off a crooked harbourmaster.

'But he did tell us something.'

Mia wrinkled her nose and frowned, as if trying to pick something useful out of the information Weston had given them.

'He told us your brother will anchor in secluded bays, and he gave us the names of a couple of his favourite islands.'

Mia didn't look convinced.

'That could be hundreds of different locations. How are we going to work out where he is right now or where he'll be in a week's time?'

'With a map and a weather forecast and a big dollop of luck.'

'Hmmm.'

'Not convinced?'

Mia shook her head, but Will was glad to see the traces of a smile on her lips.

'Okay, a very big dollop of luck.'

'It would have to be a massive dollop of luck.'

'You forget I'm a very lucky man. I survived a shipwreck and met you the very same day.'

Will was pleased to see the very beginnings of a blush creep into her cheeks.

'That was a very lucky day for you,' Mia agreed, smiling properly now. 'But maybe you used up all your luck.'

'Then I'll just have to be clever instead.'

Will offered her his arm and together they walked back towards the harbour area. He enjoyed how she leaned on him when the ground became a little uneven and how her fingers gripped his arm a little tighter.

'So you have plenty of maps and you claim to have the luck, but how on earth are you going to get an accurate weather forecast?' Mia asked.

It was the question that was bothering him. He could study the maps all he liked, but if he didn't know which way the wind was coming from or if they were due a storm he had no way of narrowing down Del Torres' whereabouts.

'I'm not sure,' Will said. 'The Captain seems quite knowledgeable, but all he can do is give me his best guess based on what normally happens at this time of year.'

'Well, if you think his best guess is good enough...' Mia said lightly.

'You've got a better idea?' Will asked.

'You could ask someone who can actually predict the moods of the sea and the changes in the weather.'

Will knew his face was a picture of scepticism.

'It's only a suggestion.'

'A fortune teller?'

'No. A wise woman.'

'A charlatan who will tell us what we want to hear.'

'As I said, it's only a suggestion.'

'And what do they base their predictions on? Whispers from God?'

'Actually it's quite scientific.' Mia paused and laughed when she saw Will's face. 'They have a lot of equipment that measures wind speed and air temperature and cloud movements.'

'These are the same women who make love potions and claim they can talk to the dead.'

Mia shook her head. 'There are some who just look at the weather. Call themselves meteorologists.'

He wasn't convinced.

'What's the harm?' Mia said. 'We could see one of these meteorologist women and then compare what she says to the Captain's predictions. Surely the more information we get the better.'

'As long as it's correct information.'

'Or we could ask the Captain to guess.'

Will contemplated for a few seconds.

'I only suggest it because I know Jorge used to be fascinated with the weather. He used to pride himself on knowing when a storm was coming.'

* * *

They stopped at the bottom of the hill and looked up at the brightly painted wooden cottage perched on the edge of the cliff.

'I'm still not sure,' Will said reluctantly.

Mia silently rolled her eyes and started up the hill. He'd half-heartedly agreed to come and Mia was convinced any moment he was going to dig his heels in and refuse to go any further. She wouldn't mind that much, but the man they'd asked for directions had described Amber Honey as a 'wild woman' and Mia was rather intrigued.

She glanced behind her and saw Will hadn't moved. Retracing her last few steps, she reached out and took his hand. His palm was a little rough against her softer skin and she enjoyed the sensation of holding his hand in hers. She pulled on his arm and Will obligingly followed her up the hill. After a few steps he pulled his hand free, leaving Mia feeling strangely bereft, then he tucked her fingers into the crook of his arm and in the process drew her even closer to him.

Mia enjoyed walking side by side with him. She could imagine for just a few minutes they were equals, a man and woman of the same social class, the same background, just enjoying a stroll together on a balmy Caribbean afternoon.

They reached the wooden gate to the property and Will grimaced again. It was painted a lovely bright yellow colour, clashing with the purple-pink hues of the house.

'Be nice,' Mia warned.

'I'm always nice', he said, the charming grin he flashed at her making Mia's knees wobble. She looked down at the offending joints and silently told them to behave.

'Good afternoon,' a voice called out from somewhere amongst the overgrown plants beside the house.

'We're looking for a Miss Amber Honey,' Mia called out.

'You've found her.'

A tall, graceful woman emerged from the greenery and opened the gate for them.

'What can I do for you two kind souls today?'

'We were hoping you might be able to give us a weather prediction,' Mia said.

'You've come to the right place,' Amber Honey said, 'I love anything and everything to do with the weather.'

'We don't want to take up too much of your time, Miss Honey,' Will said quickly.

Amber looked at him searchingly for a few seconds then nodded slowly. 'A sceptic,' she said. 'You think it's all guesswork.'

Mia started to protest on Will's behalf, but he beat her to it.

'I'm willing to be convinced,' he said.

'Come into the garden, have a seat.' Amber Honey led the way into the verdant garden. 'Maybe I can show you some of my equipment, let you decide for yourself how much is guesswork.'

Mia followed Will into the overgrown tropical garden. There were flashes of bright colour amongst the greenery and there didn't seem to be much order to anything. She rather thought Amber just picked the flowers and plants she liked and placed them in a haphazard fashion throughout the garden. There was a certain charm in the disorder and Mia paused for a few seconds to take it all in.

They reached a table with four chairs set out around it and Amber motioned for them to sit whilst she disappeared into the small wooden house.

'What do you think?' Mia asked quietly.

'She's not what I expected.'

'In a good way?'

Will shrugged, 'Let's see what she comes up with, then I'll make up my mind.'

From such a sceptic it was the most she could expect.

Will closed his eyes and turned his face up towards the sun, basking in the warm rays. For an Englishman he did seem to enjoy the Caribbean weather more than most. Mia had seen the soldiers at the fort dripping with sweat at ten in the morning or cursing when the tropical rains soaked them to the skin within seconds. Will seemed to take it all in his stride.

His natural skin colour was beginning to darken even after just a couple of days in the tropical sunshine. His hair was lightening, too. The blond locks that she had been so fascinated with during their first meeting were already a shade lighter.

Mia closed her own eyes so she wouldn't be caught staring. She could stare at Will all day. He fascinated her, and although it would be too much to say he enchanted her she definitely felt a pull towards him. He exuded a certain magnetism. He was handsome, she couldn't deny that, but Mia had met a lot of handsome men before and never felt quite so curious.

'Penny for your thoughts,' Will said.

Mia's eyes flashed open.

'Only a penny?'

'They're worth more than that? Now I really have to hear them.'

Mia stayed silent. She couldn't tell him what she was thinking; he'd think her a sentimental fool. Not that he'd tease her or mock her, he was too kind for that, though he'd probably just gently remind her they were from different worlds. She was a felon, the sister of a pirate. He was a law-abiding hero. She had no business wanting him, and he would be crazy to think of her as anything more than a source of information. Sure, he might have kissed her on the beach. She wasn't so naive to think he wasn't a little attracted to her, but that attraction was purely physical, nothing more.

'Back at the inn you were going to tell me about your brother,' Mia said eventually.

A cloud passed over his face and for a second Mia wished she hadn't asked. He opened his mouth to speak, but before any words could come out Amber ambled back outside.

'So, you want to understand the weather,' she said. 'What do you know about meteorology?'

Will looked at Mia and she motioned for him to go ahead.

'Very little,' he admitted. 'I've heard of it, but always thought the idea of predicting the weather preposterous. It can change within seconds.'

'That's very true.'

'If we could predict the weather, then ships wouldn't sail through hurricanes and farmers would know when to harvest their crops to stop them from spoiling.'

Amber nodded in agreement. 'But some people have been doing those things for hundreds of years. Experienced Captains know when to head for cover and lower the sails. Farmers watch the skies to decide when to plant their crops and when to harvest them. Sometimes they get it wrong, but a lot of the time they get it right.'

'So you're saying meteorology is just pattern recognition?'

Mia could tell Will remained unimpressed so far.

'Meteorology is part pattern recognition. The rest is surprisingly scientific.' Amber stood. 'Why don't I show you?'

They followed her further into the overgrown garden.

'We use readings from the air and ground thermometers, barometers, wind gauges.' Amber pointed each out in turn as they walked past the gadgets. 'I accumulate the data and then I look at what has happened before in similar circumstances. And it's not just isolated data, either. The rate of change from one value to another can tell you so much.'

She was becoming animated as she talked—here was a woman who clearly loved her vocation.

Mia felt a sudden emptiness inside. Looking at Amber was a stark reminder of what life could be like. The past few months she hadn't been living, she'd been existing. Barely surviving. And when Will caught her brother and his crew, which she now had no doubts he would, she would be even worse off. She doubted she'd have her freedom, let alone a life like Amber's.

'Mia?' Will asked, the concern evident in his voice, 'What's wrong?'

'Nothing,' she said with a sad smile.

'Why don't I give you a few minutes?' Amber said, looking shrewdly between them. 'I'll compile a weather report for this area for the next two weeks.'

Will started to say something but Amber cut him off.

'If you don't want to use it, that's fine, but let me

give it to you. You never know when it will come in handy.'

Amber disappeared again, leaving them alone.

'What's wrong, Mia?' Will asked again.

'Nothing, I'm just being silly,' she said, wondering how to get him to drop the subject.

'Was it something Amber said? We can leave.'

'Don't try to use me as your excuse,' Mia said sharply, 'If you want to be rude and leave, then go ahead, but don't try to make out it's what I want.'

Will looked slightly taken aback by her tone. Mia wanted to reach out to him but she knew she couldn't. Then she'd have to explain what this was actually all about: her lack of future.

'We'll wait,' Will said, turning away from her.

Mia swallowed and tried to call out for him, but something inside stopped her. She had to hold herself back from getting too close to him. In a few days he would be apprehending her brother, the only person in the world she loved, the only family she had left.

They stood in silence for a few minutes. Mia pretended to admire the different plants in the garden whilst Will just stood with a wide stance, his arms crossed in front of his chest.

'I see you two have worked it out,' Amber said

when she returned. She was carrying a couple of sheets of paper covered in text and diagrams.

'Thank you,' Will said, ignoring her comment as she handed him her predictions, 'I'm sure these will be very handy.'

Amber shrugged. 'I hope so, but I don't mind if you throw them away. If you would just wait until you're out of sight of the house, it's better for the ego.'

'I'll study them tonight,' Will insisted.

'It was lovely meeting you both.' Amber caught Mia's arm as she walked past, 'He's a good man and he likes you a lot,' she whispered in her ear. 'You just need to make him realise it.'

'Can we go to Savanna-la-Mar?' Mia asked suddenly.

They'd walked in silence all the way from Amber's house back into Port Royal. Mia had spent the time trying to decide if she wanted to go to the town her brother had raided or not. Part of her knew she shouldn't punish herself, but the other part wanted to know. If she was going to help Will find her brother, she had to accept the fact that she was going to be partly responsible for his execution. At the moment she was finding it hard to acknowledge her big brother could be the one ordering all the atrocities they'd heard about. She knew going to the town he'd sacked would help to focus her mind and decide once and for all what was the right thing to do.

'Mia, I don't think that's a good idea,' Will said, turning to face her.

'Please,' she said, 'I need to see it with my own eyes.'

'It will just upset you.'

Mia knew she had to make Will understand why she wanted to go to Savanna-la-Mar, but she was finding it hard to put her internal dilemma into words.

'I want to help you,' she said slowly, 'I really do. I know what Jorge is doing is wrong, but it's so hard to believe that my brother is the one doing all these terrible things.'

Will didn't look convinced.

'If I help you catch Jorge, then he will be executed. I will be sending my brother to the gallows.'

She looked imploringly at Will, begging him to understand.

She saw him soften.

'This will help?' he asked.

'I think so.'

She hoped it might focus her mind and help her decide what was for the best.

'Then we'll go.'

Mia watched as Will took charge, organising the hiring of a horse for the ride and getting supplies and directions from the tavern owner.

In an hour they were ready to go. Will expertly swung himself on to the back of the horse and reached down with his hand. Mia looked up at him, her heart pounding in her chest, hoping he didn't expect her to hop up behind him.

'Come on,' Will said.

'Behind you?' Mia asked.

Will looked around as if to ask where else she wanted to sit.

'Won't it be a bit dangerous?'

'It's perfectly safe.'

Mia hesitated again.

'You have ridden a horse before?' Will asked.

She shook her head.

'It's easy. All you have to do is hold on.'

The idea of looping her arms around Will's waist was tempting, but Mia still felt a reluctance holding her back.

'I promise I won't let anything happen to you.'

He said it so sincerely Mia placed her hand into his. 'I'm going to swing you up behind me,' Will explained carefully. 'Just place your hand on the horse's back and let me do the rest.'

He allowed her to get into position, then he gently pulled her up behind him. Mia clutched at his waist as soon as she was seated, wondering if she would slip off backwards as soon as they started moving.

'Comfortable?' Will asked.

Mia nodded, then realised he couldn't see her. 'I'm comfortable.'

'We'll start off slow. You just let me know if you want me to stop.'

Will nudged the horse forward and Mia felt her fingers gripping his waist even tighter as they began to move.

'You all right?'

'Fine.'

After a couple of minutes Mia felt herself relax. The rhythmic movement of the horse was quite soothing and she felt safe holding on to Will for support.

Soon they had left the busy town of Port Royal and were trotting through the Jamaican countryside. Mia allowed herself to enjoy the ride, taking in the lush forests on either side of the dusty road and feeling the warmth of the Caribbean sun on her skin. She also enjoyed being so close to Will in such an acceptable fashion. Apart from their brief encounter on the beach it had been months since Mia had experienced any form of human contact. She'd lived an isolated life in her cabin and every day had been as lonely as the last.

After a few days' ride they paused at the top of a hill to look at the town below.

'Savanna-la-Mar,' Will said. 'Are you sure you want to go down?'

'I'm sure.'

He spurred the horse forward and they trotted down the winding road into the small settlement.

Even before they had reached the centre Mia could see the damage that had been wrought upon the town. Some buildings were burned to the ground, just blackened husks and rubble to hint at what they had been before. Debris littered the street and the town was virtually deserted.

'It's like a ghost town,' Mia whispered into Will's back.

They rode on in silence, reaching the small town square. A solitary woman, dressed entirely in black, was attempting to scrub the wooden front of her house. Even from the other side of the square Mia could hear her heart-wrenching sobs as she laboured in the midday heat.

Holding on to Will for support, Mia slid off the horse and landed lightly on her feet. She slowly walked towards the woman, not wanting to scare her with a sudden approach. She wondered where all the other townsfolk were and why this single woman had insisted on staying if no one else had.

'Can I do anything to help?' Mia called when she was a short distance away.

The woman stopped her work and glanced up, her eyes clouding with fear.

'I'm not going to hurt you.'

When the woman didn't answer, Mia edged forward.

'He's gone,' the woman whispered.

'Who's gone?'

This set the woman off sobbing again. Mia reached her side and gently placed an arm around her shoulder, pulling the distraught woman towards her.

'He was only a boy.' She sobbed into Mia's shoulder. Mia could see she shouldn't immediately ask what had happened to this boy—she needed to ease the woman into it.

'Where is everyone?' Mia asked.

The woman snorted, making an effort to dry her eyes. 'Most left as soon as there was any sign of trouble. Those who stayed are behind locked doors. Not that there's any point hiding now.'

'What happened here?' Part of her didn't want to know the answer, but she knew she'd come too far to leave without the whole story.

'Pirates,' the woman said forlornly. 'They came late at night, most people were in bed. We knew it was a raid before we'd even looked out the window.'

Mia tried to imagine how petrified this woman must have been when she'd realised her town, her home, was being attacked by pirates.

'I did my best to protect him. I thought he was going to be safe,' she said, her hands wiping the never-ending stream of tears from her cheeks and her eyes pleading with Mia to understand. 'I made Roger hide in the wardrobe, made him promise me he wouldn't come out until I fetched him.'

'Roger's your son?' Mia asked.

The woman straightened and looked Mia directly in the eye. 'Roger was my son.'

Mia didn't think she wanted to hear any more, but she couldn't stop the mourning woman now.

'What happened?'

For a minute Mia wondered if she would refuse to say any more, she seemed so consumed by her grief, but when she did start speaking it was as if she couldn't wait to get the story out and share her burden with someone.

'The pirates were streaming through the town, raiding anywhere that looked like there might be something worth stealing. I was watching from the upstairs window.'

Mia glanced up at the wooden house behind her, seeing the small window that must have served the single upstairs room.

'It was sickening. If anyone was caught out in the street they shot them, or beat them unconscious. I couldn't bear to watch, but I couldn't look away.'

'There's more, isn't there?' Mia asked, sensing they were reaching the climax of the story.

'A group of the pirates had just set fire to the bakery.' She indicated a charred building across the square. 'I was sure they were nearly done—they'd taken everything of value from the town and had caused so much destruction.' Her voice wobbled for an instant, but quickly she regained control. 'I looked down into the street again and I saw Roger just outside our front door. He looked so scared out there all on his own.'

Mia tightened her grip on the woman's arm to show her support, knowing all the time that nothing would ease the pain of her loss.

'I don't know how he'd got out there, or why, but I suppose he'd heard the commotion and wanted to see what was happening for himself.' The tears were streaming freely down her cheeks now and Mia knew she was reliving every awful moment of the pirate raid.

'I ran down the stairs, I thought I could drag him back inside before anyone noticed him.' She shook her head. 'I was wrong. By the time I got downstairs he was dead. They'd shot him.'

Mia felt as though she'd been punched in her stomach.

'How old was he?' she asked quietly.

'Seven.'

She took the grieving mother in her arms and hugged her, allowing the tears to stream from her own eyes, mourning for a little boy she'd never met.

'I buried my only child yesterday,' the woman said eventually. 'What kind of animal shoots a defenceless seven-year-old?'

Mia didn't have an answer for her. Instead she tried to convey her support and sympathy, knowing that nothing she could say would ever even begin to make up for her loss.

'Can we take you anywhere?' she asked, motioning over to the other side of the square where Will was waiting with the horse.

The woman shook her head. 'I feel closer to Roger here. I don't want to leave.'

'Will your neighbours return?'

She shrugged, looking as though she didn't care if she was the only one left in Savanna-la-Mar.

'Will you let me help you?' Mia motioned to the stain the woman was trying to clean off the front of the house. As she offered she realised it was the splatter of blood from where Roger had been shot.

Silently the woman nodded, allowing Mia to lead her into the house and sit her at the table. Once she was back outside Mia began scrubbing the wood, trying to get rid of the terrible reminder of the pirate raid. As she cleaned she knew her mind was made up. Jorge was her brother and she had loved him, but she couldn't continue to protect a man who allowed a seven-year-old to be shot for no reason at all. This poor woman's life had been ruined and Roger would never get the chance to live his.

Mia knew she wouldn't be able to live with herself if she didn't do everything in her power to help Will find her brother and bring him to justice. If she didn't, it would almost be like she was killing little Roger herself.

Chapter Six

The evening was balmy, a tropical heat that made even the idea of sleep impossible for Will. He'd been sitting at the small desk in his cabin for well over three hours, studying the maps and the accounts of the sightings of Jorge Del Torres and *The Flaming Dragon*. He was trying to piece it together, trying to make a pattern, but so far he was failing. He supposed Del Torres might not follow a pattern. He might randomly sail from cove to port, terrorising merchant ships in between. Will doubted it though. Del Torres had evaded the Navy for years now. He had to have more of a plan than aimlessly sailing around the Caribbean as some pirates seemed to.

He ran a hand through his hair and sighed. He was tired and hot and wasn't concentrating properly. He needed a break.

'Just a few minutes,' he muttered to himself.

Will stood and groaned as he stretched the stiff muscles in his legs and lower back. He was a man of action, much happier in the saddle or chasing after fleeing pirates. He had gone to university more because it was expected than because of any real desire on his part, and he'd got his degree, but he'd been much more interested in the extracurricular activities. His father had paid his expenses and insisted his son get a good education. The man had been different to many of his peers' fathers; he'd wanted Will to have the same chances as his brother even though he was the second son and not the heir.

Well, not the heir at the time. Of course things were different now Richard was dead.

He flung open the door of his cabin and decided to take a stroll on deck. The ship might be small, but a few laps in the humid air might revive him a little at least.

'Evening, Mr Greenacre,' Ed Redding, the First Mate, greeted him as he emerged from below decks.

'How are things?' Will asked.

'Making good progress. You have an exact destination in mind yet?'

Will grimaced. He'd instructed the Captain to sail for St Lucia. It was an island he knew had numerous secluded coves a ship could shelter in quite happily without being observed. But they couldn't just sail from cove to cove on each island. That wouldn't get them anywhere. He needed a brainwave, or some insight into how the men on *The Flaming Dragon* thought.

'Not yet,' Will said.

'Are you looking for Miss Del Torres?' Redding asked. 'She's sitting at the prow.'

Will nodded and moved towards the front of the ship. It hadn't been his intention to seek Mia out; he'd assumed she would be asleep by now, but he wouldn't mind her company for a while.

She was perched on the wooden rail right at the front of the ship. She'd let her hair down and it was flying behind her, whipped by the wind. She looked so delicate and fragile sitting there that Will wanted to reach out and fold her in his arms.

'Mia,' he said quietly so he wouldn't startle her. The last thing he wanted was for her to fall into the churning sea.

She glanced over her shoulder and smiled at him.

'Join me,' she said after a few seconds. She patted a space on the rail beside her.

Will carefully climbed over and perched on the wooden bar. It was quite a precarious position, but he could see why she'd chosen it. With nothing but sea in front and below you could almost believe you were floating over the water.

'I thought you would be in bed,' Will said after a few minutes had passed in silence.

'No,' Mia said.

He sensed she didn't want to talk straight away so he stayed quiet. He wondered if she was still thinking about their trip to Savanna-la-Mar. She hadn't told him exactly what happened when she had gone to talk to the crying woman, but he could more or less guess. She'd been contemplative and quiet ever since.

Will could feel the salty sting of the spray on his skin and felt invigorated. After hours of sitting in his cabin this was what he needed.

'How are things going?' Mia asked eventually. 'With your maps, I mean.'

Will shook his head, 'Not well. I can't work out any pattern, any way of predicting where your brother will go next.'

'Maybe you're looking at it wrong,' Mia suggested. She glanced at him, a small smile on her lips. Will felt a frisson of excitement dart through him at her smile and had to stop himself leaning over and tracing the contour of her lips with his fingers.

'I've got no doubt I'm looking at it wrong. Otherwise I'd be making at least a little progress.'

'Maybe I could help.'

'I would love your help,' Will said slowly. 'It's just…'

She looked at him quizzically, then her face fell.

'You're worried I might send us on a wild goose chase trying to protect my brother.'

Will knew it was ridiculous as soon as she said it, but it had been exactly what he'd been thinking.

'Even you,' Mia said quietly. 'Even you are so quick to condemn me because of who my brother is.'

'I didn't mean that, Mia.'

'I've never done anything to hurt anyone. I may have had to steal when I was a child, but I've never committed a crime as an adult. Yet still everyone thinks I'm a criminal.'

'Mia, I didn't mean anything by it. It was a stupid comment.'

She looked into the distance and Will could see her jaw clenching and the small muscles of her face flicking as she pressed her teeth closer together.

'Fine. Do it on your own,' Mia said eventually. 'See how far you get.'

Will edged closer to her. He wanted to reach out and touch her, but he was very aware of the big drop to the sea below. He didn't want to startle her into falling off.

'I just meant he's family. Jorge is the only one you've got. I'd imagine it would be pretty tough helping me catch him.'

Mia turned to look at him again. Her jaw had relaxed, but her expression was sad.

'Jorge is my only family,' she said quietly. 'He's the only person in the world who actually cares a little bit about me. But I told you earlier I know what he's doing is wrong.'

Will sat quietly, he wanted her to vent all of her anger and sadness.

'And if I sit by and do nothing whilst he's hurting other people, that makes me as bad as him.'

'No,' Will said, 'that's not true.'

'That's how it would feel.' She paused. 'Earlier today, when I heard how that young boy had been killed, I knew I had to stop Jorge. He's out of control and, if he condones the killing of children, he's not the brother I once loved any more.'

Will reached out and took her hand gently. Mia

jumped a little as his skin connected with hers, but she didn't pull away.

'Fine,' he said, 'I'm sorry. I know you wouldn't lie to me to lead me down the wrong route. It was a stupid thing to say, insensitive.'

Mia looked at him for ten long seconds, then nodded. Will felt like she'd looked deep into his soul. He hoped she hadn't found him wanting.

'So what do you suggest?' he asked.

'Five more minutes,' Mia said, 'then we'll go and have a look at your maps and charts.'

He could give her five minutes. Mia had turned away from him again and was looking out into the darkness. He wondered what it was she was looking for, but didn't want to disturb her thoughts. Instead he closed his eyes and enjoyed the sound of the calm sea lapping against the ship.

Mia's hand was still underneath his and he enjoyed the physical contact. It had been a long time since he'd been with a woman. Ever since his brother had died he'd been on a one-man crusade to avenge him. Hopefully soon his efforts would be rewarded. He wondered what he would do once he'd found the men responsible for Richard's death. He'd been on the move for so long he didn't know if he could settle into the role of English lord and landowner.

He glanced again at Mia. Maybe settling down wouldn't be so bad with a good woman by his side.

He almost laughed at himself for the absurdity of the thought. It was wrong on so many levels. He didn't even like Mia like that.

He did find her attractive. She was a kind and caring person. And she made him laugh. But they'd been thrown together in the most ridiculous of circumstances. They were from different worlds in more respects than one. If that wasn't enough in itself, when this was all over Mia would be in mourning for the man he'd sent to the gallows. Add to that the fact that he wasn't used to sharing his life with anyone, the whole idea was preposterous.

No, certainly not a good idea. That didn't have to stop him from imagining what was beneath her rather tightly laced bodice.

'Shall we?' Mia asked.

Will hoped she hadn't seen where he was looking.

He swung his legs over the wooden bar and held out his hand to help her over. Gracefully she hopped back down to deck and took his arm as they walked back to the stairs leading to the cabins.

'Right,' Mia said as she flopped down on to his bed, looking much more comfortable than the last time she'd been there, 'where shall we start?'

Will resisted the urge to sit beside her; he was feeling distracted enough as it was.

'Well, this is us,' Will said, unrolling a large map of the Caribbean. He pointed out the approximate location of their ship. 'And I've instructed the Captain to make for St Lucia.'

'Why?' Mia asked.

Will ran a hand through his hair, 'Best guess,' he said eventually.

'So what else do we know?'

He reached behind him and picked up some papers from his desk.

'I've got a whole list of alleged sightings of *The Flaming Dragon* from the past six months.'

'Good. Why don't we put those on the map? I'm always much better with a visual representation.'

Will frowned. He didn't have a clue what she wanted him to do.

Mia sighed. 'Wait here,' she said and bounded out of the cabin.

He didn't exactly have anywhere else to go. A minute later Mia was back holding an assortment of hairpins in her hand.

'Okay, what type of sightings do we have?' Mia asked.

'What?' He had no idea where she was going with this. And he was rather distracted as she squeezed past him and flopped back down on the bed.

'What type of sightings?' she repeated, slower this time, as if speaking to a halfwit. 'You know, attack on another ship, raid on a town…'

'We've got six confirmed attacks by *The Flaming Dragon* on merchant ships. Three raids of small towns. Three supposed sightings in ports and one Naval chase.'

'Let's start with the attacks,' Mia said, taking over.

'Okay.' Will was unsure what she wanted him to do.

'Where and when was the first one?'

'February fifteenth. Six miles south of Basseterre.'

Mia took one of the hair pins with a red end and stuck it into the map.

'Next.'

'March twentieth. Ten miles south of Puerto Rico.'

'Next.'

'April twenty-fourth. Forty miles west of St Lucia.'

'Next.'

'May thirtieth. Twelve miles east of St Kitts.'

'Next.'

'July fourth. In the middle of the Greater Antilles strait between Haiti and Jamaica.'

'Next.'

'August eighth. Fourteen miles south of Puerto Rico.

'Right,' Mia said sitting back to admire her handiwork. 'Let's move on to the raids.'

'March tenth, Road Town, Tortola, and July twentieth, Santo Domingo, Dominican Republic...' He paused. 'And August thirtieth. Savanna-la-Mar.'

Mia took three pins topped with a fake pearl and stuck them into the map. A picture was forming. It didn't make any sense at the moment, but Will had to admit it was easier to picture the route of *The Flaming Dragon* when it was laid out on the map like this.

'Right, how about the Naval chase?' Mia asked.

'That was on June the first. The Navy sighted *The Dragon* close to the island of St Martin and gave chase east before losing her somewhere near Puerto Rico.'

Mia stuck a plain hairpin in at the location of the start of the chase and where the Navy had lost them.

'So just the random sightings left.'

He recited the dates and locations and Mia stuck the last pins into the map. When they had finished she inched up the bed and admired her handiwork. With her head tilted to the side she looked so pensive Will didn't want to disturb whatever thoughts were running through her head.

'Clever boy,' she murmured.

'Excuse me?'

'I'm not talking about you,' Mia said, still staring at the map.

'Your brother?'

She nodded her head.

'Come over here.' She patted a space on the bed beside her.

Will moved slowly. He was aware of how close they would be sitting, and tonight Mia was affecting him in a rather strange way.

'Come on,' she repeated impatiently.

He sat down beside her. They were so close their thighs were touching. Mia had tucked her feet up underneath her again and Will knew if he looped his arm around her waist she would be in his lap in a second, two at the most. He felt the blood start to pulsate in his temples. His hand brushed against her arm and he felt the thrill of such close contact.

'Look at this,' Mia said, leaning over the map. As she leaned forward Will found himself looking at the mounds of her breasts rather than the map.

'You're not looking,' Mia said, her voice an octave higher than usual.

'I am looking,' Will murmured, his eyes moving up her body to her face.

He knew he had to have her. It didn't matter that it wasn't a good idea. It didn't matter that their relationship would never work out in the real world. Will couldn't think straight. All he could see and feel and smell was Mia. It was as if she'd taken over every one of his senses and he just needed to devour her.

Her breathing had quickened and the delicate skin of her cheeks was a little flushed.

'Mia,' he murmured.

'We can't,' Mia said quietly.

Will agreed, but he leaned forward anyway.

'Mia,' he said again. He'd lost the ability to say anything apart from her name.

Gently he brushed his lips against her, testing for any resistance. At first she didn't respond, but just as Will was about to pull away she let out a faint moan and shifted very slightly forward. He reached a hand up and caressed the back of her neck, trailing fingers over her silky soft skin.

Without a thought for the consequences Will hooked his other arm around her waist and pulled her into his lap.

He could feel the heat radiating from her body as she pressed herself into him. He deepened the kiss, flicking his tongue into her mouth and enjoying how she whimpered as he dropped his mouth to her neck. He peppered the smooth skin with tiny kisses before rising up again to kiss her lips.

'Mia,' he murmured into her neck.

He could feel his hardness pressing into her, straining the lining of his trousers. He wanted to throw her on the bed and ravish her, the consequences be damned.

He raised a hand and trailed it along the edge of her bodice, causing Mia to shiver in anticipation. Slowly he dipped his head to her breasts, kissing the exposed skin, all the time wanting more.

Mia suddenly froze, then pushed his head away.

'Stop,' she said quietly. 'We have to stop.'

Will raised his head reluctantly.

'We have to stop,' Mia said. 'We can't do this.'

'I know. But I want to.'

Mia shook her head, not moving her eyes from where her gaze was locked. Will followed the line of her sight and saw what had made her reconsider. She was staring at herself in the small mirror on his cabin wall. As he glanced over he saw how dishevelled she looked. Beautiful but dishevelled. It looked as though he'd ravished her ten times over.

She stumbled up from the bed and headed towards the door, pulling at her dress, trying to straighten herself out.

'Mia,' Will called after her. 'Wait.'

She didn't even pause. Instead, she wrenched at the handle and staggered out into the corridor.

He knew he had to leave her alone; going after her now would make things so much worse. He cursed loudly and slammed his fist into the soft mattress.

Will couldn't believe what he'd instigated. Normally he prided himself on his self control. He'd always been able to resist the advances of women if the circumstances didn't suit him and Mia hadn't even made the first move.

He flopped back on to the bed, wondering what to do. He'd ruined everything; they'd been doing so well. Mia had been on to something and now he didn't even know if she'd ever speak to him again.

'Good work,' he told himself and closed his eyes. Not only had he sabotaged his working relationship with Mia, he felt completely frustrated now, as well.

Chapter Seven

She'd lain awake all night and now that the early morning rays were streaming through the tiny window in her cabin Mia knew she had no chance of getting any sleep. The first half of the night she had spent cursing her stupidity and the second half she'd tried to devise ways to avoid seeing Will ever again.

She felt completely confused. There were two things she knew for sure: one, she was undeniably attracted to Will Greenacre, and, two, a romantic involvement with him on any level would be the worst idea she'd ever had.

He was chasing her brother, and when Will caught him he would return to whatever life he had back in England and she'd most likely spend the rest of her days rotting in a cell. There was no future for them.

When she'd seen herself in the mirror in his room it was her mother looking back, in the arms of one of the men paying for the pleasure of her company. Mia refused to give up her integrity no matter how much she wanted him. She wasn't so naive she insisted on marriage before giving up her virtue, but she at least wanted love. She'd promised herself a long time ago she would only ever make love to the one man she fell in love with.

With a groan she got up from her bed and splashed some cold water left over from the night before on to her face. She looked in the grimy mirror above the sink and grimaced. There were faint black circles under her eyes and her skin had lost a little of its colour. She looked a mess. She pinched each cheek for a few seconds, trying to encourage the blood flow, but in the end decided nothing was going to hide the fact she hadn't slept a wink that night.

Mia pulled her dress over her head and got to work fastening the bodice, pulling the laces through herself as she had learned to do in the months she'd been living alone.

She ran her fingers through her hair, trying to tease out the tangles, before pulling it into a loose bun at the nape of her neck.

With one last look in the mirror she left her cabin and made her way up to the deck.

'Good morning, miss,' Ed Redding said as she emerged into the sunlight. 'Did you sleep well?'

Mia gave him a small smile. 'Unfortunately I found the motion quite disconcerting.'

'Why don't you have a walk about the deck and I'll get one of the men to bring you a cup of tea?'

'Thank you,' Mia said.

'Not a problem. It looks like you had a rough night.'

Mia looked at him sharply, wondering whether he was hinting he knew what had gone on in Will's cabin the night before. But he had already moved on, shouting orders to the men around him.

Mia shook her head and told herself to stop second-guessing herself.

She walked across the deck, smiling at the seamen as they went about their work. Mia loved this time in the morning when the sun wasn't yet hot, just a warm caress on the skin. She liked it when the mist hadn't quite lifted, the last few wispy tendrils still lingering in the sky. This was the time of day she felt was the Caribbean at its best, since so often as the afternoons closed in the temperature soared and the clouds rolled in.

Leaning against the wooden rail, Mia closed her eyes and let the sounds of the ship fade into the background. She was strong. She'd always been strong. She had coped with losing her mother and leaving her home and learning her brother was the most notorious pirate in the Caribbean. If she could cope with that, she could cope with the aftermath of kissing Will. She would just have to ignore the butterflies she got every time she caught sight of him and the way her pulse raced when he happened to touch her.

Mia groaned. Who was she kidding? She wouldn't last five minutes trying to ignore him. Maybe it was better to have it out with him. Tell him she was attracted to him, but that she knew they had no future, so no matter how much she wanted it would he please not kiss her again.

'Mia.'

She spun around. Will was standing a little way away as if uncertain whether to come closer.

'Will.'

They stood looking at each other for half a minute, neither wanting to be the first to start talking.

'I'm sorry,' he said eventually, 'for last night.'

Mia nodded, unsure how to reply.

'It was unforgivable.'

She nodded again even though she didn't exactly agree. It was awkward and embarrassing, but it wasn't unforgivable. She'd wanted it as much as he had.

He fell silent and took a few steps towards her, pausing when he was an arm's length away.

'I don't want things to be awkward between us,' he continued.

She agreed. The last thing she wanted was for things to be awkward between them, but she didn't see how they could avoid it. She felt she could barely meet his eye.

'I'm sorry,' he repeated, seemingly at a loss as to how to proceed.

He stepped up to the rail so he was standing beside her. She watched as he leaned forward and looked out to sea, as if he was searching for the answer on the horizon.

'I...' Mia started, but found the words wouldn't come out.

Will turned around to look at her, his expression hopeful. She realised he must be thinking he'd taken advantage of her, seduced her to near abandonment. He was feeling guilty and thought she blamed him for their kiss when in reality she blamed herself.

She had shamelessly flopped down on to his bed and had noticed when he'd edged closer. She could have created some distance between them right then, but she hadn't. She'd wanted him to kiss her. She'd been thinking about nothing else for two days and when he'd finally pressed his lips to hers she'd been in heaven.

Part of her wished she could just give in to her desires, but Mia had never been the type of girl who would give herself to anyone. She'd never even kissed a man before Will's delirious attempts on the beach. Mia reminded herself that when she gave herself to someone it would be to the man she intended to spend the rest of her life with. The man she loved.

A thought flitted through her brain and she pushed it away. She most certainly did not love Will Greenacre. She had barely known the man for a few days, certainly not long enough to fall in love. Perhaps if they had met in a different place, a different time with very different circumstances, perhaps then he was a man she could fall in love with. But most certainly not here and not now and not like this.

'I'm sorry, too,' Mia managed to say.

'You've got nothing to apologise for.'

'I have,' Mia pushed on to say. 'I wanted you to kiss me. I wanted it so much I allowed it to happen even though I knew better. I knew it wasn't a good idea.' The words were tumbling out so fast Mia didn't think she could stop. 'I knew it wasn't a good idea and I let you kiss me anyway. I'm sorry.'

He looked rather surprised. Mia supposed he'd expected to come out to apologise and for her to act all indignant as if he had forced himself on her and she hadn't enjoyed a single moment. Nothing could have been further from the truth.

'You wanted me to kiss you?'

Mia wondered if that was all he'd heard from her jumble of words. Slowly she nodded. 'I wanted you to kiss me even though I knew nothing could happen between us.'

He turned so he was looking out to sea again.

'So I want to kiss you and you want to kiss me,' he said.

Mia wasn't sure she liked where this was leading.

'But it would be a very bad idea,' she said.

'I suppose it would.'

'It would.'

They stood side by side in silence for a few minutes. Mia desperately wanted to reach out and touch his arm, just make some sort of physical contact, but she knew she mustn't. He might take it the wrong way.

'Fine,' he said eventually. 'We can do this.'

Mia looked at him questioningly.

'You're not the first woman I've been attracted to and I'm sure I'm not the first man you've wanted to kiss.'

Mia didn't bother correcting him. There were certainly men who'd tried to kiss her over the years, mainly drunken sailors or arrogant shipbuilders, but none she'd wanted to kiss back. No one had ever made her feel like she would burst into flames by just looking at her like Will did.

'So we acknowledge it and we carry on. We both agree it would be disastrous if we allowed our baser instincts to take over.'

Disastrous was maybe a little strong, but she agreed with the general sentiment.

'We work together and we spend time together, but no more.'

Mia nodded her agreement. It was exactly what she wanted, so she wondered why his words hurt quite so much.

'Last night,' Will said after a few moments, 'before we kissed, you'd worked something out.'

Mia nodded.

'What was it?'

Back to business. Just like that. She swallowed her sadness and her confusion and smiled at him.

'It'll probably be easier to show you.'

She followed him back across the deck and down the stairs. He hesitated a moment before leading her into his cabin. Mia nearly laughed out loud. He'd made it very clear he wasn't going to lose control again so she wondered if he was worried about her trying to ravish him.

'Have a seat.' Will pulled out the chair from the desk and waited for her to sit down. He leaned across her to retrieve the map with all of her hair pins still in place. She felt the warmth of his body as he hovered just over her skin and wondered how long it would take before her heart learned not to race when he was near.

She waited until he had sat back on the bed, then turned to face him, holding the map in front of her.

'Look,' she said, pointing at the pins with the red ends. 'Concentrate on the attacks on merchant ships. We know this information is accurate. The Captains keep detailed logs so the date and the location are going to be pretty much spot on.'

Will nodded his agreement.

'If we look at each one in chronological order, the pattern might become a little clearer.'

He leaned forward, eager to know what she had worked out.

'The first attack and the fourth attack took place close to the island of Antigua. So let's imagine that's our starting point.'

Mia traced her finger over a route she'd worked out the night before, linking in all the assorted attacks in the order they happened. The route went from Antigua to Tortola to St Lucia, back to Tortola and then west towards Jamaica. With the attacks that they knew about, Del Torres had navigated the route three times in the past six months.

'A couple of the sightings don't fit,' Mia admitted, 'But I'm guessing if Jorge had information about a well-stocked ship or needed to dock for repairs after a fight he'd have to deviate from the plan.'

Will was looking at her with admiration in his eyes.

'How did you work it out?' he asked.

Mia shrugged. 'I told you, it's easier when you can visualise it. Plus I knew Jorge would have a basic route, he always used to like having a plan as a child. People don't change all that much.' Mia suddenly thought of the boy who had protected her when they were young and her eyes welled up with tears. 'Or maybe they do.'

Will looked as though he wanted to reach out and comfort her, but he didn't move. Mia understood, but she would have liked the consolation.

'So now we just have to work out where he's going to be next on his route,' she said, swallowing her moment of grief for the boy her brother once was.

'Well, we know he was in Jamaica five days ago. If he's sticking to his normal route, *The Dragon* should be headed towards Tortola now.'

Mia nodded. She was convinced of her theory. Many pirates sailed haphazardly through the waters of the Caribbean, waiting near known trade routes for the merchant ships to pass, but her brother would be different. He'd know the key was to keep moving. And the course he'd chosen took *The Flaming Dragon* backwards and forwards over many of the main trade routes of the Caribbean.

'Tortola,' Will murmured. 'Where on Tortola would he be?'

He jumped up from the bed and leaned over her again, this time his excitement making him forget he was trying to keep his distance. His arm brushed the bare skin just above Mia's clavicle. They both froze, then Will pulled away as if he'd been burned.

He took a step back and cleared his throat.

'Would you be so kind to pass me the map of Tortola?'

Wordlessly Mia rifled through the pieces of paper until she found the detailed map of Tortola. It showed all the inlets and bays and places a ship could anchor around the island.

'And the merchant ship sailing schedules.'

Mia flicked through the papers again until she found a list of all the major merchant ships in the area and their dates and ports of departure. She watched him as one by one he traced their route on the map.

'We've got four potential targets,' he said excitedly. 'If your brother sticks to the same sort of time gap in between attacking the merchant ships, we've got about three days until his next attack. There are four ships sailing close to Tortola in the next week.'

'So if we're right about Jorge's pattern of sailing, he'll attack one of those.'

Will nodded. 'The only problem is we've got no idea which he'll go for. We could be waiting for one merchant ship to pass whilst he's off attacking another.'

Mia thought for a moment before speaking, 'Then we need to narrow down where he will be before the attacks.'

'Go on.'

'Well, we know he often shelters in secluded coves and bays and we think he's going to attack a ship off Tortola or one of the neighbouring islands in the next week.'

'So he's most likely anchored somewhere just off the coast of Tortola, resting his crew before their next attack,' Will finished the thought for her.

They turned back to the map of Tortola.

'It's only small, and would probably only take us a day to sail around.'

'That might be the only way,' Mia said hesitantly.

'You've got another idea?'

'You won't like it.'

He raised his eyebrows, waiting for her to continue.

'We could check the weather report.'

Mia waited for a laugh or his quick disagreement.

'I suppose we could check it,' he said eventually, 'There might be something in there we could use.'

Well, that was unexpected.

Mia picked it up from where he'd dropped it on the desk the day before and began reading. After a minute she realised he was looking at her, his head cocked to one side.

'What?' she asked.

'How do you know how to read?' he asked her.

It was a fair enough question. Most daughters of a runaway slave and a sailor wouldn't be able to tell their a's from their b's.

'My mother hated not being able to read. She paid a man to teach us when I was about six. Jorge could never see the point, but I loved how suddenly a jumble of lines became something intelligible.'

She pushed away the memory of her and her brother sitting on Señor Hermes's front porch, arguing over which book they were going to struggle through next.

'Wind speed is picking up over the next few days, strong gusts, mainly east to west.'

Will didn't respond. Mia decided she would just push on.

'No storms for the next few days. In fact, it looks like it's going to be pretty perfect weather.'

He looked dubious, 'There were some clouds bubbling up this morning....'

Mia put down the weather report and turned to face him, 'There's no point in continuing if you're not going to take it seriously.'

Will opened his mouth as if he were about to say something, but then a thought must have occurred to him because his face lit up.

'Strong winds you said, east to west.'

Mia nodded.

'Then if *The Dragon* is planning on sheltering in a quiet bay it would make sense to choose one on the west of the island, protected from the wind.'

He was right. Mia leaned forward so she could see the map of Tortola on the bed.

'Here—' Will pointed '—there are three possibilities.' He pointed out three bays on the west coast of Tortola. 'And it looks like one of them would be too shallow for a ship of *The Flaming Dragon*'s size.'

'So we're down to two,' Mia said, sensing Will's excitement.

She didn't feel excited, she felt dread. Dread that the closer they got to Tortola the sooner she would have to confront her brother and tell him she'd betrayed him. She wasn't having second thoughts, she knew she couldn't let him continue to rob and kill people and keep a clear conscience, but she most certainly wasn't looking forward to seeing him again.

Chapter Eight

'So what's the plan?' Lieutenant Glass asked as he strolled up behind Will on the deck.

Will took a second to temper his reply before answering. He didn't like the Lieutenant. He wasn't sure exactly why. Certainly the man had an abrupt way about him and he looked down on everyone who wasn't his social equal, but that described about half the men of Will's acquaintance. No, there was something else Will didn't like about him that he just couldn't quite put his finger on.

'The plan?' he asked.

'Yes. What are we to do when we reach the first bay?'

He really didn't want to share his strategy with Glass. It wasn't a big secret; he'd talked it through with Mia the night before, but he felt as if he wanted to keep something up his sleeve when it came to the Lieutenant.

'There's not much to it really,' Will said. 'We'll approach the bay by hugging the coastline. If *The Flaming Dragon* is anchored there won't be much time for the pirates to come about and make a dash for it. We'll have them trapped.'

'They do have superior firepower,' Glass said sceptically.

'I'm not planning on giving them much chance to fire on us.'

'We should call in the Navy.'

Will had feared this might be what Glass wanted. The Navy man was there to keep an eye on things and no doubt if he thought there was a chance they would actually come upon *The Flaming Dragon* he would call upon the full force of the Navy to swoop in and take some of the credit.

'This is just a hunch,' Will stated slowly. 'I wouldn't want to cry wolf. We're right at the very beginning of the hunt, and I'm not expecting to apprehend Del Torres in a couple of days. Yes, it'd be a bonus if we did, but I'm not expecting it.'

Glass seemed to accept that. He could hardly quibble; the Navy had been after Del Torres for nearly two years and had nothing to show for it.

Will saw movement out of the corner of his eye. Mia had emerged from below decks and had started to walk towards them before pausing. She hesitated a second before turning around and making her way to the back of the ship. He didn't blame her—if he could have avoided being cornered by Glass he would have. Nevertheless he wished she'd come over. He wanted to talk to her.

Things had been rather uncomfortable between them even after their talk yesterday. Her words just kept circling in his mind: she'd actually wanted him to kiss her. Yes, she'd followed that with some other thoughts on the matter, but the thing that stuck was that she'd wanted to be kissed.

That had made it even harder to resist. He knew he'd acted quite strangely whilst they'd been looking at the maps, but he'd felt awkward. He tried so hard not to touch her, not to give himself any temptation, that it must have been obvious to Mia. Then when his arm had brushed her skin he'd reacted badly, as if he'd been burned.

Mia had looked hurt and he didn't blame her. If she'd acted as if touching him was that toxic, he'd be upset, too.

He wanted things to go back to how they were before he'd kissed her. Well, before he'd kissed her for the second time. Maybe without so many lust-ful thoughts on his part. He had a job to do and the delightful Mia Del Torres was proving to be a distraction. Will wasn't used to a woman get-ting under his skin like Mia was. He'd never been someone who had needed others to entertain him, often quite happy in his own company. This con-stant desire to know where Mia was and what she was doing was a new experience for him.

Will turned back to Glass. 'Was there anything else?' he asked.

'If you're sure about not involving the Navy…'

'I'm sure.'

He pushed himself up from the rail and ambled towards the back of the ship.

'Good morning,' he said as he came up behind Mia.

'I didn't want to disturb your intimate chat with Lieutenant Glass,' Mia said with a smile.

Will was pleased she was looking more relaxed today, more her normal self.

'How kind of you,' he said drily.

'What did he want?'

'He wanted to call in the Navy.'

Mia laughed. 'Of course he did.'

'I refused.'

'Good.'

Will stood for a few seconds looking at the view. Tortola had been sighted at dawn. They were approaching from the west, but the Captain had turned slightly so they were heading to the southern tip of the island. From there they would head up the coast and check out the two bays they'd decided on the day before. If they didn't find *The Flaming Dragon* sheltered in one of those two bays, they would make a lap of the island, checking out all the other possible anchorages.

'It's beautiful, isn't it?' Mia said quietly.

It was beautiful. The sloping lush green interior was a perfect contrast to the white sand of the beaches. There were a few houses dotted about on the hillsides, but all in all the island looked peaceful and idyllic. The finishing touch was the cloudless Caribbean sky.

'I've never left Barbados before,' Mia said. 'I've spent all my life so close to hundreds of beautiful islands and I've never seen any of them.'

'Most people don't explore what's on their doorstep. Look at me, I've been all over Europe, the Caribbean, even parts of India, but I've never set foot in Cornwall. Or Wales.'

'Wouldn't it be nice to spend a lifetime exploring

these islands, sailing from one to another, spending each day discovering a new paradise?'

He loved how her eyes lit up as she talked about her dreams and felt a pang of sorrow that once he'd caught her brother he wouldn't be spending his days with her. She'd probably return to Barbados and he'd be expected to go back to England, his brother avenged, to run the family estate.

'How long until we reach the first bay?' Mia asked.

'A couple of hours, three at most.'

'Are you nervous?'

Will wondered that himself. He'd been in lots of skirmishes. He'd risked his life time and time again and he'd never suffered too much with nerves. He had certainly experienced the surge of adrenaline as he'd charged into danger and on numerous occasions he'd known it was a fair chance he wouldn't escape with his life, but he'd never really been a nervous person.

So the faint sensation of a rat gnawing at his gut was unfamiliar to him. He wondered if it could be nerves—maybe he was losing his edge—but he wasn't sure. He always told himself there was no point in feeling nervous. Either he would live or die and no amount of apprehension would change that.

'No,' he said, not sure if he was lying. 'Are you?'

'I'm petrified.'

He reached out to touch her. He wanted to caress her cheek, pull her body close to his and hold her tight, but he knew he couldn't. Instead he patted her firmly on the upper arm. The safe zone.

It felt so inadequate. He could tell she was hurting, terrified at the prospect of seeing her brother and him finding out she'd aided in his capture. A mere pat on the arm wasn't going to do anything to comfort her.

Mia looked at him sadly. She looked so vulnerable he just wanted to protect her from everything that was to come, but that was impossible. The next few days were going to be the hardest of her life and because he'd overstepped the line and kissed her he couldn't even comfort her as a true friend should.

'How did you become a pirate hunter?' Mia asked him suddenly.

He wondered if she was just changing the subject because she felt awkward. Probably, but there was real curiosity in her eyes, as well.

He debated how to answer. Normally he wasn't one to confide in others. He nearly made some glib comment to avoid the question, but he realised Mia deserved more than that. It would take her mind off what was to come, even just for a few minutes, and that would be worth baring a little of his soul.

'I've always been good at finding people,' he started, 'even as a child. My brother, Richard, refused to play hide-and-seek with me after a while, said I must be cheating. I wasn't.'

Mia smiled as if she could imagine a younger version of him playing with his brother.

'I just worked out how to read people and the trail they left.'

And that was how it had all started. Throughout school he'd been a bit of a loner. He'd always had friends, people to talk to when he wanted, but he had chosen to spend a lot of time alone.

'A boy went missing whilst I was at school. The masters all tried to find him, even called in the authorities. He was missing for five days. We had a free afternoon on a Saturday—I found him within two hours.'

'How?'

Will shrugged. It was difficult to explain. It was just a talent he had.

'I'd watched him in the weeks before he disappeared. I watched everyone. He was unhappy. A couple of the boys in the older years were bullying him. That's why he left.'

'And that knowledge helped you find him?'

'There was more. I sneaked into his room one night and checked what he had taken with him.'

'What had he taken?' Mia was engrossed in his story. His plan to distract her had definitely worked.

'Hardly anything. So it had been a spur-of-the-moment decision. Which meant he couldn't have got far. Not without warm clothes and hardly any money.'

'But how did that lead you to where he was actually hiding?'

He shrugged. He wasn't quite sure how to explain it. He had a natural instinct for these things—sometimes he could look at situations and just know where people had gone.

'There weren't really many options. My theory was he was hiding nearby until the commotion died down and he could sneak back in and get some of his things and, more important, some money. Then he would go and throw himself on the mercy of some relative or other who would have been sufficiently worried by his disappearance they wouldn't send him back to school straight away.'

'So where was he?'

'In the games shed at the end of one of the fields.'

'Hadn't the schoolmasters searched them?'

'They searched a few of the buildings close to the school, but everyone assumed he'd run away and therefore wouldn't be hanging around close by.'

'Everyone but you.'

Will nodded.

'So you took him back to school?'

Will laughed, 'No. That would have been cruel. I sneaked him out some warm clothes and gave him some money so he could get on his way.'

Mia nodded as if she approved.

'So how did you go from finding missing schoolboys to hunting pirates?'

It was a question Will often asked himself.

'Up until two years ago I was living in London and I spent most of my time hunting for missing people. Sometimes the authorities would come to me for help, more often it would be the families. But normally I wouldn't return the person to their family…not if they were the reason they'd run away.'

'You're a real-life hero, aren't you?'

Will looked at her to see if she was joking. Her face remained completely serious.

'No,' he said slowly, 'I just think people shouldn't have to live their lives in fear.'

'That's the description of a good man,' Mia persisted. 'But you still haven't told me what led you here.'

'My brother, Richard, was the eldest. He was the heir to our father's estate. And when our father died he became a fantastic Lord of the Manor.' Will paused, taking a few seconds to remember his brother, the man he'd looked up to. 'He owned land out in the Caribbean and he'd heard rumours that slaves working on the estate were being mistreated. Richard set sail for Jamaica two years ago.'

He remembered waving his brother off, thinking nothing of his trip across the globe, knowing Richard would be absent for a year but expecting his brother to return home in the not-too-distant future. Will had spent a bit of time travelling himself so thought nothing of a sea voyage and a foray into unknown lands.

'His ship was attacked by pirates. They took Richard captive—I think they recognised he was a man of some means.' Will paused, feeling his voice catching in his throat. 'He died before a ransom demand could be made.'

He looked down at the wooden rail and tried to

compose himself. Even after all this time he found it upsetting talking about how his brother had met his end.

'How did he die?' Mia asked gently.

'Fever. Richard never had the most robust health.'

Will closed his eyes. He felt Mia moving closer to him, hovering as if she couldn't decide whether to reach out and touch him. She placed a soft hand on his bare arm.

'You loved him,' Mia said quietly.

Will nodded.

'And that's why you're here?'

He nodded again, not trusting himself to speak.

She moved even closer, her hand still resting on his arm. He could feel the heat of her body as it brushed against his and for a second he just wanted to lose himself in her arms.

'Was it Jorge?' she asked eventually.

He didn't know how to answer. The truth was going to hurt her, make her realise the sort of man her brother had become.

'I believe so.' He saw her face fall and felt the need to explain further. '*The Flaming Dragon* was sighted in the area where my brother's ship was attacked.'

'It could have been a coincidence.'

'And his body was delivered to our Jamaican estate with a note.'

Mia shook her head in disbelief. 'Why would they do that?'

'It was a taunt, a warning. A warning to all the nobility in the Caribbean that the waters weren't safe for the rich or the poor.'

She withdrew her hand from his arm and hugged her own body.

'I'm so sorry,' she whispered, 'I had no idea.'

'Mia…' Will started to say.

'No. Please.' Her voice broke. 'I can't make excuses for my brother any longer. For years I've buried my head in the sand and tried to remain ignorant of what he's doing. I'm so sorry. I wish I could bring your brother back.'

'I wish that, too,' Will said. 'He was a better man than I, a better Lord of the Manor.'

'You haven't taken up the title?' Mia asked.

'Not until Richard is avenged.'

'I'm sure your brother was a good man, but I don't believe he was a better man than you,' Mia said quietly.

'He was kind,' Will explained, 'and sensitive. He'd always know instinctively if something was wrong.'

He felt Mia's eyes searching his face, but found he couldn't look at her. The temptation to seek solace in her arms would be too much.

'He knew what was right and what was wrong, and he expected others to respect the same values.'

'I think you're probably more like your brother than you give yourself credit for.'

His eyes rose and met hers and Will knew if he wasn't careful Mia could make him forget everything: the pain he felt over Richard's death and the rage he felt towards the men who'd taken him. And whilst part of him wanted her to soothe his pain, he knew he needed the rage to drive him on and succeed in his mission to avenge his brother.

Chapter Nine

'Land, ho,' the sailor up in the crow's nest shouted from his perch.

Mia stepped away from Will. It wasn't good for her sanity to be too close to him for too long.

They both peered over the side of the ship into the distance. She strained her eyes trying to make out the outline of the island, but at first couldn't see anything. It was only after a few minutes that a shape started to form, as if emerging from a haze.

'Tortola,' Mia murmured.

She wondered if this was going to be where they apprehended her brother and his crew. Part of her hoped for a quick resolution to their hunt—she was feeling guilty about betraying her brother even if he was a murderous pirate. The rest of her wanted this voyage to run on for months, months of sailing the Caribbean Sea with Will as her companion

'The population is tiny,' Will said.

'Hmm?' Mia wondered if she'd missed the beginning of the conversation whilst she was daydreaming.

'The population of Tortola,' Will said again, 'it's tiny, so if your brother has anchored off the coast it shouldn't be too hard to find someone who has seen him.'

'What I don't understand is why the Navy couldn't find a trace of him.'

Will inclined his head towards Lieutenant Glass. 'Would you tell a pompous fool like Glass anything?'

Mia laughed.

'I suppose not. I'd probably dislike him so much I'd send him in entirely the opposite direction.'

'Exactly. The Navy have failed not because the pirates are supernaturally good at hiding from them, but because they are generally disliked by most of the people of the Caribbean.'

Mia gazed out at the tropical paradise that was growing closer by the second. She could see the lush interior rising up to a peak in the middle surrounded by golden sandy beaches.

'I wish...' Mia started to say, then realised she

was speaking aloud thoughts that should be kept private.

Will looked at her with interest. 'Yes?'

She didn't know what to say. She couldn't tell him the truth, that she wished their hunt was over and they were stranded on a tropical beach. Just the two of them. Preferably for a very long time. With very little clothing.

'What do you wish, Mia?' he asked her softly, his voice seductive and low.

She swallowed convulsively as she felt her cheeks starting to burn. There was no way she was going to come up with a convincing lie; her mind had gone completely blank.

'Sometimes I wish life were simpler,' she stated, wondering if that was going to satisfy him. He stayed quiet, indicating for her to continue. 'I was thinking it would be wonderful to live secluded from the world, in a tropical paradise.'

'And would you be living there on your own?'

Mia glanced up at him and wished she hadn't. She hadn't realised he was standing quite so close. Momentarily she forgot how to speak.

'Yes. No.'

'Which is it?' Will asked, turning to face her

properly and closing the gap between them even more.

'No.'

'Who would you like to join you in your little paradise?'

Mia started drumming her fingers on the wooden rail, trying to channel all her pent-up emotions into physical movement.

'Erm, well…' She wished she could pull herself together and utter more than a few barely coherent sounds, but she felt as though her brain had taken a holiday and had left her with only the fire that was burning inside her. A fire of desire.

'Maybe there's a friend,' Will said, 'or a maiden aunt. Or one of the girls you used to work with.'

He covered her hand with his own and stilled her drumming fingers.

'I really hope it isn't a Spanish admirer or an Italian lover.'

'Why?' Mia managed to whisper.

'Because then I would be very, very jealous.'

'Mr Greenacre,' the Captain said as he walked towards them, 'what are your instructions, sir?'

Will tore his eyes away from hers and immediately Mia felt bereft. She burned for him, wanted him with a passion and a force she'd never experienced before. She felt drunk, and every minute she spent in his company the sensation was growing stronger. Then when someone else took his attention she felt empty.

'Stay within one hundred yards of shore where possible,' Will instructed the Captain, 'and we'll take each bay in turn. Any of your men not occupied on deck are to be ready and waiting with the cannons.'

The Captain nodded and walked away.

Will turned back to her and smiled, but there was a hint of sadness in his eyes.

'We probably won't chance upon *The Flaming Dragon* today but I'd feel much less worried if you went below decks.'

Mia felt a flutter of warmth inside at his concern.

'I'm not going to hide,' she said softly, 'and below decks is not much safer than above.'

He must have seen the resolute expression on her face because he didn't argue any further.

'At least stay well back from the sides of the ship so stray bullets aren't going to get you.'

'I'm sure I can do that.'

She watched as he walked away and then she took a few steps away from the rail and sat herself on an upturned barrel. As the crew hustled around

her Mia only had eyes for Will. She was in dangerous territory and she didn't know how she could
extricate herself. Her plan to acknowledge her attraction for him but overrule it with all the reasons
they couldn't be together worked well in theory.
But when he covered her hand with his and their
bodies swayed together it was as if all common
sense and reason fled. She wanted him more than
she had ever wanted anyone. She wanted to kiss
him and caress him and writhe underneath him.

The irony was she could have all of that, but she
wanted more. She wanted love and respect and a
shared life. There was no way she could fool herself into thinking that was ever going to happen,
no matter how often she wished it. Will was a focused man and she was a means to an ends. With
her help, his job of finding *The Flaming Dragon*
was much more likely to succeed.

Mia wondered if she should just give in to her
desires, allow herself a few days of intimate bliss
with Will, something that would keep her going
through all the lonely years ahead. As she felt her
resolve slipping, the image of her mother, welcoming another paying lover into the house, surged into
her mind. In the image her mother was smiling,

but it didn't quite reach her eyes. Mia knew to give herself to anyone but the man she loved would be a mistake, one she would have to live with for ever.

She resolved not to think about it any more. But that was a difficult undertaking when Will strode past her resting place every few minutes all tanned and muscled and confident, shouting instructions to the crew. He was so confident and in control the men followed his commands without question.

Instead of thinking about Will she tried focusing on the scenery, the sky—which was remarkably cloudless and boring—and the other sailors. It wasn't long before she was comparing every man to Will and finding them all coming up short.

Stop it, she told herself firmly. In the end she rested her head back against a mast pole and allowed the sun to warm her skin.

'Miss Del Torres.' Lieutenant Glass's clipped tones woke her from a contented doze.

He was towering over her and blocking out the sun. Mia shivered.

'How can I help you, Lieutenant?' She tried to sound as polite as possible, a difficult task when she hated the man.

'I just wanted to come and have a talk with you,' he said. 'Mr Greenacre seems to find you fascinating company. I thought I would find out what the attraction is.'

Mia immediately felt the hairs on her neck stand up.

'I'm merely assisting Mr Greenacre with his search for *The Flaming Dragon*.'

'And your brother.'

'And my brother,' Mia repeated, trying not to grit her teeth.

'How do you see this all ending for you, Miss Del Torres?' Glass asked.

Mia stood, not liking the disadvantage she was at with her sitting and him towering over her.

'How do you mean, Lieutenant?'

'When we have captured your brother, what do you think will become of you?'

Mia chose her words carefully. 'I would hope Mr Greenacre and yourself would convey how helpful I have been in the search for *The Flaming Dragon* and put in a good word for me with the Governor.'

'You'd like me to speak on your behalf to the Governor?' Lieutenant Glass asked, giving her a smile that didn't reach his eyes.

'And Mr Greenacre,' Mia added.

'What would I get out of this…favour?'

Mia leaned back, suddenly realising his intentions.

'Help finding *The Flaming Dragon*.'

'And?'

Mia felt sick. She couldn't even begin to contemplate what the Lieutenant was suggesting.

'There's got to be more in it for me than that—surely you must agree. Some extra little incentive to speak favourably of you.'

Mia opened and closed her mouth a few times, trying to think of a suitable response. She was in an impossible situation. If she rebuffed the Lieutenant completely, he would speak against her when they returned to Barbados. The other option made her skin crawl. Glass was a snake. Although not physically unattractive, he repulsed her and she realised she'd rather risk a harsher penalty than even contemplate what he was suggesting.

'I'm sorry, Lieutenant, I'd better get below deck,' Mia said without offering an explanation why. She smiled as blandly as she could manage and hurried away.

Closing her cabin door behind her, Mia felt her heart pounding in her chest. She flicked the lock and tested the door. She wouldn't put it past Lieutenant Glass to follow her down to her cabin and reiterate his offer more firmly.

Mia shivered despite the sunlight streaming into the little room. Sometimes she hated being a woman, being subjected to men's whims and fancies. If she were a man, Jorge's brother rather than sister, Glass would never have thought to offer a favourable word in exchange for intimate moments.

Will's face popped into her mind, calming the churning of her stomach. If she were a man, Will Greenacre would not trace his fingers over her skin or hold her gaze those extra few seconds. Maybe being a woman wasn't all that bad.

Chapter Ten

Will thanked another of the crew for their hard work and tried to keep the smile fixed to his face. It had been a long day. They had been circling Tortola, hugging the coastline, since mid-morning. Although they had come across plenty of sheltered coves and secluded bays, none of them had been hiding *The Flaming Dragon*.

He wasn't sure why he was so despondent. It wasn't as if he'd expected success on their first real day. It would have been more than lucky to come across Del Torres in the first location they scoured.

Despite this knowledge Will still felt like the day had been a failure. He wanted some proof, some sign they were on the right track.

He looked around the deck in the fading light and realised it had been a long time since he'd seen Mia. Initially he'd been pleased when he had glimpsed her heading down to her cabin in the late morning, but as the day had worn on he'd missed her presence at his side. He had got dangerously close that morning to leaning in and kissing her again, on the deck of the ship with all the crew's curious eyes watching. He needed to be careful and demonstrate at least a little self-restraint.

With these thoughts in mind he strode across the deck and hurried down the wooden stairs into the darkness. He knocked on Mia's cabin door and waited for an answer. After a few seconds he heard her quiet footsteps approaching the door.

'Who is it?'

'It's me, Will.'

The lock on the door turned and Mia peered out.

'I missed you,' Will said simply. 'On deck.'

'I didn't want to get hit by any stray bullets,' she said with a smile.

'I have to admit there wasn't much chance of that today.'

'So we weren't successful.'

Will shook his head.

'We weren't likely to come across *The Flaming Dragon* on the first day searching,' Mia said practically. 'The Navy have been looking for years.'

'Ah, but the Navy don't have you as their secret weapon.'

'I'm not sure I like being called a weapon. Is it a compliment?'

'Most assuredly.'

Will was beginning to feel better about the day already.

'We've anchored near a small settlement. Doesn't look big enough to be called a proper town, but apparently it's Tortola's capital.'

'So are we going to wait until tomorrow and then go and talk to the locals?'

Will felt the mischief flashing in his eyes.

'Why wait until tomorrow?' he asked, 'when tonight lips will be loosened by alcohol.'

As he said it Will felt his gaze drawn towards Mia's own lips, luscious, full, just a little moist and very warm and inviting.

'You're going to row over now?' Mia asked, sounding excited by the idea.

Will nodded.

'And how are you planning on getting back?'

'Tubs, one of the men, reckons he can find his way to row back to the ship in absolute darkness.' Will grinned at her dubious look. 'And if not I'm sure there are plenty of beds if you have the right-coloured coin.'

'Are you going on your own?' Mia asked.

'I was planning on asking the Lieutenant if he'd like to join me for an intimate drink by the light of a candle,' Will said, 'but if you really wanted to get your feet back on dry land I expect Glass won't mind postponing our date.'

'I don't want to spoil your plans.'

'That's settled. Let's leave before Lieutenant Glass finds out and insists on chaperoning us.'

'It would be more fun without a chaperone,' Mia murmured quietly.

Will felt his heart pound in his chest. A whole evening alone with just Mia. He couldn't think of anything more wonderful, or more tempting. Their eyes locked for an instant and Will felt a jolt of excitement rush through his body.

He watched as she hurried into her cabin to fetch a shawl to keep her warm after dark. He felt like he was watching her all the time. Every minute of the day he had an awareness of where she was, catching glimpses of her out of the corner of his eye. And when she disappeared he felt bereft. Although they'd only known each other for a short time Mia was becoming the person he turned to if he felt unsure, the one he wanted to share every success with and dissect every failure.

'Shall we make our escape?'

Will offered her his arm and led her on to the deck and towards the back of the ship. Tubs, a sailor with leathery skin and a toothless grin, was waiting for them and silently nodded a greeting.

'Watch your step, sir,' he said, 'there's a bit of a drop from the ship to the boat.'

Will peered over the side. A rope ladder was swinging against the side of the ship, hitting the wood with a soft thud every few seconds. The small boat below rocked gently in the current and Will could see there was a few-foot gap between it and the ladder.

'Will you be all right?' he asked Mia.

'If you catch me.'

He felt a surge of guilty pleasure at the thought of a legitimate reason for holding Mia in his arms again.

'Of course.'

He swung his legs over the rail of the ship and began his descent. Climbing down the rope ladder was harder than he expected; it was a flimsy thing and every time he shifted his weight the ladder swung precariously from side to side. As he reached the bottom rung he glanced beneath him. The boat seemed quite a distance off and he hoped he landed squarely. Letting go of the ladder, he dropped down, bending his knees instinctively on impact and finding his balance immediately.

'You make it look so easy, Mr Greenacre,' Mia shouted down from her position above him.

He watched as she daintily swung her legs over the rail and carefully tested out the rope ladder. He tried not to stare at the honey-coloured skin of her ankles as she lifted her skirt so it wouldn't get caught beneath her feet. From her ankles his gaze moved up her legs to the shapely backside making its way towards him. He had an overwhelming urge to reach up and squeeze her buttocks through the thick layers of her dress, but somehow managed to restrain himself.

'Are you ready for me?' Mia asked, looking dubiously at the drop from her position at the bottom of the ladder into his arms.

'Ready and waiting.'

Mia craned her neck one last time to check his position, then without any hesitation pushed herself from the ladder and into his arms. In the milliseconds it took for her to drop through the air Will felt a surge of elation. She trusted him. She trusted him enough to believe he'd catch her no matter what.

Then she landed.

'Oof,' Will groaned.

He'd caught her—actually, he'd caught her quite magnificently. His arms encircled her waist and slowly he lowered her feet to the floor.

With his arms still around her Mia turned to face him. Will enjoyed the closeness of her body pressed against his and let his arms linger for just a few seconds longer.

'Oof?' she asked.

Will frowned.

'Am I that heavy I knock the wind from you?'

He grinned. 'You must be. I felt quite stunned.'

She raised a hand and swatted him gently on the shoulder.

'You really know how to compliment a lady.'

Will was about to say something very charming and witty in reply when Tubs called down, 'Watch out below.' Will was forced to let go of Mia as they shuffled apart to make way for the old sailor.

'You get yourself sitting down, sir, otherwise a little boat like this will capsize,' Tubs said. 'Leave all that romance nonsense for dry land.'

Suitably chastised, Will edged around the seaman and took a seat next to Mia.

Quickly they moved away from the ship. Tubs's skinny arms belied their strength and in a few minutes they were closer to shore than the ship.

Will felt Mia shift on the wooden bench.

'Are you comfortable?'

She nodded. 'Just a little cold.'

The change in temperature as the sun went down was surprising. Balmy and hot in the daytime, the Caribbean air certainly had a slight chill about it in the evening. Will cursed himself for not bringing an overcoat—he would have gladly given it up to make Mia more comfortable.

'Come closer,' he said quietly, so Tubs wouldn't hear.

Mia looked at him with indecision in her eyes.

'I promise not to ravish you,' he said, trying to keep his tone cheery and light, 'but it might make you a little warmer.'

As she scooted her bottom closer to his he silently cursed his promise not to ravish her. He was finding it increasingly difficult to keep chaste thoughts when Mia was close.

Her left thigh pressed into his right and slowly Mia relaxed into his body. Gently he placed his arm around her shoulders and little by little she allowed herself to fold into him.

'Better?' he asked softly.

'Better.' She sounded content and comfortable and Will had a sudden urge to tell Tubs to turn around and head out into the open sea and keep going. He wanted to be alone with Mia, outside the constraints of society, not under pressure to complete the task he had set himself. Just man and woman and their mutual desire. There was no way they could be together in the real world, their lives following such different paths, but for a few moments in his imagination he could see a future with him and Mia happy without the judgement of society.

It was a strange thought for Will, who for so long had assumed he would spend his life alone, but Mia was getting to him, making him re-evaluate what he thought was important. Maybe he *could* open up his heart and his life enough to share it with someone else.

'There we are, sir,' Tubs said, pulling the small boat up alongside the wooden jetty.

'Thank you, Tubs.'

Will reluctantly stood and hopped out of the boat,

reaching down to take Mia's hand and help her on to dry land.

'I'll wait for you here, sir.'

'If you'd be more comfortable back on the ship...' Will started to offer.

'Don't you worry about me, sir, you go ahead and enjoy yourself with the lady. I don't mind waiting all night, if you catch my drift.'

The old man gave him a leery wink, then settled down in the bottom of the boat and promptly closed his eyes.

Mia giggled quietly.

'Don't encourage him,' Will said. He picked up her hand and slotted it into the crook of his arm and set off down the jetty.

The town rose up the gentle hill before them. There were a few welcoming taverns along the waterfront with lamps lighting up the exterior. Most of the rest of the small settlement was in darkness. Tortola didn't have a raucous reputation like Jamaica and Barbados, but he hadn't expected it to be quite so sleepy.

'So what's the plan?' Mia asked him as they walked past the first of the taverns.

'I was going to choose one of these fine establishments to buy my lady a drink.'

'How very generous of you.'

As they passed the second of the taverns the door swung open. A woman with arms the size of two fat logs and a chest an opera singer would be proud of heaved a drunken man through the door and out into the street.

'Maybe not that one,' Mia whispered, earning her a glare from the beefy barmaid.

The third tavern they reached seemed quieter and slightly more salubrious. The wooden sign hanging above the doorway declared this was the Golden Chest.

They entered and the whole tavern suddenly fell silent. Thirty pairs of eyes regarded them as they walked through the warm interior and found an empty table.

'I don't think they get many visitors,' Mia whispered.

Will checked the faces staring at them. They didn't look openly hostile, just curious at who these intruders into their tavern were.

'Good evening,' Will said with a cheery smile.

One by one the conversations started up again until there was a quiet background hum.

'What can I get you?' a young woman in her early twenties asked as she came sauntering over, eyeing Will up and down and giving him a winning smile.

'A pint of ale.' Will turned to Mia.

'Rum,' she said sweetly.

'Anything else takes your fancy you just let me know,' the barmaid said flirtatiously.

'You've got an admirer,' Mia said as the barmaid went to fetch their drinks.

Will looked at her carefully. He was trying to assess if she was jealous. He wanted her to be jealous, just like he would be if a man started vying for her attention.

'You from that fancy ship?' an old man at the next table asked, leaning over towards Will.

There was no use denying it, a town this size probably didn't get more than one strange ship anchor each night. He wasn't sure Captain Little's vessel counted as fancy, though.

'Yes.'

'What's your business in Tortola?'

Straight to the point. Will wanted information, but he didn't think coming out and asking about *The Flaming Dragon* directly was going to get him very far. He was saved from answering by Mia.

'I'd heard the men of Tortola were the handsomest and strongest and bravest in the Caribbean,' Mia said, 'And I forced him to bring me here.'

This got a murmur of approval from the mainly male occupants of the tavern.

'I wanted to see these marvellous specimens of manhood for myself.'

'You can see my marvellous specimen of manhood, darling,' a voice called from the other side of the tavern.

Will felt his temper rise, but squashed it back down. He knew Mia was doing this for him, gaining the men's trust so they would be more likely to talk about *The Flaming Dragon*. He just wished she'd do it in a less suggestive way.

'I wonder…' Mia pondered aloud. 'If I wanted to meet the bravest, strongest, most handsome man in Tortola, who would that be?'

'You're looking for me, miss,' a brawny man in his mid-thirties yelled, standing up and thumping his fist on the table, 'I've fought twenty men and never lost.'

Mia smiled at him sweetly, then addressed the rest of the room. 'So is this fine fellow the bravest amongst you?'

'He wishes.' Another man jumped to his feet. 'I've wrestled a shark and lived.'

'Lies,' the first man shouted. 'You got those shark teeth you're always harping on about from a dead shark down on Cane Garden Bay.'

'Are you calling me a liar?' The shark wrestler turned red in the face.

'Boys, no fighting, please,' Mia said with enough charm and authority to shut them up. 'Are there no other contenders for the title?'

'Aye, girl, I be the bravest man amongst this sorry lot.'

Mia turned to see a small man in his forties stand up and address her. He was a wisp of a man with just skin on his bones and a pale complexion.

'You may be brave, Pablo, but you definitely aren't strong or handsome,' another voice called out from across the tavern. Everyone laughed.

'Tell me, Pablo, impress me with your bravery.'

'I told the bloodthirsty pirate Del Torres he could get right off my land.'

Will tried not to react to the comment and waited to see how Mia would handle this information.

'Del Torres is a scary man. I think you're right, you are the bravest man in this tavern. Come and sit with me and you can tell me all about it.'

Will watched as the skinny man proudly strode over to Mia and squeezed on to the bench beside her. Will felt a bubble of anger as the little man stole a glance at her chest and leaned in a little closer than was strictly necessary. He tried to control himself, knowing the information this man had could only help their mission, but all the same he wished Mia wouldn't smile at him so encouragingly.

'Keep your hands to yourself,' Will growled.

'Who's he?' Brave Pablo asked Mia.

'Just my grumpy guardian,' she said with a smile. 'Ignore him.'

Will frowned and was just about to haul the weasel-like Pablo from his seat when he received a sharp kick in the shins from Mia. Folding his arms across his chest, Will restrained himself.

'So tell me about your encounter with the notorious Del Torres,' Mia said, refocusing the conversation.

'What is my reward?' Pablo asked.

Will had to hand it to the scrawny chap, he knew when to bargain with a lady.

'A place in my thoughts as the bravest man of Tortola for ever more.'

'Anything more…physical?'

Mia pretended to look shocked, then leaned towards Pablo and whispered something in his ear.

Pablo's eyes widened to the size of coconuts. Will nearly expired on the spot. He didn't know what Mia had offered for his story, but he was sure he wouldn't approve. This sewer rat of a man didn't deserve to breathe the same air as her, let alone get to enjoy whatever *physical* reward had made his eyes pop out of his head.

Will stood, ready to throw Pablo out into the street. Mia glared at him with such force he immediately sat down again.

'I run a small plantation over on the other side of the island,' Pablo confided proudly to Mia. 'I'd seen that big old pirate ship anchored in Smuggler's Cove, but hadn't paid it much attention. Every few months it seems to anchor up there for a day or two.'

Will marvelled at the Navy's incompetence. They'd spent two years searching for Del Torres and *The Flaming Dragon*. If they'd swallowed their pride and actually asked the locals, he had no doubts they would have caught these pirates months ago.

'I was checking on the boundary wall for the plantation, thought it might have been damaged by one of the storms. I just sat down to rest my

legs for a few minutes when this man came striding towards me.'

Will rather suspected he'd sat down to fall asleep
somewhere away from the watchful eyes of the
plantation owner.

'And that was Del Torres?' Mia asked.

'Well, I didn't know it at the time. I yelled at him
that he was on private land. He just laughed. Came
up to me and asked whether I knew who he was.'

'What happened next?' Mia asked.

Will had to admire her determination. Pablo
wasn't getting away with any detail of this story
untold.

'I told him I didn't care who he was, this was still
private land and he'd better get off it quick.'

Will watched as Pablo turned from centre-of-at-
tention hero to the scared man he must have been
when he realised who he had been talking to.

Slowly the skinny man lifted his shirt. Will
craned his neck to see what he was showing Mia.

'The bastard kicked my ribs in. I was lucky he
didn't puncture a lung.'

Will watched as Mia tried to maintain her composure. Her face lost some of its healthy glow and
the light in her eyes flickered and died.

'He did that to you?' she asked, gesturing at his

deformed ribcage. 'Just for telling him to get off the private land.'

Pablo nodded. 'I thought he was going to kill me.'

'Pablo,' Mia said sincerely, 'I truly think you're the bravest man I've ever met.'

She leaned forward and placed a quick kiss on his lips. The men of the tavern roared their approval. Before Pablo could react, Mia stood and hurried outside.

Will dropped some money on the table and strode after her.

Chapter Eleven

Mia gulped at the salty air as if she were drowning. She'd been so happy with her plan, her little game to draw out any man who might have information about her brother. She hadn't realised she didn't want to know any more about his exploits.

She had wanted to impress Will, make him see she really was committed to helping him. And she was. She'd got more information out of the tavern of locals than Will could ever have done on his own no matter who he bribed.

She just wished she hadn't heard the story about her brother, or seen what he'd done to that poor man's ribs. Every time she sought information about the kind of man Jorge had become she was disgusted.

She jumped as Will placed a hand gently on her shoulder. He had come up behind her so silently she was only aware of his presence when he reached out and stroked the bare skin of her neck.

'Mia' he said, his voice thick with emotion, 'I'm so sorry.'

She wanted to cry and scream and pummel at his chest. She wanted to show the world quite how angry and upset she was, but more than anything she wanted to take comfort in Will's arms. The one thing she couldn't do.

'We know now where to wait for *The Flaming Dragon*,' Mia said, her voice flat.

'I'm sorry you had to see that,' Will persevered. 'I never want you to be upset.'

She felt a hysterical giggle building up in her throat. This whole situation was madness. She was betraying the only family she had, helping to catch her own brother and send him to the gallows, and she was glad about it. Everything she'd learned about her brother in the past few days had confirmed her worst fears. The little boy she'd known and loved was dead already, replaced by a monster of a man.

'Mia,' Will said, as if lost for words.

She turned to face him and looked up into his eyes. Immediately she wished she hadn't. He looked so upset for her, so pained that she'd had to hear those terrible things about her brother. Will was such a good man and she wanted him so badly.

She reached up and stroked his cheek, feeling the stubble under her fingertips, sending shivers over her sensitive skin.

'I wish I could make all of the bad things go away for you.'

He wasn't making resisting him any easier.

'Will you hold me?' Mia asked.

He hesitated, but only for a second. His strong arms enveloped her, folding her into his chest. Mia felt safe and secure and shielded from the world. She wished she could stay wrapped tightly in his arms for the rest of time and not have to face the real world again.

She felt him move his head and drop a gentle kiss on her hair, lingering for a few moments before taking his lips away.

'I know we can't...' Mia struggled to find the right words '...be together, but I really don't want to be alone tonight.'

What she wanted was to kiss him and touch him all over his body. To feel the muscles beneath his shirt and run her fingers all the way down to what lay beneath his breeches. She wanted to writhe beneath him as if they were husband and wife and wake in the morning knowing she would never have to be alone again.

Will swallowed. 'Are you sure it's a good idea?'

'Please,' Mia said, 'just hold me tonight. Nothing more.'

She wanted so much more. She wanted to possess him body and soul. She wanted to be the first thing he thought about when he woke up and the last thing he saw at night. She wanted to spend every moment of every day of every year of the rest of her life with him.

'Just one night,' she said.

He looked torn and for a moment Mia thought he might refuse her.

'How?' he asked, his breathing heavy and his body tense.

'One of these taverns will have a room.'

She couldn't believe she was being so forward and brazen. She'd always prided herself on her maidenly reputation in an environment where there was temptation at every turn.

He grabbed her hand and pulled her towards the next tavern along the waterfront.

'Wait here,' he commanded, disappearing inside the building.

It felt as though he was gone for ages. The minutes stretched out in front of Mia as if tormenting her. She wondered if she might change her mind in his absence, suddenly come to her senses and realise what a bad idea it was to spend the night in close proximity to the man she wanted so badly. Instead the desire to be close to him built and built. She wanted to rest her head against his chest and hear his heart beat after they'd ravished each other to exhaustion.

After a few minutes Will emerged, took her hand, and wordlessly tugged her into the tavern. They sped through the seating area and up a narrow staircase. He paused outside the first door they came to.

'Are you sure about this?' he asked.

'What's the harm of one night?' Mia asked. 'I just don't want to be alone.'

Will dug the key from his pocket and unlocked the door to the room. He pulled her gently inside and quickly locked the door behind them. Two candles were burning on either side of the bed, but otherwise the room was in darkness.

Now they were inside, just the two of them, Mia didn't know what to do with herself. Will took her hand and led her to the bed.

'If you want to undress a little,' he said, his voice

unusually husky, 'I can turn around, or go outside. Whichever you would prefer.'

Mia knew she shouldn't. Her clothes were a barrier between her and forbidden pleasures, but she couldn't imagine getting any rest whilst still wearing her dress.

'You don't have to leave,' she said.

Slowly she unlaced her dress, aware of Will's eyes following her every move. When the bodice section was sufficiently loose she turned around to preserve a little modesty and lifted the material over her head.

She heard Will's breathing become more ragged.

'You don't know what you do to me, Mia,' he said quietly.

Mia wrapped her arms around herself, suddenly very self-conscious. She was still clad in her white undergown, which reached her mid-thigh, but she might as well have been naked the way Will was looking at her.

Slowly she slipped into the bed, pulling the sheet up to cover her breasts, aware her nipples were hard and most likely visible through the thin cotton.

'Your turn,' she said.

Will looked at her as though she were mad, then slipped his shirt off over his head.

Mia couldn't even pretend to look away. She had run her fingers over his chest just a couple of days ago when they had both lain exhausted on the beach. Back then she'd thought he had the finest physique of all the men of her acquaintance. Now she corrected that to the finest physique of all the men in the world. His chest was taut and toned and his abdominal muscles defined. She just wanted to touch them, feel the hardness beneath her fingers.

'And your breeches?' Mia asked.

Will laughed. 'That I can't do,' he said. 'Trust me.'

Mia's eyes drifted down to the coarse material of his trousers and widened as she realised there was a sizeable bulge.

'Are you sure about this, Mia?' he asked again. 'I can still get another room.'

'What's the harm in holding me?' she asked.

He didn't answer. She knew the harm. Holding could lead to touching, which could lead to much, much more. Something they might regret in the cold light of day.

'I promise to behave,' Mia said.

'It's not you I'm worried about.'

After a final moment's hesitation Will lowered himself into the bed and slipped under the sheets.

Already Mia could feel the heat radiating from his body. She wanted to press herself up against him, feel his bare skin against hers.

'Mia,' Will said quietly.

'Yes?'

She looked up at him.

'I want you to know I want you. I know I can't have you, but I want you.'

She nodded, not trusting herself to speak.

Slowly he lifted an arm and placed it around her shoulder, pulling her into his chest. She allowed herself to relax and rest her cheek on his velvety skin. He stroked her hair and Mia realised she could hear his heart beating in his chest.

She moved closer to him, allowing her legs to push up against his thighs. For a moment she let herself imagine this was her life. That every night she would slip into bed with Will and curl up beside him. It sounded like heaven.

She was aware of every little movement he made. Even the rise and fall of his chest as he breathed seemed exaggerated. After a few minutes Mia relaxed a little. She was in bed with Will. He was holding her and it felt right. She felt as if she were safe and cared for. Gradually her body began to feel heavy and her eyes fluttered closed. Surely she could just rest for a few minutes, then be fully able to enjoy her night in Will's arms.

Chapter Twelve

Torture. Pure and simple torture. It had been the worst night of his life and perversely also the best. He hadn't slept a wink. Mia had awoken a beast inside him as she stripped off in front of him. Through the thick cotton that made up her chemise he'd seen every womanly curve of her body and every detail upon it. He fancied he could even make out the exact berry hue of her nipples.

He groaned at the thought of her nipples. Someone was torturing him and it just wasn't fair.

Then she'd invited him into bed, pressed herself up against him and proceeded to fall asleep. It was as if she were oblivious to his discomfort.

He'd lain perfectly still all night long, watching her as she slept, fantasising about all the wicked things he wanted to do to her. And there were many wicked things, enough to keep his mind churning and his loins in a state of readiness all through the long night.

Mia murmured something in her sleep and snuggled in closer to him. He didn't move. She mumbled something else, frowning slightly and creasing the skin between her perfectly shaped eyebrows.

Will hadn't thought this torture could get any worse, but when Mia inched even closer and hooked her leg over his he thought he might die from the pure agony of desire.

Her smooth thigh rubbed against his trousers and was getting dangerously close to his manhood. The very same manhood that had stood to attention all night, aroused by the woman beside him.

Mia murmured something again and as he looked down at her face her eyes fluttered open.

Her first reaction on seeing him was to smile, a contented smile of someone who doesn't quite grasp the implications of what they are seeing.

'Good morning,' Will said.

Mia's eyes widened as she realised she was draped over him in such a provocative fashion. Quickly she sat up, blushing slightly as she readjusted her chemise to try to preserve some modesty.

'Good morning,' she said a little sheepishly.

'How did you sleep?'

'I think that was the best night's sleep I've ever had.'

Will couldn't help but smile. He'd imagined all manner of conversations when Mia had woken up to find herself in bed with him. Although it had been her suggestion the night before, he thought she would be regretting it deeply this morning.

'How about you?'

'Not bad,' he lied.

They sat in silence for a few minutes, neither sure what to say to the other.

Mia smiled sadly. 'Thank you,' she said.

'What for?'

'I didn't want to be alone….' She paused as if unsure whether to go on. 'And I wanted to spend a night with you, even if we weren't together intimately.'

Will wanted to push her back into the pillows and ravish her right there. Her words brought such a fire to his heart he thought his whole body might go up in flames. It was as if she felt she were not good enough for him. This wonderful, kind, beautiful woman. He wanted to claim her for his own and make it so no other man could have her.

Yet the sensible part of him knew she was right.

It wasn't that she was not good enough for him, just that they would never have a future. She was a prisoner in his custody and in a few weeks he would be returning to England to take over the running of his estate. He would once again be alone, as he had always been, but he wondered if he would be quite so content with only his thoughts for company after spending this time with Mia.

She would remain in Barbados, serve out what short sentence the Governor thought fit and then return to her work and her friends. If he took her now, laid her back and made love to her like he wanted to, it wouldn't be fair on her. He'd seen how important her virtue was when he'd kissed her before. He had no right to take her virginity from her. She deserved to save that for marriage.

Will also knew he wasn't the right man for Mia, for any woman. He'd spent so many years in his own company, he couldn't imagine sharing his life, each and every day, with someone else. Or at least he hadn't been able to imagine it until he met Mia.

Getting out of the bed he had shared with Mia was probably the hardest thing he'd ever done.

Stiffly he stood and pulled on his shirt.

'I'll wait for you downstairs,' he said.

Mia nodded. He saw the rejection in her eyes and

felt like a cad. He was trying to do the right thing, but at the same time he was hurting Mia, making her feel rejected and unwanted. Surely she could see he wanted her more than anything else.

Before his resolve could falter Will slipped out of the room and down the stairs. He found the landlord cleaning up from the night before and nodded a silent greeting, then he pushed through the tavern doors and exited into the warm morning air.

Minutes later Mia joined him, looking as fresh and beautiful as ever. He dreaded to think what he looked like. After a sleepless night where he'd been racked by unfulfilled desire he doubted he was at his best.

'We forgot about Tubs,' Mia said quietly.

'I'm sure the old boy's absolutely fine.'

They walked in silence along the waterfront, the gap between them strange to Will after their closeness throughout the night.

'What are you planning on doing next?' Mia asked after a few minutes of silence.

Will remembered Mia's artful questioning of Brave Pablo and his revelations about *The Flaming Dragon* anchoring in Smuggler's Cove.

'We should head over to Smuggler's Cove,' he said, glad to have something to distract him once again. 'I'm sure someone must live around there. They'll likely be able to tell us more about the ship and when it anchors in the cove.'

'Good morning, sir,' Tubs said as they approached the end of the jetty. The old sailor looked content and rested. 'Hope you had a satisfying night.'

Will ignored the innuendo and stopped just short of the boat.

'Miss Del Torres and I had a very productive evening, thank you,' he said. 'We've uncovered some information which might help us in apprehending the pirates.'

Tubs looked as if he were about to make another suggestive comment so Will ploughed on.

'We shall be going across the island to Smuggler's Cove, if you would row back to the ship and inform the Captain. We shall be back later in the day.'

'You enjoy your trip, sir.' With a suggestive wiggle of an eyebrow the old seaman even made that innocuous sentence seem dirty.

'We will. Thank you, Tubs.'

Will abruptly turned and led Mia back down the jetty.

'We're going on our own?' Mia asked.

'Yes.'

In truth he hadn't thought that part through. Another few hours with just Mia for company. It would be torture for sure, but exquisite torture.

Mia looked down at the stretch of golden sand and smiled. She'd been feeling on edge all morning, unable to relax with Will within hand's reach but still so out of bounds. The bright blue of the Caribbean waters lapping up against the golden sands wasn't enough to make her forget about the man standing beside her, but it was enough to make her smile.

'It's beautiful,' Will said.

They started walking down the hill towards the beach. The owner from the tavern where they'd stayed had arranged for one of the local men to drop them off in his cart. He'd left them on the hill just above the beach and had promised to return in a few hours to pick them up. He had also pointed out the small cottage perched on the hillside overlooking the cove.

They walked in companionable silence. Most of the awkwardness of earlier that morning had evaporated on the journey to the quieter side of the island and now Mia was left with a deep longing once again.

She stole a glance at Will. He looked deep in thought. She wondered if he was thinking about her. It was more likely he was deciding how to proceed with questioning the man who lived in the cottage.

She'd asked the impossible of him last night. She had needed him to hold her, knowing that physically he desired her, but nothing could come of it. Mia had expected him to refuse, any lesser man would have, but he'd seen she was distressed and he had sacrificed his own comfort for hers.

They reached the cottage and Will raised a hand to tap the door. It opened immediately and a tall man with skin the colour of the night's sky peered out.

'I don't want any trouble,' were the first words he uttered.

'And I don't want to bring you any. We're here to ask you for help.'

He looked them up and down suspiciously.

'Who are you?'

'My name is Will Greenacre and this is Mia.'

'I didn't ask your names. Who are you?'

'I'm a pirate hunter and this lovely lady is Mia Del Torres.'

Mia thought he was going to slam the door in

their faces, but eventually he stepped outside. It wasn't quite as good as being invited in, but she doubted many people would ask the sister of the infamous Captain Del Torres into their homes.

'No one likes pirates,' the man said slowly, 'but I don't want any trouble.'

'No one has to know we've spoken to you.'

Then man snorted. 'It'll be all over the island by now.'

'Then what's the harm in helping us?'

The man contemplated this and after a few seconds held out his hand to shake Will's. 'My name is Alberto.'

Mia saw Will relax a little as he shook the other man's hand.

'What makes you think you can catch Del Torres?' Before Will could answer he asked another question. 'That is the plan, isn't it? To catch him?'

Will nodded.

'And you're helping him?' he asked Mia.

She felt her throat thicken up. It wasn't as though he was accusing her of betraying her brother, but his incredulity was just like an accusation.

'I'm helping him,' she said simply.

'The Navy have been all over the island, threatening people,' Alberto said.

'I bet no one had seen or heard of *The Flaming Dragon* then.'

'They have a way of putting people's backs up.'

Mia thought of the arrogant Lieutenant Glass waiting for them on the ship and silently agreed with Alberto.

'Help us,' Will said. 'Del Torres and his crew have been terrorising these waters for long enough.'

Alberto seemed to think about Will's request for a good few minutes.

'If Del Torres returns to Tortola before you catch his ship, I'm a dead man,' Alberto said.

'Then help us catch him before he returns.'

He studied Will's face and eventually nodded. 'What do you want to know?'

'We've been told *The Flaming Dragon* anchors in this cove every so often. Anything you can tell us about what the crew do, when they were last here, if there is any pattern to their arrival, would be an immense help.'

Alberto smiled wryly. 'They left at dawn yesterday.'

Mia felt her pulse quicken. They'd just missed them on their lap around the island. A few hours earlier and this could all have been over. Her brother would be in custody and she would be on her way back to Barbados for a life without Will. She felt the tears starting to sting her eyes and quietly turned away so neither man would see.

'They'd been anchored for four days, which is about normal for them. They had been making some repairs on one of the masts—must have got damaged when some poor merchant ship tried to fight back.'

'Did they come ashore?'

'A party of ten men came as far as the trees beyond the beach—I think they must have been sent for a few bits to help with the repairs—but no one ventured further than that.'

'And did anyone from the island approach the boat?'

'It's pretty quiet over here. I'm the only one living in this part of the island. I'm not sure anyone else knew *The Flaming Dragon* was anchored here. If they did, I doubt anyone would approach it.'

So they didn't take on supplies in Tortola.

'How often does the ship anchor in the cove?'

Alberto shrugged. 'I haven't really been keeping note. Perhaps once every six weeks or so. Sometimes sooner, sometimes longer. And sometimes they're only there for a day and other times four or five. It's as if they're waiting for something.'

Mia thought of the merchant ships now resting at the bottom of the Caribbean Sea and knew immediately what they were waiting for: their targets to get into position so they could sneak up and attack.

'Thank you, Alberto,' Will said, shaking the other man's hand vigorously. He had a fresh gleam in his eyes and looked excited, as if he had caught a whiff of the scent of his prey and knew he was closing in.

'No one around here likes pirates,' Alberto said with a shrug. 'We had a raid on Road Town a few months ago. The town was trashed and two women were taken. If the Navy weren't such pompous fools, I would have talked to them.'

Mia couldn't meet his eye. Her brother was probably responsible for raiding the island this man so clearly loved.

'And now if that's everything I think I will make myself scarce for a few weeks. No point making it easy for Del Torres to find me.'

Without another word Alberto strode off up the hill away from the beach.

Mia turned to Will to find he was grinning like a little boy.

'We're closing in,' he said excitedly. 'I can feel it, Mia.'

She smiled, too, trying to share his enthusiasm. She did want to catch up with *The Flaming Dragon* and help Will apprehend her brother and the rest of the pirates, but she was dreading it, as well. More than that, though, she was dreading the thought of never seeing Will again. In a matter of days they would probably be making their way back to Barbados and Mia would have to face a lifetime on her own. She knew that no other man would interest her now she'd known Will. She wouldn't want to kiss another man, pledge her heart to him, when she would know deep down it was a lie. Will Greenacre, a man she'd shared only a few intense days with, would always be in possession of her heart.

Mia wanted more. She knew she could never be with Will like she wanted to, but if her memories were going to sustain her for the rest of her life she wanted no regrets about the time they spent together.

'When we get back to the ship we'll be able to figure out where *The Flaming Dragon* is likely to be headed next. We're going to find them.'

'I never doubted you.'

Mia slipped her hand through his arm and looked up at him.

'When we get back to the ship we will get all the maps out and work out where my brother is likely to be…' she paused '…but we've still got a couple of hours until we're picked up for the ride back to Road Town.'

Will looked down at her curiously. 'You say that as if you had a plan in mind.'

'We are in the Caribbean,' Mia said, gesturing at the beach stretching out in front of them.

'You want to go and paddle? After the last time we were in the water together?'

'You're a brave man. I'm sure you can cope with it.'

'Who am I to deny a lady her wishes?'

Mia nearly grinned. If he wasn't going to deny her, this might be easier than she'd first thought. She knew now she had to have Will—all of her misgivings about giving herself to him had fully evaporated. They might not ever live together as man and wife, but she had realised this was nothing like her mother's situation. She cared for Will and was following her heart, and if there was one thing she'd learned in life it was to seize the moment. She might never be completely alone with Will again.

She pulled him down the gentle path that led to

the beach. As they reached the sand Mia bent down and slipped off her shoes, enjoying the warm sand beneath her toes.

The bay wasn't large by Caribbean beach standards, but the sand was golden and the water a clear blue. Palm trees fringed the beach and hung over the edge, providing a few small patches of shade on the otherwise sun-kissed sands.

'The water looks so inviting,' Mia said.

It wasn't a lie. The waves lapped calmly at the shore and you could see a gentle sloping of the sands as they disappeared into the sea.

'You do actually want to paddle, don't you?' Will asked, slightly incredulous.

'No,' Mia said. 'I want to swim.'

Before he could object or she could lose her confidence, Mia started to unlace her dress. As he looked on in disbelief she slipped it over her head and placed it on top of her shoes on the sand. Clad once again just in her thin cotton undergown, Mia resisted the urge to cover her body with her arms. That would defeat the point. She wanted Will to look and she wanted him to see her.

'Mia,' he said.

She wasn't sure if it was a warning to stop or a plea to carry on.

Telling herself to be brave, Mia grabbed hold of the bottom of her undergown and lifted it over her head.

She lifted her chin and looked Will straight in the eye. Or at least tried to—Will's eyes were devouring her body, taking in every inch of her nakedness.

'Mia,' he repeated, seemingly unable to say anything else.

'You're not going to make me swim alone, are you?'

Chapter Thirteen

Will watched as Mia spun around and slowly walked towards the sea. He was mesmerised by her. His eyes trailed down her back, taking in the two little dimples near the base of her spine and then carrying on to the delicious curve of her bottom. Then further. To the space between her legs he wanted to possess and invade and then her shapely thighs and slender calves. He wanted all of her, every last inch. He wanted to lay her down in the sand and never let her get up again.

He almost ripped off his clothes and ran after her, but his mind was in too much of a spin. Surely she knew what she was doing to him. She'd said herself nothing could happen between them, she wasn't going to become his mistress for a few short days, she deserved more than that.

Mia paused at the water's edge and dipped a toe into the water.

'It's lovely and warm,' she said, looking back over her shoulder at him.

She watched as he stood paralysed. His body and his heart were telling him to throw his clothes on top of hers, scoop her up in his arms, and deal with the consequences later. His mind couldn't really get past the sight of Mia naked.

'Am I going to have to come and get you?' Mia asked.

Will didn't move. She shrugged, turned around, and walked back towards him. This time he was treated to the sight of her beautifully rounded breasts, nipples hardening to little points. His eyes trailed down her abdomen and he knew if he didn't stop them his self-control would break.

Mia reached him and started to untuck his shirt.

His arms moving of their own accord, he reached out and touched the soft skin on her shoulders.

The contact was delicious and Will knew instantly he was lost. Mia could ask anything of him and he would comply.

She pulled his shirt over his head and placed her hands on his chest, tracing small circles on the tanned skin, her touch like a tiny electric current.

Her hands dropped to the waistband of his breeches and slowly started unfastening them. He hesitated, then placed a hand over hers.

'Mia,' he said, his voice rasping with unconcealed desire, 'are you sure about this?'

'I want you.'

'But you said…'

'Forget what I said.'

'If we go any further, I won't be able to stop,' he said, trying to give her ample opportunity to change her mind.

He wanted her so badly. She was beautiful and curvaceous and seductive, but more than that. She was kind and clever and he wanted to possess her mind as well as her body.

'I won't change my mind,' Mia said and slipped a finger below his waistband.

With a groan of surrender Will gave in. He crushed Mia to him and sought her lips with his own. Frantically he kissed her, pulling her ever closer, wondering if at any moment she would come to her senses and stop him.

She fumbled with his breeches, trying to undo them whilst kissing him. He didn't come to her aid. His hands were too busy exploring every inch of the perfect body she had bared for him. He felt her shiver as he traced his fingers from her shoulder down her arm, then across her abdomen. He teased her, refusing to go lower even though she trembled in anticipation.

His fingers moved up towards her breasts and gently he cupped them, enjoying the sharp intake of breath as he gently grazed a thumb across one hard nipple.

'Something tells me you liked that,' he said in between kisses.

He flicked his other thumb over her other nipple and enjoyed the same reaction.

'Would you like me to do that again?'

'Mmm.'

He smiled possessively. He liked that he was the only man to do this to her.

Slowly, deliberately, he brushed her nipples, pulling away from their kiss to watch the reaction on her face.

'Lie down,' he commanded. He wanted to take his time and peruse every part of her.

Mia obeyed. She sunk to the ground and watched as he lowered himself on top of her, trousers still firmly in place.

'There are so many things I want to do to you,' he

said, peppering her with quick kisses. 'How about I give you a list and you can decide?'

Mia moaned. He took it as her agreement.

'Well, I want to kiss every inch of your lovely body,' he said, holding up one finger. 'And I want to lavish attention on your beautiful breasts.' A second finger joined the first. 'And I want to touch you right here.' The third finger touched her most sensitive place and Mia gasped.

He waited, looking at her expectantly.

'Which would you like?' he asked.

'I have to choose just one?'

'My lady is greedy,' Will said with a wolfish smile.

He dipped his head and sought her mouth out, kissing her long and hard and deep. When he pulled away she moaned, but looked at him with eager anticipation.

'Where shall I start?' he asked.

Sliding away from her, he took one slender ankle in his hand and started to dot kisses up her leg. As he reached her thigh he stole a glance at her face and saw her biting her lip, trying to control herself, to stop herself begging for more. His lips reached the fold where leg met abdomen and he couldn't help himself, he planted a long kiss on her most private place. Mia gasped in surprise, but Will was pleased to see her hips thrust towards him rather than wriggling away.

'Greedy and impatient,' Will said. 'I suppose I will have to teach you patience is a virtue.'

With that he drew away and picked up her other leg, starting at the very bottom and working his way up. Again as he reached her thigh Mia tensed and pushed her hips towards him. He gave in and again pressed his lips against her, making her squirm in pleasure.

Reluctantly he drew away and continued his exploration of her body. His lips brushed over the firm muscles of her abdomen and Will once again positioned himself on top of her. This time he was straddling her completely, pinning her down by the hips and leaving her powerless to wriggle away from his affections.

'Now what was number two on the menu?' he asked, pausing for a second to brush a kiss against her lips.

'Breasts.' Mia said, her voice heavy with desire.

'Breasts. Well, that does sound delightful.'

Without another word Will dipped his head and caught one of her nipples between his teeth. He heard Mia gasp and her hips moved instinctively towards his. He ran his tongue over the delicate bud and revelled in the moan of pleasure that escaped her lips.

'You like that, do you?'

'Yes.' Mia panted. 'Please.'

He loved the sound of her voice when she was aroused and loved that he was the one doing this to her, making her feel such pleasure.

'Yes, please? Who am I to refuse such a polite request?'

Will dipped his head again and nipped at her other nipple, running his tongue in small circles around the darkened skin and gently grazing her with his lips.

'I need you, Will,' Mia said, looking straight into his eyes. 'I need you now.'

He was suddenly overcome with an urgency. He had to have her, too. He wanted to possess her and pleasure her all at the same time. Tugging at his trousers, Will paused only to smatter kisses over her lips and breasts.

When he was finally free from his breeches he positioned himself against Mia.

'Are you sure?' he asked one final time.

If she refused him now, he didn't know if he could stop. He wanted her so badly, had driven himself nearly insane with arousal during his slow enjoyment of her body.

'I want you.'

It was exactly what he wanted to hear. He pushed gently against her and slipped inside. He felt himself meet the resistance of her maidenhood and paused, reminded of what a gift she was giving to him.

'This might hurt a little,' he warned, hoping he could take away any pain he did cause her and replace it with pleasure.

She gasped as he pushed inside her and, once he was fully buried, he stopped to check she was comfortable. Before he could ask the question Mia started to rock her hips backwards and forwards, shifting him ever so slightly inside of her.

Will felt close to ecstasy, but he wanted to try to give Mia some release first. He started slowly, drawing nearly all the way out of her before plunging back in. Every time it felt as though he was deeper inside her. After a few strokes he picked up the pace. Mia's hips rose to meet his at every thrust and soon her breathing became heavier.

'It feels so good,' she whispered.

Will wanted to give her more than good, he wanted to give her perfection. He wanted to look into her eyes as an orgasm flooded through her body and she experienced that pleasure for the first time.

He continued his thrusting, well aware he was close to finishing himself, and reached down to touch her clitoris with his fingers. He rolled the nub between finger and thumb and felt the electric jolts of pleasure as Mia writhed beneath him. Her eyes glazed over as he thrust into her one last time and her muscles contracted around him. A low, long groan escaped her lips as she climaxed for the very first time.

The sight of her losing control was enough to send Will over the edge. He felt the inevitable pulsation and held himself deep inside her as the waves of pleasure reached a peak and slowly began to subside.

Chapter Fourteen

Will rolled off her and lay down in the sand with an almighty sigh.

'Is it always like that?' she asked, still unable to uncurl her toes completely.

'No.'

She turned her head to look at him.

'It's better with you,' he said simply.

Mia giggled. 'You make it sound like we've done this many times.'

'It's better when it's someone you care about,' he corrected himself.

She reached out a hand and brushed a stray strand of hair from Will's eyes.

Mia knew she would never be the same again. On the outside she might look like the same old Mia Del Torres, but on the inside she was a changed woman. His woman.

She stretched her legs out and raised her arms above her head. She knew she should be feeling self-conscious, acutely aware of her nudity, but she found she didn't care. She'd given herself to Will completely and it felt right she should be lying there naked in the sand next to him.

Will's breathing was returning to normal as Mia shuffled over closer to him. He pulled her gently on to his chest and tenderly kissed the top of her head.

'I don't know what made you change your mind, Mia Del Torres, but I'm very happy that you did.'

Even in this post-pleasure moment of bliss she daren't tell him the truth: that she cared for him so deeply she knew he was the only man who would ever possess her heart and she'd promised herself to only make love to the man she truly loved.

She nearly giggled at the absurdity of everything. Will had only come into her life a few days ago and in no time at all she'd fallen in love and lost her virginity. She reminded herself to enjoy this moment because she was sure there would not be another. When they returned to the ship all Will's focus would be on catching her brother and once that was accomplished he would disappear back to his English estate. So this would be the sum total of all her lovemaking in her life, for she knew she couldn't ever love another man like she did Will.

Mia felt a sudden overwhelming desire to tell him. She wanted to shout her feeling from the highest hill on Tortola so everyone could hear. Even though she knew he couldn't reciprocate her feelings.

Instead she bit her tongue and allowed herself to enjoy a few more minutes of the fantasy world she'd fallen into.

'We'd better get dressed,' Will said reluctantly when they'd been lying on the beach for about half an hour. 'Wouldn't want anyone to come across us in such a state.'

Mia half-heartedly agreed. Part of her wanted to spend as long as possible naked in Will's arms before they had to rejoin the ship's crew, but she also acknowledged she didn't want the old man with the cart catching sight of her in the nude.

She felt strangely self-conscious as she picked up her clothes and went about getting dressed. She'd been so brazen just an hour earlier, stripping naked in front of Will to seduce him, but now she felt the need to cover up again. It was as if they had been in a separate world for the last sixty minutes where normal rules didn't apply and Mia had forgotten to feel embarrassed that Will had seen her naked and touched her in places no one else had ever seen.

Will helped her to secure her dress and brushed as much sand from her hair as he could. She thought she still must have looked a complete state, but there wasn't much she could do about it.

'Thank you,' Mia said as they started to climb the hill back to where they were due to be picked up.

Will looked at her with a frown. 'What for?'

'I wanted you to make love to me, just once,' Mia said. 'I wanted something I could cherish.'

He looked slightly uncomfortable at her words.

'It was perfect,' she finished.

Will looked as though he didn't know how to react. Mia knew it was unusual to thank a man when he'd taken your virginity and didn't plan on marrying you, but she wanted him to know all the same. She didn't want him regretting it, or chastising himself for allowing himself to go against his principles and take her virtue.

As they walked, Mia stole a glance at Will every few minutes. He looked troubled and deep in thought. Every so often his lips would move as if he were trying to work through an argument in his head.

Eventually Mia felt compelled to say something. He'd been silent for a full twenty minutes and she was worried he might never speak a word to her again.

'I know what we just did has changed things,' Mia said, 'but I hope we will still be friends.'

Will looked at her with such incredulity Mia thought she might cry. Obviously the idea of them being friends seemed ludicrous to him.

He stopped walking and turned to face her, taking both her hands in his own.

'Mia,' he said, 'if you would deign to have such an awful man as myself as your friend I would be honoured.'

Will was kind, caring, intelligent, witty. Anything but awful.

'You're not awful.'

'I should not have...' He let the sentence trail off.

Mia smiled sadly. 'I didn't give you much choice in the matter.'

'I should have been stronger. A true gentleman and a true friend would not have taken advantage of you like that no matter what temptation was dangled in front of him.'

'You didn't take advantage of me, Will,' Mia said slowly, hoping he might actually understand. 'I seduced you because I wanted you. I knew exactly what I was doing and I knew the consequences.'

'I don't understand.'

Mia took a deep breath and looked up at the man she loved.

'I love you, Will. And I wanted to make love to the man in my heart, just once.'

She saw each and every emotion flash over his face: confusion, elation, disbelief.

'You love me?' he asked, incredulous.

'I love you.'

A tiny part of her was waiting for him to say it back. She knew it wouldn't happen and she knew it could never be, but still there was just a sliver of hope.

He hesitated, stepped back slightly and Mia's hope died.

She smiled at him again, this time trying to hide her disappointment, and patted him awkwardly on the arm. Before he could say anything at all a cart lumbered round the corner and the old man who was taking them back to Road Town raised a hand in greeting.

He didn't know what to say. Suddenly his relationship with Mia had gone from friendly flirtation to fantastic sex to a declaration of love to this awful awkwardness. She'd told him she loved him. He hadn't known how to react. What did a man say in response to such a declaration? 'Thank you very much' didn't really seem to cut it and most other responses were pretty inadequate, too.

When she'd said it he'd wondered if she'd expected him to tell her he loved her, too. He'd been too stunned to say anything at all. In truth, he didn't know how he truly felt about Mia. She seemed to occupy his thoughts every waking moment of the day. He either wanted to discuss an idea with her, make her laugh or rip her clothes off and ravish her. He hadn't thought about a single other woman since he'd met her.

He certainly cared for her. Never before had he wanted to look after another person quite so much. But love was a big word, a big emotion. Will had never felt love for a woman before. Lust and desire undoubtedly, but love?

For as long as he could remember, Will had been on his own. Certainly he'd had friends, family who cared for him and whom he'd loved back, but no one who had taken over his world like Mia. He'd always assumed he would be on his own, a bachelor until the end—it was just in his nature. He lived alone and worked alone. It was just how it was, how it had always been.

A rebellious part of him asked whether it really had to be that way in the future. Maybe sharing a life with someone else would be more fulfilling.

'Lieutenant Glass won't be happy we upped and left without taking him with us,' Mia said cheerily as if she hadn't just rocked the foundations of his world a few minutes earlier.

'Mmm.' Will had never been great at holding a conversation whilst deep in thought. When his mind was stuck on one thing he found it difficult to engage with another. At the present time his mind was very much locked on trying to untangle his feelings for Mia.

Even if he did love her, did that change anything? They didn't have a future. In a few weeks if all went well with his mission they would be on opposite sides of the world. He would have returned to England to run the family estate, once again alone.

'He might have called in the Navy,' Mia persevered.

'Mmm.'

'Or maybe he's jumped into the sea and got eaten by the kraken.'

It took a couple of seconds for her words to sink in and another few to process them.

'We can only hope,' he said with a grin.

They emerged over the top of the hill and started the descent back to Road Town. Mia seemed quite content to sit in silence for the rest of the ride, allowing Will further time to ponder on his feelings. The problem was there was no easy answer. He rather thought a man should know when he fell in love, so maybe he didn't love Mia. On the other hand, he cared for Mia more than he had anyone in the world since his brother and that was after just a few days of knowing her. If they were in each other's company much longer, he could only see his feeling growing.

It would be easier not to love her, Will decided. If he loved her their inevitable separation would be agonising. He glanced over at Mia sitting serenely beside him and realised if the mere thought of being apart from her was agonising, the reality would be pure hell.

Chapter Fifteen

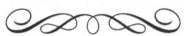

'Where the hell have you been?' As soon as they'd stepped back aboard the boat, Lieutenant Glass had sought them out, looking extremely angry.

'Gathering intelligence,' Will said calmly. And making love to Mia. And probably breaking her heart.

Glass looked the pair of them up and down and his lips curled into an unattractive sneer.

'Gathering intelligence. I see.' He took a step towards them. 'And this occupied you through the entire night.'

Will felt the anger boil up inside him. Normally he could control his emotions so well, but Glass had a way of bringing out the worst in him.

'I understand why you are here aboard this ship, Lieutenant, but can we get one thing clear? I do not report to you or your precious Navy. I am a free agent brought in to do a job you have been struggling with for far too long. So whilst I am very pleased to share any intelligence I uncover, I will not report my every move to you. Is that clear?'

Glass stepped back as though Will had slapped him.

'Is that clear?' he repeated, his voice dangerously low.

The Lieutenant nodded and looked around him. Nearly the whole crew had stopped what they were doing to listen to the exchange. Humiliation and hatred flared in Glass's eyes and Will realised he'd just made a powerful enemy.

'We found where *The Flaming Dragon* has been sheltering,' he said in a conciliatory tone.

'Good.'

'And it seems we just missed it when we sailed around the island.'

'Wonderful.'

'But it does mean we can get an idea of Del Torres' schedule. It feels like we're closing in.'

'Wonderful.' Each word was delivered in a flat monotone by the Lieutenant. 'Unfortunately whilst you were off "gathering information", *The Flaming Dragon* has attacked another merchant ship.'

Out of the corner of his eye Will saw Mia shift uncomfortably.

Lieutenant Glass turned to face her. 'It seems this time your brother has killed twelve of their crew.'

The pain was so apparent in her eyes Will wanted to reach out and embrace her. Normally Mia's face was brimming with happiness and barely controlled mirth, but now all he could see was misery.

'What a lovely family you come from, Miss Del Torres,' Glass said with a sneer.

Will felt the fingers of his hand bunch into a fist and it was all he could do to stop himself punching Glass squarely on the jaw. Mia must have seen the miniscule movement as he clenched the muscles of his arms and stepped to his side, resting her hand on his sleeve in a restraining manner.

'If we have the coordinates of where my brother has attacked the second ship…' Mia trailed off as Will spun to look at her.

'Genius!' he exclaimed and couldn't help planting a kiss firmly on her forehead.

Glass looked puzzled by their interaction. For an instant Will had the urge to exclude him from their discovery, but he knew that was petty and would only bring trouble in the future.

'We have the position of *The Flaming Dragon* yesterday morning and her position today. From that we might be able to work out where she's heading next and when we have a chance of intercepting her.'

A look of comprehension dawned on Glass's face and for an instant he looked almost excited.

'Meet mc in the mess room in two minutes,' Will commanded, and hurried off below decks to his cabin to fetch the maps.

When he reached the mess room Glass and Mia were sitting in uncomfortable silence. Mia looked close to tears and he wondered what hurtful things the Lieutenant had said in the few minutes he'd been absent. Half of him wanted to pick Glass up by the collar and pummel him until he apologised to Mia. Will hated seeing Mia upset, but he knew now wasn't the time to set things straight with Glass. Time was of the essence; they might have a real lead on where Del Torres was and a chance to catch up.

He spread the map of the Caribbean out on the dining table and placed a finger on Smuggler's Cove in Tortola.

'We know *The Flaming Dragon* was here yesterday morning. Lieutenant, where was the merchant ship attacked?'

Glass checked the coordinate readings on the top of the map and then placed a finger just west of the island of St Martin. Both Will and Mia broke out into wide smiles. They had him.

'Care to share your revelation?' Glass asked frostily.

'From past sightings and attacks we've worked out a proposed route Del Torres might take through the Caribbean, places he may shelter, that sort of thing.'

Glass sneered. 'Del Torres doesn't follow a route. If he did, the Navy would have recognised the pattern and caught him.'

'He follows a route,' Mia said quietly. 'My brother likes to have a plan.'

Will pushed on. 'We've got two points of reference and two sets of timings. We can work out the direction Del Torres is heading in and how far he will be from his starting point.'

'Sounds very unlikely.' Glass remained unimpressed.

Will turned to Mia and together they pored over the map. She was standing close to him, so close he could smell her sweet scent radiating from her skin. He had a sudden flashback of when she'd pulled her dress over her head and given him his first view of her beautiful naked body. He swallowed and tried to banish the image from his head. Mia naked wasn't a picture that helped him to concentrate.

Her arm brushed against his and the soft contact conjured more pictures in his mind. Mia lying back in the sand, gasping in pleasure as he touched her breasts and giving herself to him completely as they climaxed together.

Mia coughed, startling him from his memories.

'I said we can probably intercept *The Flaming Dragon*,' Mia said slowly.

Will nodded, trying to focus on the mission ahead.

He did a few quick calculations of speed and direction, then leaned closer to Mia. He plucked one of her hair pins from her head, allowing a few silky strands to fall free, and placed it triumphantly into the map.

Glass looked at him as though he'd grown two heads. Mia self-consciously tucked the stray strands of hair behind one ear. Will had to resist the urge to reach out and stop her. He wanted her to shake her entire head of hair free from its constrictions.

'There,' he said triumphantly.

Glass snorted with amusement. 'You truly think you can waltz in and pinpoint the whereabouts of Del Torres after a couple of days? You're deluded. Or mad.' The last part was said under his breath, but loud enough for Will to hear.

He just grinned. 'Maybe,' he said, 'but it's a damn sight closer than the Navy have been in two years.'

The Lieutenant turned bright red and his eyes narrowed. He'd suspected it before, but now Will knew—he'd made an enemy for life.

'Go on your wild goose chase,' Glass said, his voice dangerously low. 'And when you've spent all the Governor's money wasting time sailing around in circles whilst you bed this whore, let's see who the saviour of the Caribbean is then.'

Will felt the insult like a physical punch. He'd called Mia a whore. His body reacted instinctively, his right hand balling into a fist and drawing back. He felt the power in his arm as it began to straighten on its way to make contact with Glass's jaw.

'Stop,' Mia said calmly and placed a gentle hand on his right arm. He felt the power being sucked out of his punch and let the arm drop to his side.

'He's not worth it,' Mia said, her eyes holding a gentle plea.

'He insulted you.'

Mia shrugged. 'I've been insulted many times before,' she said with a small smile. 'I'm sure my pride will survive.'

'Apologise,' Will commanded, turning to Glass.

'For telling the truth? Never.' With that the Lieutenant stalked out of the room.

Will was all set to follow him and make him apologise.

'Leave it,' Mia said. 'Honestly, he's not worth it.'

'He called you a whore.'

'I've been called much worse.'

Anger and indignation on Mia's behalf boiled up inside him.

'By whom?' he asked, picturing himself hunting down every person who'd ever insulted the wonderful woman standing beside him.

Mia laughed. 'By too many people for you to fight.'

Will felt some of the anger melt away at the sound of her laugh.

'Sit down,' Mia commanded, 'or I won't relax, thinking you're going to run off after the charming Lieutenant at any second.'

He sat and felt Mia sit down in the chair beside him.

'You're not a whore,' Will said, turning towards her. 'You know that, don't you?'

'I know exactly what I am,' she said, 'and comments from idiots like Glass don't bother me.'

He wondered how much she was saying to calm him down so he didn't go and beat Glass to a pulp for insulting her.

'I'm the daughter of an Afro-Caribbean runaway slave and a Spanish sailor and I'm the sister of a Bajan pirate. But that's not who I am. I'm Mia Del Torres, I care about other people, I like to laugh and I'm kind to animals.'

Will grinned at her assessment of herself.

'You're much more than that,' he said. 'So much more.'

He felt his body inch towards hers and had the overwhelming urge to kiss her. He remembered the sweet taste of her lips and wanted nothing more than to press his lips against hers and get lost in the heady sensation that overcame him every time their bodies became entwined.

Will reached up and tugged the strand of hair he'd set loose earlier from behind her ear.

'So soft,' he murmured.

Mia's mouth opened just slightly and he knew she wanted to be kissed. He twirled the strand of hair between his fingers, wondering if he could pull out all the pins and set her hair free before Mia realised what he was doing and stopped him.

He leaned forward and was dismayed to see Mia pull away from him.

'We'd better tell the Captain,' she said, her voice husky and her cheeks flushed, 'Otherwise we'll never get to the interception point on time.'

Will felt his response get stuck in his throat.

'I'll tell him,' Mia said resolutely, then stood up and promptly fled the room.

Will looked after her with shock. He didn't think a woman had ever physically fled from him before. Yes, he'd had his fair share of flirtatious rebuffs, but Mia had run as if she were being chased by six wolves.

He sat in stunned silence for well over a minute, trying to figure out why she'd reacted like that. They'd kissed before. Only a couple of hours ago they'd been doing much more than kissing on the sands of Smuggler's Cove. He thought about her declaration of love and his silent response and cursed. How could he expect to kiss her again when she'd told him she loved him?

He was a fool. A damn stupid fool. Will knew he should stay away from Mia, but he felt as though every time he saw her she drew him closer in. He wanted to kiss her. More than that he wanted to lay her down every night and make love to her.

'Idiot,' he murmured. He'd always prided himself on being so self-possessed, his every action well thought out, yet now all he wanted to do was throw caution to the wind and sail off into the sunset with Mia.

Chapter Sixteen

Mia felt her heart pounding, but wouldn't allow herself to stop and catch her breath. He'd nearly kissed her again. She had seen the unmistakable look in his eyes as he'd inched closer.

'Captain,' Mia called as she emerged into the Caribbean sunshine, 'we've got a new destination.'

The Captain smiled and gestured at the brooding figure of Lieutenant Glass leaning over the rail.

'I gathered as much. Although the Lieutenant informed me I was about to set off on a wild goose chase.'

'I think this may be it,' Mia said, her hands shaking with trepidation. 'When we arrive at our destination I think the men should know to be prepared.'

The Captain looked at her thoughtfully and nodded. Mia gave him the new coordinates and he set about organising his crew.

'We should be there at first light tomorrow,' he informed her. 'Make sure you get some rest before then.'

She was left alone on the deck as the crew busied themselves, readying the ship for departure. She was torn between wanting to stay on deck and feel the sun on her face or retreating to her cabin. If she stayed on deck, there was the risk Glass might seek her out and she was sure Will wouldn't leave her sitting on her own for long, either. What she wanted right now was some space to think. To assess and plan for the events of the next few days and make her peace with them.

So she turned on her heel and headed back below decks. It seemed dark out of the direct sunlight and Mia shivered at the loss of the sun's warmth.

Back in her cabin she closed the door firmly behind her and sank on to her narrow bed. Over the last few days she'd been thinking increasingly about what would happen when she laid eyes on her brother. She hadn't seen him for so long she wondered if she would recognise him.

Mia dreaded his reaction, the shock at being betrayed by his own sister, the anger that he couldn't even trust his own flesh and blood to stand strong with him. She wondered again if she was doing the right thing, but immediately dismissed the doubt in her mind. Her brother was no longer the little boy she'd known and loved, he was a ruthless killer.

She'd meant it when she had told Will there was more to her than her parents and her brother. She was her own person and she could make her own decisions, decide what was right for herself. And she knew helping Will catch Jorge and his crew was the right thing to do, even if a pang of guilt sliced through her every time she thought about it.

Mia closed her eyes and allowed her head to flop back on to the thin pillow. It had been a tiring few days. One didn't often save a man from drowning, get arrested, and commence a hunt for a pirate ship all in one week, let alone fall in love.

She tried to push thoughts of love from her mind—they weren't helping anyone. She was pleased she'd told Will she loved him, otherwise in the long years of loneliness she might regret her silence and wonder how he would have responded if she'd just been brave enough to declare her love. There was definitely no regret in her mind, but she had wanted him to respond. Maybe not with a declaration of love in return, that would have been too much to ask, but with something. She needed to know how he felt about her. Mia thought it was more than simple lust; she saw caring and concern in his eyes when he looked at her and he was always seeking out her company even when there were other people around.

'Enough,' she told herself, knowing mulling the matter over in her mind would just make her feel worse.

Instead she tried to clear her head and get the well-advised rest the Captain had recommended.

Mia stirred, stretching her legs out and allowing her eyes to flutter open. She felt a pang of hunger and realised she hadn't eaten all day. Her lips were dry with thirst, too. She opened her eyes to find the cabin in complete darkness. With no idea what time of evening or night it was she sat up and moved to straighten her dress. Someone would be up on deck keeping watch, she was sure they would point her in the right direction to find some bread and something to drink.

A noise just outside her cabin made her pause. It sounded like someone was approaching quietly. For a second she had a stab of panic as she wondered whether she'd locked her door, then told herself not to be so silly. No one on the ship wanted to harm her—it didn't matter if she hadn't locked the door.

Nevertheless she waited for a few seconds for whoever it was outside to walk on past. The sound of retreating footsteps never came and Mia began to wonder if she had imagined it all in the first place.

She was just about to get up from her bed when she saw the handle to her cabin door turning very slowly. She froze, eyes locked on the handle, wondering if it were just a trick of the light. Her answer came when the door clicked open and swung inwards. She nearly screamed, but caught herself.

Mia peered into the gloom, wondering if it was Will coming to pay her a visit. She felt a thrill of excitement at the thought.

A silhouette came into the room and quickly closed the door behind them. Mia could tell it wasn't Will by the way he walked and immediately she felt a chill run down her spine.

'Who is it?' she asked in a whisper.

'So you are awake.' The unmistakable condescending voice of Lieutenant Glass froze her to the spot.

'Get out,' Mia said, raising her voice slightly.

'That's not very hospitable, my dear.' He took another step towards the bed.

Mia realised he was drunk, very drunk if the overpowering, sweet smell of rum could be trusted.

'Get out or I'll scream.'

'Go ahead. Everyone else is in the mess room eating. No one will hear you.'

Mia calculated the distance between her cabin and the mess room. He was probably right, but there was no way she was just going to sit here and let him do whatever he had planned.

She opened her mouth to scream. Before a single sound could come out Lieutenant Glass launched himself across the room and clapped a hand across her mouth.

'Now, now,' he said, swaying closer to her.

Mia bit down on the fleshy skin of his hand. Glass howled in pain and momentarily withdrew, giving Mia a few seconds to take in a breath and let out a scream. It only lasted half a second, one at the most, but Mia hoped it would be enough.

Glass raised a hand and slapped her hard across her cheek.

'Shut up, you stupid whore,' he said, looking round for something to silence her with.

He grabbed a washcloth from the stand beside her bed and shoved it into Mia's mouth. Roughly he pushed all the material inside, making her gag as the damp cloth hit the back of her throat. Instantly he pinned her arms to her side and stopped her struggles.

'Be quiet and this might not end badly for you,' he instructed.

Mia had no such intentions. She thrashed her body from side to side, trying to break free from Glass's grip so she could pull the cloth from her mouth and shout for help.

'Stay still.'

He climbed on top of her, pinning her hips to the bed whilst still holding her hands by her side.

'I don't know why you're struggling, whore,' he said. 'I know you like it.'

Mia felt sick. She was pinned to the bed completely, barely able to move, and the cloth in her mouth meant she couldn't even shout for help. She needed to do something quickly or Glass would hurt her. Badly.

He grabbed both of her hands in one of his and held them above her head. Mia realised with panic this meant he had a spare hand to do whatever he pleased with.

She started bucking wildly, hoping to throw him off balance so he might at least release her hands. Again and again she thrust her hips in all different directions but he was just too strong and too determined.

Mia thrashed her head from side to side and tried to clench her legs together as Glass used his free hand to push up her skirts.

'You've been letting that arrogant bastard Green-acre take you all week. Why don't we see how you like it when a real man makes you scream?'

Mia started trying to work the washcloth from her mouth with her tongue. She felt a sob of despair trying to escape. It seemed hopeless. He had her pinned down and at his mercy and no one was going to come to her rescue.

She eyed up the washbasin on the stand beside her bed. It was made of some sort of ceramic material. If she was able to dislodge it the resulting crash when it hit the floor and shattered might be enough to bring someone to investigate. If only she could pull one hand free, she'd have so much more of a chance, but Glass's grip was a strong as any iron manacle and she doubted it would weaken any time soon.

Glass started loosening his breeches and pushed one knee between her thighs. Mia resisted with everything she had, still trying to thrash from side to side. She knew if he got himself positioned be-tween her legs she had no hope.

'Don't pretend you're not enjoying this,' Glass said, 'I know your sort. Make out you are all sweet and innocent when we all know what lies beneath.'

He shoved his knees so hard against her thighs Mia thought she might pass out with the pain. She would certainly be bruised tomorrow. That was if she survived until tomorrow.

'You don't deserve to live,' Glass spat at her. 'You should be swinging from the gallows with crows pecking at your eyes.'

Mia didn't know where all his hatred for her came from, but she realised he wanted to hurt her so badly she would wish she was dead.

Now firmly in position in between her legs, Glass reached to push his trousers down a few inches further. As he did so Mia felt his balance teeter slightly and grabbed her opportunity. She rolled to one side, engaging every muscle in her body in her attempts to dislodge him. Glass rocked with her and to Mia's dismay he didn't fall off, but she did feel his hand loosen its grip on her wrists above her head. She wrenched her arms free and felt a bubble of elation as she ripped the cloth from her mouth and let out an ear-splitting scream.

At the same time her other hand lashed out, knocking the ceramic washbasin to the floor where it landed with a loud crash.

Glass froze for an instant, anger and surprise mingling in his face. Then he slapped her again, this time with such a force Mia felt her teeth slam together and her brain rattle inside her skull. She jerked backwards and felt the even harder blow of her head hitting the wooden bed frame. Everything spun as she frantically tried to keep her grip on the conscious world, knowing if she accepted the welcoming darkness Glass would win.

Valiantly she tried every trick she knew of to ward off unconsciousness, biting her tongue to try to make herself feel something, but the seconds stretched out before her and the darkness marched on.

Mia's last thought before she fell into oblivion was a hope Will wouldn't have to see her like this.

Chapter Seventeen

Will froze. His heart nearly jumped from his chest and it felt as though his whole world had imploded.

The scream had only lasted a second or two, but it was enough. It was a woman's scream, and on a ship full of men it could only mean one thing: Mia was in trouble.

He jumped into action, hurtling across the deck and down the narrow stairs to the passageway below. The silence that followed the scream and the crash was more worrying to his ears than further sound of a struggle would be. He dreaded what he was going to find when he reached Mia's cabin and the thought she might be hurt made his blood freeze in his veins.

Will thrust open the door to her tiny cabin and saw red. Lieutenant Glass was sat astride a prostrate Mia. He had one hand raised and the other was clutching her two wrists like a manacle.

Without thinking Will launched himself into the room and let out a primal roar of anger. Glass looked around with wide eyes as if stunned to see Will hurtling towards him.

'Get off of her,' Will shouted, ramming his shoulder into Glass. He grabbed the Lieutenant by the material of his jacket just below his shoulders and lifted him in the air. Unceremoniously he flung Glass across the room and bent over Mia.

He felt his heart shattered into pieces. She was lying motionless, her skirts gathered just above her knees, bruises already starting to develop around her wrists.

'Mia,' he pleaded, gently stroking her hair. 'Open your eyes, Mia, please.'

Will heard a commotion in the corridor behind him but didn't turn around. His whole attention was focused on the woman lying on the bed in front of him.

'Please wake up.'

He studied her, not knowing what to do for the best, his eyes roaming over her face and dishevelled body. Will leaned in closer, holding his cheek just inches from her mouth and waited, praying he would feel the warmth of her breath against his skin.

He almost shouted with happiness when her exhalation came and with it he noticed the steady rise and fall of her chest.

'What happened?' the Captain asked, pushing his way into the room.

'That animal attacked Mia,' Will said, still not taking his eyes off her face.

'Is she breathing?'

Will nodded. He took her hand and ran a finger over the smooth skin, willing her to wake up. Her fingers were warm, another positive sign her heart was still pumping the vital blood around her body, but none of this was enough to reassure Will she was truly okay.

He turned to the Captain, aware of the crowd gathered outside the cabin.

'Take him to the brig,' he commanded, pointing at Glass. 'I'll deal with him later.'

The Captain hesitated, clearly not wanting to throw a Naval Officer in the inhospitable cells of the brig.

'He attacked Miss Del Torres, attempted to rape her and has knocked her unconscious.'

The Captain gave a quick nod and motioned for two of the crewmen to step forward.

'Touch me and your career's over,' Glass warned.

He had regained some of his composure and looked ready to fight for his freedom.

Captain Little shook his head in disgust. 'Even the Navy won't protect a man who attacks women.'

'This will be the end of all of you,' Glass shouted, slurring his words slightly. 'Who will believe you over a respected Officer of the Navy?'

Will had heard enough. He stood, crossed the tiny cabin in two steps, hauled Glass on to his feet, and swung his fist back. As his clenched hand struck Glass's jaw Will felt the force reverberate through his body.

The Lieutenant sagged in front of him. Will's instinct was to reach out and lower the man to the floor, but he forced his arms to remain by his side and let the man hit the wooden deck with full force.

'Take him to the brig,' Will said again as he turned back to Mia.

Somewhere behind him he heard Captain Little shoo away the rest of the curious crew. He sat on the edge of the bed and took Mia's wrist in his hand. He felt for the pulse just below the bones of her hand and felt the reassuring steady thump.

'I'll take her to my cabin,' Will said, 'she'll be more comfortable there.'

'I'll send someone to fetch some water for her.'

The Captain paused and looked her up and down, 'And maybe something to dress her wounds with.'

Will nodded in agreement, then scooped Mia up in his arms. Even as a dead weight she wasn't that heavy, but he found it difficult to manoeuvre in the confines of the cabin. Being careful not to knock her head or legs on the door, he sidled out into the corridor. Slowly he walked towards his own cabin, kicked open the door with his foot and laid her gently down on his bed.

All through the trip she didn't stir at all and Will felt his heart pounding in his chest as he once again checked she was still breathing. When he had reassured himself she was still alive he started to check her over. He found the cause of her current state of unconsciousness almost immediately. A large lump was forming on the back of her head. He supposed she'd either jerked her head back into the wooden headboard behind the bed trying to get away from Glass or he'd propelled her into it.

Will felt the rage building again and he knew if Mia didn't wake up he would be hanged for murder. He would not allow her death to go unavenged.

The thought of Mia dying hurt him more than he ever could have imagined. He didn't want to envisage a world without her in it; she made everything so much better.

His macabre thoughts were interrupted by a knock on the door.

'Come in.'

The door opened and Ed Redding entered the room. He carried a jug of water in one hand and a wooden box in the other. He set the water down on the desk and the wooden box beside it.

'How is she?' he asked, studying Mia's peaceful face.

'No change, still unconscious. She must have hit her head.'

'I never liked the Lieutenant, but I wouldn't have ever imagined...' Redding let the sentence trail off.

Will realised he was equally as shocked. He knew Lieutenant Glass had felt contempt towards Mia and pure dislike towards himself, but he wouldn't have pinned him as a man who forced himself on unwilling women.

'Just shows you never know who to trust,' the First Mate said. 'I've brought you our medical box. There's not much in it, I'm afraid, but you might find something useful.'

Will doubted there would be anything in it that would help Mia in her current state. On a ship full of hardened sailors they were unlikely to find smelling salts. He suspected time would be the only thing to heal Mia. He just hoped her recovery would happen sooner rather than later.

'Thanks,' he said.

'Just shout if you need anything,' Redding said, 'or if you want someone to come and sit with her.'

Will nodded in gratitude, but knew he wouldn't be leaving Mia's side until she woke up, however long that might be.

Redding left the room and Will diverted his attention back to Mia. He wondered if she was comfortable enough. He had placed her down in the middle of the bed with a single pillow under her head. Maybe two would be better. Or maybe none at all.

He decided to leave her where she was. Then his eyes fell on the jug of water Redding had left. Were you meant to give water to someone who was unconscious? He wasn't sure, but looking at Mia's lips he thought they could be a little dry.

Will stood up, glad of having something to do. He grabbed a glass off the little table beside his bed and into it poured a small amount of water. Next he perched on the bed beside her head and contemplated how best to go about giving her the drink. Gently he slipped one arm behind her neck and lifted it off the pillow ever so slightly. With her head in a more upright position he held the glass of water to her lips and trickled a little into her mouth. Or at least he was aiming for her mouth. He doubted a single drop of the water made it past her lips. Instead it dribbled down her chin straight into her cleavage.

Cursing, he put down the glass and looked around for something to dry her with. The last thing she needed was to wake up with wet clothes. Finally he settled on a corner of the sheet and delicately dabbed at the skin of her chest, soaking up the droplets of water that had fallen between her breasts.

When she was dry he contemplated giving the water a second try and decided against it. She'd probably choke and end up with pneumonia.

He looked around the room, trying to think of something else to do to speed her recovery. He hated this waiting, especially hated feeling so impotent, knowing that he could do nothing to make her better.

Will was normally a man of action. He saw someone in distress and he helped them out. Now, when it was the woman he loved lying unconscious beside him, he wanted to be a man of action again and knew he would do anything to help her.

His brain froze as he realised what he'd just thought. The woman he loved. That's how he'd thought of Mia. Did he love her? His subconscious obviously believed so.

He told himself he couldn't possibly love Mia Del Torres; they could never have any kind of a future together. To love her would be to invite a whole world of pain into his life. Surely leaving the woman you loved on the other side of the world was worse than never loving at all.

Why leave her? his rebellious brain asked. Will reprimanded himself immediately. He couldn't take her with him—the idea was preposterous. He was an English Lord. He was expected to marry an heiress and sire a brood of pure-bred children.

But he didn't want to marry an English heiress, he realised. In fact, he didn't want to contemplate a life without Mia.

Even with this revelation he knew it would still be impossible. They weren't just from opposite ends of the earth geographically, their whole lives were different. He could never expect Mia to leave everything she'd ever known behind for a cold and distant shore. And he'd been so sure he would remain a bachelor for ever, the lone man prowling his estate or searching for lost people.

'Will?'

All thoughts of the future were banished from his mind the moment he heard his name.

'Mia.' He felt the relief flooding over his body and knew he was grinning like a madman. 'My darling Mia.'

'What happened?' she asked, looking around in confusion. 'Why am I here? Why does my head hurt?'

She winced as her fingers found the tender lump on the back of her head.

'You don't remember?' he asked.

She shook her head.

'What happened?' She sounded a little panicked now.

Will took her hand in his own and gently stroked her skin. 'You were attacked,' he said gently. 'By Glass.'

Mia screwed her eyes tight as if trying to remember.

'I was?' she asked, as if barely able to believe it.

Will nodded.

'Why?'

It was a good question. One he hadn't quite

figured out the answer to yet. He suspected the stink of rum that emanated from Glass when he'd punched him might explain some of his behaviour. Explain, but certainly not excuse.

'Did he…?' Mia trailed off and Will saw the look of revulsion cross her face.

'No. You fought him so bravely, my darling.'

Tears started to flood down her cheeks and her body shook. Will realised she must be in shock and scooped her up into his arms again, holding her body close to his.

'Shh,' he soothed, 'I've got you now. I won't let anything bad happen to you again.'

Chapter Eighteen

Mia felt her whole body shudder as the tears streamed down her face and she gasped for breath. She couldn't breathe properly. Every time she tried to inhale it was like there was an apple stuck in her throat.

'Shh,' Will said soothingly, stroking her hair with one hand whilst cradling her like a small child with the other. 'You're safe now. Just breathe.'

She gasped, sucking air into her lungs, but it didn't feel like anywhere near enough to sustain her. She gasped again, lungs ready to explode, but still her head was spinning.

'Breathe in and out,' Will instructed calmly, rubbing her back as he encouraged her.

Mia tried to make her body relax and some of the air she'd been storing up gushed out through her lips.

'Good girl. Just breathe slowly.'

Mia felt his strength infusing her and slowly she took a deep breath in and let it out again.

'I don't remember anything,' she said after a few minutes.

'That's perfectly normal,' Will said. 'You've had a concussion.'

It sounded so dramatic.

She didn't know how she should be feeling right now. Glass had attacked her, that much was evident from the bruises across her body, but she didn't remember a second of it. She found it hard to be angry or scared when it felt as if it had happened to someone else.

Mia let her head drop forward on to Will's shoulder. She felt safe in his arms and knew she didn't want to leave. He smelled wonderful—she could detect a mixture of the salty sea air mixed with his own masculine scent—and she nuzzled into the folds of his shirt ever so gently.

'I've got you,' Will said reassuringly.

She wondered if she could freeze time and stay in this moment for ever. Despite the fact her body ached from top to toe, sitting on Will's lap, cradled in his arms, seemed just about as perfect as life could get.

'Would you like me to let you sleep?' Will asked.

'No,' she answered quickly. 'Don't leave me.'

He responded by tightening his grip and pulling her closer to him.

'I'm so sorry I let this happen, Mia,' he said after a few seconds' pause.

Of course the silly man was blaming himself. It was exactly the chivalrous, ridiculous sort of thing he would do.

She tipped her head up and looked into his eyes. She could see the guilt emanating from them and shook her head in amazement.

'You blame yourself?' she asked.

'Of course. I should have seen what he had planned.'

'How could you?'

'I knew he disliked you. I should have seen that it was so much more.'

'There's no way you could have predicted what the Lieutenant was going to do. He probably didn't even know himself until he was making his way to my room.'

'You're far too generous, Mia.'

'You think he sat in his cabin and planned it?'

Will shrugged. 'I don't know. I can't pretend to

understand a man who tried to force himself on an innocent woman, on any woman.'

'That's because you're one of the good ones,' Mia said.

He looked down at her fondly. Their faces were only inches apart with her head resting upon his shoulder. She wanted to stretch her neck up and brush her lips against his, but she knew any movement and every muscle in her body would scream. Plus they hadn't really talked since she'd told him she loved him. He probably wouldn't want to encourage her by kissing her.

Nevertheless it was ever so tempting.

'What are you thinking?' he asked softly.

Mia felt the blush creeping over her cheeks.

'You're looking at me very strangely,' Will murmured.

'I was thinking I wanted to kiss you,' Mia said, 'but my neck hurt too much to move.'

'Now that is a dilemma.'

'Isn't it?' She let his shoulder take the full weight of her head and tilted her face up towards him.

'I suppose I could blow you a kiss,' he offered. 'Would that satisfy?' The gleam in his eye told her he knew full well it wouldn't satisfy.

'It's a start.'

He brought his lips together and kissed the air.

'Strangely unsatisfying,' Mia reported.

'Well, I can't leave a lady unsatisfied.'

'That sounds like a promise, Mr Greenacre.'

'I can just about reach the top of your head from here,' Will offered. 'Maybe that will please you more.'

'There's only one way to find out.'

He bent his head forward and planted kiss on the top of her head.

'Marginally better.'

'Only marginally? My pride is sufficiently dented.'

'Let's just say there is room for improvement.'

'Ah, constructive criticism,' Will murmured. 'I do like to learn from my mistakes.'

'Maybe a kiss where there is a little less hair and a little more skin,' Mia suggested.

He pulled an expression of mock shock. 'You mean you don't enjoy being kissed here?' he asked, kissing her on each eyebrow, one after the other.

Mia pretended to contemplate his question for a second or two. 'It's not that I don't enjoy it. I just think your lips could be better employed elsewhere.'

She saw his eyes slip to her breasts and he grinned wolfishly.

'I agree,' he said.

'*I* was thinking about my lips,' Mia said, 'although I can see your male mind was focused elsewhere.'

Will shrugged and shook his head. 'Alas, I am cursed with a male mind.'

Before she could think of any reply Will dipped his head and kissed her. He was gentle, as if he didn't want to hurt her. Ironically Mia's lips were one of the only places she didn't hurt. She deepened the kiss, passionately running her tongue along his lips as he had before.

She felt one of his hands slip down her back and cup her bottom, squeezing gently. She let him fondle her, enjoying the attention. Then felt herself stiffen and grimace as he brushed against a bruise.

'How are you feeling?' he asked, breaking off the kiss.

Mia considered her answer carefully. She was feeling sore and confused and her head was pounding, but at the same time she felt a contentment she'd never have imagined was possible.

'I don't know if I want to remember what happened,' she said, 'or if I'm grateful I can't.'

Will nodded solemnly.

'Will you hold me?' Mia asked.

Will tightened his grip around her waist and slid her bottom off his lap so she was on the bed. Gently he rolled her on to one side and shuffled in beside her. He looped one arm around her waist and pulled her closer towards him.

'How's that?' he asked.

'Perfect,' Mia murmured.

And it was. She could feel his reassuring presence behind her and felt safe and secure. His body was gently moulded to hers and she could feel the rise and fall of his chest. The warm breath from each and every exhalation tickled the back of her neck and sent little shivers down her spine.

She tilted her head back as he reached up and stroked her hair.

'I wanted to say thank you, Will,' Mia said quietly.

'You shouldn't be thanking me.'

Mia could tell he still blamed himself for not foreseeing the attack by Lieutenant Glass and she wished he would believe her when she told him it wasn't his fault.

'I wanted to say thank you for the past few days. They've been the happiest of my life.'

She felt his body stiffen behind her and his hand stopped stroking her hair. At first he didn't say anything, but Mia didn't mind; she'd accepted now he didn't love her. She knew he cared for her and that would have to be enough. And she'd made plenty of memories with him these past few days—she just hoped they were enough to last a lifetime.

'I never expected this,' Will said after a few minutes of silence.

Mia waited for him to elaborate.

'I came to the Caribbean to avenge my brother and catch the people who had abducted him. I never expected to meet someone like you.'

Mia didn't know what to say.

'You are a truly remarkable woman, Mia, and I'm blessed to have met you.'

He didn't explain any further, but Mia couldn't stop smiling. He cared for her, she knew he did. Maybe not quite like she cared for him, but there were definitely some strong feelings there. She didn't push him any further; she sensed it had taken a lot for him to admit so much to her. He was a private person who didn't often talk about his feelings.

Mia felt her eyes drooping and allowed herself to enjoy the warmth and safety of Will's embrace. She knew that as long as he held her nothing bad would happen, she just wished he never had to let go.

'Tomorrow might be our last day together,' Mia said sleepily. 'But I want you to know I will never forget the time I have spent with you.'

Chapter Nineteen

Will hadn't slept a wink. Mia's last words to him before falling asleep had rattled around in his brain for hours.

'Tomorrow might be our last day together.'

The very thought was making him feel sick. He didn't want to give her up. He felt like he'd only just found her. Surely they deserved a little more time together. He even thought about going to Captain Little and asking him to sail around in circles for a few days. Then he thought of his brother and a horrible wave of guilt washed over him. He was meant to be focused on bringing his brother's killers to justice, not indulging his passions in bed with a beautiful woman.

Still, he didn't think he would be able to say goodbye to Mia. She had come to mean so much to him.

Restless, Will resisted the urge to roll over in bed. Mia was sleeping soundly beside him and it wouldn't be fair to disturb her just because he was fretting about the future. After a few more uncomfortable minutes he decided to get up. There were still a couple of hours until dawn, and he wanted Mia to be rested for the day ahead as it was likely to be mentally and emotionally draining for her.

He slipped away, pausing to lean over Mia's sleeping form and plant a kiss gently on her forehead. She looked so peaceful and he marvelled at how well she had coped with being attacked earlier that evening. It was true she still couldn't remember the events, but finding her body bruised and beaten must have been a huge shock.

Silently Will left the cabin and padded down the corridor. The ship was quiet. A few men would be up and about, wordlessly going about their duties, but the rest of the crew were resting, in anticipation of the day to come.

Will emerged into the balmy night air and felt his eyes adjusting. It was quite a clear night, with the stars twinkling brightly in the sky, and after a few moments he could see the men dotted around the deck.

'Mr Greenacre,' Ed Redding said, quietly coming up beside Will, 'how is Miss Del Torres?'

'Awake,' he said, 'or at least she did wake up. She's sleeping now.'

'She must be very distressed.'

He remembered holding her shaking body against his.

'She can't remember anything,' he said. 'I think she's concussed, but she was still in shock.'

'I would never have imagined the Lieutenant would do such a thing,' Redding said. 'He's an arrogant, dislikable man, but I didn't peg him as being capable of such a foul act.'

Will felt the same. He'd disliked Glass, but he hadn't thought of him as dangerous. A pang of guilt ripped through him; maybe he should have realised the sort of man he was. Then he might have been able to protect Mia better.

'I'm going to speak to him,' Will said decisively. 'Now he's sobered up I want to see what he has to say for himself.'

Redding looked dubious.

'I won't kill him,' Will promised, knowing he might not be able to stick to it.

'He's not worth a one-way trip to the gallows.'

Will knew Redding was right, he wasn't worth a

death sentence, but somehow he wanted the man to pay for what he'd done to Mia.

'I'll come with you,' the First Mate said. 'Just until I'm sure you're not going to kill him.'

It was as good as he was going to get.

Redding led the way back below decks and through the maze of corridors. They went into the very bowels of the boat to reach the brig. The First Mate selected a key from the ring he was carrying and opened the door leading to the cells.

It was gloomy inside, with no natural light entering the confined space to illuminate it. Will stood in the doorway for a few seconds, allowing his eyes to adjust. Eventually he could see a small cell, lined on three sides by thick iron bars and a huddled shape in the corner. Apart from the cell there was little else in the room, just a solid wooden bench and an empty jug on the floor just outside the bars.

'Come to gloat, Greenacre?' Glass said.

Will strained his eyes and saw the huddled shape move slightly.

'I'm not here to gloat,' he told the Lieutenant.

'So you're here to dish out your own personal form of justice,' Glass moved from his position in the corner and pressed his face up against the bars so Will could see him properly. 'It will be a comfort in my last moment to know you are on your way to the scaffold, too.'

'He's not going to kill you,' Redding said, darting a nervous glance at Will.

'I'm not going to kill you,' Will confirmed and was surprised to find he spoke the truth. 'You're not worth ruining my life over.'

He was thinking of Mia lying peacefully asleep in his bed and he realised he couldn't do something that would take him away from her. He imagined the anguish on her face as she watched him take his last walk, that short distance from the cart to the gallows, and realised he never wanted to do anything to hurt her.

'If you're not going to kill me, why are you here?' Glass asked.

Will stepped further into the small room and sat down on the wooden bench.

'I want to know why.'

The Lieutenant let out a short snort of laughter.

'Why did you attack Miss Del Torres?'

For a second Will thought Glass wasn't going to reply.

'You've ruined your life,' he prompted. 'The Navy will throw you out. Your connections may save you from any harsher consequences, but your life as you know it is still over.'

'I wouldn't be so sure about that,' Glass said cockily. 'Not everyone puts such high value on a pirate whore as you do.'

'Miss Del Torres is neither a pirate nor a whore,' Will said, trying to keep his anger from bubbling over. 'She has been indispensable with helping us track down her brother and his crew.'

'You speak as though you have already captured them.'

Will ignored this comment. He was pretty confident he would have Del Torres in a couple of hours so it wasn't worth arguing about.

Redding shifted on his feet and Will glanced at him, 'I'd better go,' the First Mate said. 'Don't kill him.'

He handed Will the key to lock the door to the brig behind him when he left, but took the key to Glass's cell with him.

'Tell me,' Will said again, 'why you attacked Miss Del Torres.'

Glass hesitated for just a second, then started speaking. 'She's worthless,' he said. 'She's the illegitimate child of a runaway slave and the sister of a pirate.'

Will shook his head in disbelief. 'That's not who she is. She's a woman in her own right, a woman who jumped into the sea and saved a stranger from drowning. A woman who is helping us track down her own brother because she knows it's the right thing to do.'

'Lovesick fool....' the Lieutenant spat. 'She's got you wrapped around her little finger.'

Will took a deep breath and calmed himself. 'So you think she's worthless, but that still doesn't explain why you attacked her.'

'I saw the way you look at her, like a man bewitched. It was obvious to everyone on this ship what you'd been doing on your little trip to the other side of Tortola.'

Will had hoped no one had noticed their slightly dishevelled appearance, but it seemed he had been a little naive.

'Every time you even glanced at her you smiled. It was sickening.'

An awful realisation began to dawn on Will and he stood suddenly. He leaned forward, hands grabbing the bars of the cell.

'You did it to hurt me?' he asked.

Lieutenant Glass laughed, lounging back out of Will's reach against the far side of the cell.

'You attacked Mia to hurt me?'

'Not just to hurt you,' Glass said, 'but that certainly was a big incentive.'

Will thought about every comment he'd made to the Lieutenant, every time he'd excluded him from their plans. He felt sick at the idea Glass had picked Mia as his weakness. He had wanted to get his revenge for being sidelined on this mission and had struck out at Mia.

Will realised it had worked. Nothing Glass could have done to him would have been worse than attacking Mia. At least he could have defended himself against a physical attack.

'You said not just to hurt me,' Will repeated. 'Why else?'

Glass shrugged, 'She might be a pirate whore, but she's an attractive pirate whore.'

Will pictured Glass' hands roaming over Mia's body as she struggled beneath him. All night he had been trying to contain his imagination—he didn't want to even contemplate what would have happened if Mia hadn't screamed. The idea of Glass raping her was Will's worst nightmare.

'You're a sick man,' he said, taking a step away from the cell.

'She'd given herself up to you. I'm sure she would have enjoyed it once I'd got started.'

Will saw red. Anger and hatred surged through him and he smashed a fist against the bar of the cell. Glass just laughed. He knew in his current position and without the key to the actual cell there wasn't much Will could do.

'Laugh now,' Will said, calming slightly. 'When we get back to Barbados I will make sure your life as you know it is over.'

Glass shrugged. 'You're welcome to try.'

He seemed all too confident and untroubled for a man who would at the very least lose his career and could lose his liberty or his life.

'The reality is I'm well connected, with an exemplary military record. The Navy will most likely sweep this under the carpet. I'll get a rap on the knuckles, a few months' posting to an undesirable part of the world, then all will be forgotten. It's not as if she's anyone of consequence.'

She was of consequence to Will.

'You're not the only one with contacts, Glass,' he warned him. 'I may not be able to touch you whilst you're in the Navy, but one day you'll want to retire and I expect you'll want to return to your family in England. I can make it so all of society knows what kind of man you are.'

Some of the colour drained from the Lieutenant's face. He shook his head in disbelief and tried to put on a good front.

'There are other places to live,' he said. 'And after a few years no one is going to be bothered I groped a foreign whore anyway.'

Will agreed there were other places to live, but the second half of his statement wasn't quite true. After his career in the Navy he had no doubt Glass planned to return to England a hero and try to bag himself a nice heiress. No society mama worth her salt would allow their precious daughter anywhere near a man with even a whiff of this kind of scandal.

'I would worry about sorting your own sorry mess of a life out rather than ruining mine,' Glass said.

'My life is fine.'

'Really? What's the plan, then? You catch Del Torres and return to run your estate with a pirate whore as your mistress? Or you leave her behind, never knowing if you have an illegitimate child on the other side of the world?'

Will's eyes glazed over. Glass was right, he did

have a decision to make. A decision he hadn't even known was there. He could take Mia back with him to England. She wouldn't be society's idea of an acceptable wife, but what would that matter? They could retire to his estate, hidden from the rest of the world's cruel jibes, and have a family together.

The thought of children with Mia made his heart swell. He wanted to populate a nursery with her, have hoards of giggling children with honey-coloured skin and dark, bottomless eyes.

He didn't care if he could never show his face in his London club or attend another society ball again. It wouldn't matter; he would have Mia.

Suddenly everything became clear. It was as if a huge weight had been lifted from his shoulders. He loved Mia. Of course he did. He couldn't delude himself any longer that the happiness that diffused through his body every time he laid eyes on her was anything other than love. He loved Mia Del Torres and he was going to marry her.

If she would have him. A momentary stab of panic lanced through his heart. What if she didn't want him? Then he remembered her declaration of love, undemanding of a vow in return, and knew she wanted him. And if she protested that a marriage between two such different people couldn't work he was sure he could persuade her. In fact, he thought persuading her might be rather fun. Even if she didn't want to go and live in England he wouldn't care. He would hire a man to run the estate and they could spend their days on Caribbean beaches, walking barefoot in the sand and making love on the shoreline.

He grinned, looking at Glass. 'Mia won't be my mistress,' he said, 'she'll be my wife.'

Will pushed himself away from the bars of the cell and spun on his heel. He heard Glass shouting something after him as he closed the door to the brig, but didn't bother to pay attention. He was too happy to be brought down by the petty, cruel Lieutenant. He was in love.

He strode along the corridor and took the wooden steps two at a time, rising out of the darkness of the bowels of the ship to the open air of the deck. With a spring in his step he hurried towards his destination. He needed to see Mia, he couldn't wait to tell her he loved her. Will could picture the moment; he would sweep her into his arms and declare his love before smothering her with kisses. He would ask her to become his wife, to spend the rest of her life with him and to become the mother of his children.

'Mr Greenacre,' Captain Little called quietly, stepping into his path.

Will almost didn't stop, he was so eager to get to Mia.

'We've sighted a ship.'

He halted suddenly.

'In the exact location you gave us.'

He knew it was *The Flaming Dragon*. It had to be.

'How long have we got until dawn?' Will asked.

'Ninety minutes.'

He knew their best chance was to sneak up on the pirate ship in the darkness. It would be at its most vulnerable in the hours before dawn. The men assigned night watch would be weary and, if they were lucky, maybe even sleeping. They would probably be able to get pretty close before the alarm was sounded.

'What do you think, Captain?' Will asked, knowing it was Captain Little's men he was sending into danger and his ship that was going to take the battering.

'This is the best chance we'll get. We can be within cannon's range in forty minutes.'

'Are the men ready to fight?'

'Redding is rousing everyone as we speak. They'll be at their stations within minutes.'

Will looked into the distance, straining his eyes to try to make out the outline of the ship they were hunting, even though he knew it would be too far away to see in the darkness. This was the moment he had been waiting for. He felt the adrenaline surge through his body to prepare him for the fight.

'Gather the crew in the mess room,' he said. 'I will speak to them.'

The Captain nodded in agreement and hustled off to arrange his men.

Will took a deep breath and steeled himself. He needed to inspire the men. The fight ahead would be a tough one. Del Torres's crew were renowned throughout the Caribbean as ruthless fighters and he had no doubt they would fight to the death before surrendering their ship.

He tried to push his thoughts of Mia from his mind. This wasn't the right time. His declaration of love would have to wait, for now he had to focus on the next few hours and bring her out of this safely. Then he could tell her his feelings and they could make their plans for the future.

Chapter Twenty

Mia opened her eyes and stretched. For an instant she couldn't work out why her muscles were so sore, but then the events of the previous night flooded back to her. She still couldn't remember exactly what had happened. If she closed her eyes, she could see flashes of activity, but even with these short memories she felt strangely detached from the incident.

What had occurred later that evening was another matter entirely. She remembered every minute of Will comforting her and holding her. She knew for sure that part had happened.

Mia reached out a hand and patted the empty spot on the bed beside her. She was disappointed it was cold, Will must have left her some time ago. She wanted nothing more than to snuggle up to him and spend a lazy morning in bed.

Footsteps in the corridor outside brought her to her senses. They must be approaching dawn, which meant soon they would find out if *The Flaming Dragon* was where they had anticipated it to be. She felt a coil of dread form in her stomach and suddenly Mia wanted to be anywhere else but here on this ship that was about to attack Jorge.

More footsteps along the corridor outside and frantic whispering was enough to alert her—something was going on. She pushed herself out of bed and started to straighten her clothes. Her dress looked more like an old rag than the simple but elegant ensemble it had once been. In the past few days she'd been thrown in a cell in it, discarded it on a beach, been attacked in it and now had slept in the battered material.

She gave up trying to make her dress look presentable and instead focused on her hair. Sometime in the night it had fallen free and now cascaded over her shoulders. Most of the pins had been misplaced during her adventures of the past few days and she knew it was pointless trying to pin it up. Instead she ran her fingers through the loose curls and let it fall over her shoulder. When she was satisfied there was nothing more she could do to look presentable, Mia poked her head out of the cabin.

The corridor was deserted, but somewhere in the distance she could hear Will's voice. It sounded like he was making a speech.

She followed the sound. It wasn't hard to do; the rest of the ship was silent and Mia smiled as she could start to make out the words. He was rousing his troops.

'A ship has been sighted,' Will said, 'and we believe it is *The Flaming Dragon*.'

Mia paused for a second and told herself to breathe. She had known this moment would come. Now it was here she needed all her strength and courage to infuse her so she could survive the next few hours.

'We are approaching the pirate ship as we speak. The darkness is our ally and I am hopeful we will get within cannon range before they even realise we are there.'

Mia pushed the door of the mess room open and her eyes immediately fixed on Will. He was standing on one of the tables, the crew gathered around him. He looked magnificent.

'They will fight,' Will warned, 'and they will fight dirty. If they lose, they die.'

The assembled men nodded and murmured. Mia couldn't tear her eyes away from Will.

'We have the advantage,' Will said. 'We have surprise. They have no idea we are coming for them.'

Mia felt a sudden surge of panic. What if Will was injured? He would no doubt be at the forefront of the fighting. He wasn't the sort of man to command his men from the rear. He would be the first to fire upon *The Dragon* and the first to board. That meant there was a real chance he could get hurt. She felt a lump form in her throat, making it hard for her to swallow. She couldn't lose him like this. She'd only just found him.

'We will win. Their luck has finally run out. Fight for all the innocent men and women and children they've killed, all the towns they've plundered. Fight to stop them taking one of your loved ones away.'

Will's eyes met hers and she heard his silent addition. He would be fighting to avenge his brother.

The men let out muted cheers, all savvy enough to know too much noise could travel to *The Flaming Dragon* and alert the so-far unsuspecting pirates.

'To your stations, men,' the Captain commanded. 'Make me proud.'

The crew dispersed quickly, each man heading off silently to prepare for the battle ahead. Mia was swept along in the crowd and carried on to the open deck. A few minutes later Will emerged, deep in conversation with Captain Little and Ed Redding.

He saw her watching him and gave her a half smile. Mia responded with the same and watched as the men planned their strategy. She didn't know how to feel. So many emotions were vying for her attention. She felt nervous about the battle to come—whatever happened, she would be losing someone she cared about today. She felt scared at the notion of having to face her brother, to see his face fall as he realised his sister had betrayed him. And she felt suddenly lonely, because no matter how the day turned out she would be going back to Barbados to spend whatever remained of her life alone.

'Mia,' Will said quietly as he came up behind her.

She spun and couldn't help but smile. Just being close to him made her happy.

'How are you?' he asked.

'Scared.' There was no reason to lie to him.

'I won't let you get hurt,' he said.

'It's not me I'm worried about.'

He raised a hand and stroked her cheek, then let his fingers tangle in her hair.

'I will try to take your brother alive,' he said, 'so he can stand fair trial.'

Mia nodded. It didn't matter much. He would be condemned for his crimes at trial and sentenced to hang in front of a jeering crowd. Perhaps it would be kinder for him to die fighting.

'And you?' she asked.

He looked puzzled.

'Will you be safe?'

He looped his free arm around her back and pulled her closer to him.

'I'll be just fine,' he promised. 'I've got something to fight for.'

In full view of the whole crew he dipped his head and kissed her passionately on the lips. Mia recovered from her initial shock and kissed him back, never wanting the embrace to end. There was a small chance this was the last time she would ever kiss him.

'Everyone's looking,' Mia murmured as he pulled away.

'I don't care.'

Redding hurried over and coughed quietly. 'Sorry to interrupt, but the Captain wants your advice,' he said.

'I'll be right there.'

Mia felt his arm slip from around her waist and suddenly she felt very alone.

'After this is all over,' Will said, catching her hand in his, 'we need to talk about the future.' Then he planted one last quick kiss on her lips before striding off after Redding.

The future? Mia felt her head spin at the idea. Surely they had no future, that was the whole point. The way he had said it made a spark of hope flare in her heart. He had kissed her in front of everyone, claimed her as his own. Then he had told her they needed to talk about the future.

Immediately Mia began to weave a fantasy in her mind. She saw herself strolling the crowded streets of Bridgetown on Will's arm, not caring who saw them together. She saw him in her bed night after night and making love to her until she begged for mercy. And she saw a cherubic little boy, with golden hair and tanned skin, climbing up on to Will's shoulders as the three of them fell about laughing.

Maybe that was a step too far, but surely she was allowed to dream. She wanted the whole dream, but in reality any little part of it would do. As long as Will remained in her life she would be happy.

She wondered if she could be satisfied with being

his mistress and immediately knew the answer. If that was the only way she could be with him, then of course she could. It would break her heart every time he left her, not knowing if one day he would put her aside, but every day with him would be a gift.

'Perhaps you would like to go below decks now, miss,' Ed Redding suggested, quietly coming up behind her. 'We will be within cannon range in five minutes.'

Mia shook her head. There was no way she was going to hide below decks when they attacked. She was part of this mission and she wouldn't cower in her cabin as the men she loved fought.

'I'll stay up on deck,' she said. 'If you could just point me to somewhere I won't be in the way.'

'If you stay up here, I can't guarantee your safety, miss,' Redding said, his brow furrowing with concern.

'I know.' Mia smiled at him.

He looked at her for a few long moments, then nodded as if he'd made up his mind.

'If you'd follow me, Miss Del Torres.' He led her up on to the raised platform where the navigation took place. She followed him behind the large wooden ship's wheel and smiled in encouragement to the young sailor who stood there.

'You should be out of the way here,' Redding said, 'but still able to see everything that's going on.'

'Thank you.'

He hesitated as if he wanted to say more and after a few seconds lifted her hand to his lips.

'It's been a pleasure knowing you, Miss Del Torres.'

Before she could reply he had hurried off below decks, no doubt to supervise the men manning the cannons.

They were sailing silently through the early morning darkness, making good speed towards the ship they supposed to be *The Flaming Dragon*. Mia could see the outline of the mast against the inky blackness of the sky and wondered what her brother was doing. Probably he was fast asleep. Jorge had never been an early riser, even as a boy, and she doubted the pirate life, heavy in copious amounts of rum and revelling, had done much to remedy that.

She could feel the nervous anticipation emanating from every man quietly preparing for the attack. As she watched them she wondered who would survive the upcoming battle and who would fall. Mia wished there was something she could do to avoid the bloodshed, but she knew it was hopeless. Men on both sides would die today, men who had been kind, law-abiding citizens and men who had given their lives to piracy and lawlessness.

She watched as Will stepped up to the prow of the ship and raised the telescope to his eye. He stood completely still for at least a minute, surveying the ship, then whispered something to Captain Little. The Captain took the telescope from him and looked for himself.

Silently Will turned and held up a hand. Around the ship Mia saw the crewmen return his signal. They all understood: they were coming up upon *The Flaming Dragon* and at the first sign of life on board the pirate ship they were to attack.

Her heart pounding in her chest, Mia waited. She held her breath as every second took them that little bit nearer. She wished Will would step away from the prow—surely he was a very obvious target to anyone who glanced over from the pirate ship. She couldn't bear it if he got shot down in the first minute of the battle.

Suddenly she heard a shout from across the water and all hell broke loose.

Chapter Twenty-One

Will heard the shout as the pirate lookout finally stirred from his sleep and spotted the big ship bearing down on *The Flaming Dragon.*

'Fire!' Will shouted.

The order was relayed across the ship and Will heard the telltale thud of the cannons being readied. Within seconds the cannons fired, one after another in quick succession. He watched as the cannonballs flew through the air. Three hit their targets, but the others fell short. He could imagine Redding below decks, adjusting each cannon as the men reloaded, ready for the next onslaught.

They were close enough now Will could see the activity on the pirate ship. Men were swarming about on the deck, no doubt responding to Del Torres's orders for retaliation. They seemed calm given the circumstances—from what he could see the Captain of *The Flaming Dragon* ran a disciplined ship.

The cannons fired for a second time and this time most of the balls hit their mark. One of the masts of the pirate ship was hit, and even from across the water Will could hear the unmistakable groan of splintering wood.

Despite the barrage of cannonballs the men on *The Flaming Dragon* seemed to be getting themselves organised. To Will's dismay he could see hatches opening and the tips of cannons poking out. They were going to be attacked.

He heard the first boom and shouted, 'Brace for impact.'

The pirates were skilled, he had to give them that. The very first cannonball hit its mark and rocked the ship as it punched through the wood.

Will felt a blinding panic. He'd seen Mia standing up near the wheel just seconds before *The Flaming Dragon* had fired. He spun to check she was still there and still upright, knowing he wouldn't forgive himself if she was harmed.

Mia stood next to the young man at the wheel. She wasn't cowering or ducking as the cannonballs thudded into the ship, instead she stood proud and tall. Will had an awful premonition; she was going to get hit. Surely she presented too much of a target for the pirates to miss. He could see her silhouetted against the rapidly lightening sky, her hair blowing free around her shoulders.

The ships were two or three minutes away from each other now. He had to get Mia to safety before they were able to board.

He strode across the deck, resisting the urge to duck every time he heard the boom of the cannon. He saw Mia turn towards him and felt his heart leap. She was still safe.

Will took the stairs up to the small deck where the young man continued to steer faithfully towards *The Flaming Dragon*, seemingly ignoring the cannon fire. He barely flinched when the wood a few inches from his head splintered, sending jagged shards flying in every direction. Will admired Captain Little's crew. They were experienced and well trained and had accepted this mission with the cool certainty they would prevail.

'Mia,' Will shouted over the booming, 'you need to get to safety.'

'I'm staying here.'

'You could get hurt.'

Mia smiled at him sadly. 'We all could get hurt.'

'Please, go below decks,' he begged her, knowing his heart would split in two if she was injured.

'Don't worry about me,' Mia said bravely. 'Focus on the men you're going to lead into the fight.'

She stood on her tiptoes and kissed him hard on the lips, then planted a hand on his chest and pushed him away. 'Go,' she commanded. 'Make me proud.'

Will hesitated, but he saw she wasn't going to budge. He glanced over his shoulder and saw they were nearly upon the pirate ship, in the next minute or so they would be able to jump aboard. And the pirates would be able to jump to theirs. Most of Del Torres's crew wouldn't know who Mia was, but he hoped they wouldn't kill a woman not involved in the fight when there were more than enough combatants to keep them occupied. He was more worried she might get hit by a stray bullet or crushed by a falling mast.

Realising there was nothing more he could do, he darted back to the main deck and called the men to his side. They were waiting with planks of wood, ready to push them over to *The Flaming Dragon* as soon as they were close enough to board the pirate ship. The best thing he could do for Mia was to keep as many of the pirates on *The Dragon* as possible and engage them there.

'Ready, men?' he asked.

His question was met by a collective roar. They waited, every second dragging as the ship inched closer. Will checked his pistol one last time and placed a hand on his sword. He was quick with both, but he had never been up against bloodthirsty pirates before. He would need every ounce of skill and swordsmanship he could muster.

'Now,' he shouted.

The men responded immediately, pushing the planks of wood across. Will was the first to cross, nimbly hopping across the gap, making sure he didn't fall into the churning sea below.

The sight what met him was terrifying. Dozens of ferocious pirates roared as he and his men boarded their ship. A few of the wooden planks were pushed free and Will heard the cries of men as they plunged into the sea below.

As he set foot on the deck of *The Flaming Dragon* he fired his pistol twice in quick succession. Two pirates fell. Then he was in too close quarters to use the gun and he drew his sword. With a battle cry he surged into the fight, only hoping the rest of the crew was behind him.

Will engaged a giant of a man, covered from head to toe in crude tattoos. Will was faster than the giant and nimbly sidestepped quite a few of his strokes. As the man began to tire Will plunged his sword forward and heard the man scream in agony.

There was no time for remorse, or even to check if the large man was still alive. His next assailant was upon him immediately. They fought hard and fast, using their fists when in close proximity. Eventually Will was close enough to headbutt the other man and as he fell to the floor Will expertly stepped over him and surveyed the scene.

It was difficult to tell who was winning. Clusters of men were fighting and there were dead and injured men littering the deck. He glanced back over his shoulder at the pirates who were flocking over to the ship where he'd left Mia unguarded. He hoped he had left enough of Captain Little's crew to hold off the pirates and for a second he doubted himself. Knowing that attitude would get him killed, he pushed Mia from his mind and set about his real mission. He needed to find Del Torres. If he could take the Captain he was sure the rest of the pirates would lose their nerve and maybe even surrender. They were outnumbered and it looked like they had taken significant losses during the bombardment with cannonballs. Now Will had to break their spirit by capturing their Captain.

The problem was he didn't have much idea what Del Torres looked like. All reports of the infamous pirate Captain were made by survivors following an attack on a town or a ship. If they were to be believed, Del Torres was approaching seven feet tall, had hair like a jet black lion's mane, and was both devastatingly handsome and devilishly horrific at the same time.

Instead of looking for a man fitting this fantastical description, Will looked for someone who bore a resemblance to the woman he loved. His eyes scanned the deck of and alighted on a handsome young man who was getting the better of two of Little's crew. Will knew instantly this was Del Torres. He fought with the conviction of a Captain and the ferocity of a man who has everything to lose.

For an instant their eyes locked and Will felt a shiver run down his spine. He had no doubt only one of them would leave this ship alive.

He started to approach Del Torres, sidestepping pairs locked in mortal combat, deflecting pirates who ran at him roaring with anger and rage. Del Torres was doing the same. Slowly he was making his way towards Will, fighting anyone who got in his way.

As Will progressed across the ship he saw Captain Little's crew were slowly prevailing. The fighting was still going strong, but the pirates were outnumbered and one by one were being subdued. He felt a flurry of anticipation; if he could take Del Torres this would all be over.

Will and Del Torres stopped only when they were a couple feet apart. Will studied the man he was preparing to kill and Del Torres regarded him with interest in return.

'Surrender,' Will demanded.

Del Torres laughed. Will found himself smiling. It probably was a bit of a naive demand.

'Who do I have the pleasure of fighting today?' the pirate Captain asked.

'My name is Will Greenacre.'

Del Torres narrowed his eyes as he recognised the name, but obviously couldn't quite place it.

'You abducted my brother,' Will said, helping him out.

'Of course. He died.'

'He died.'

Del Torres nodded in understanding and raised his sword.

'I must congratulate you,' he said, 'The Navy have been after us for years and have never even been close to finding us. Do you mind if I ask how you did it?'

Will was fascinated by his voice. He had the same tone as Mia and the same inflection. For a pirate he sounded quite well educated.

'I had a little help,' Will said cryptically and lunged.

Del Torres parried easily and the fight began.

Will could tell from the very first this man was an excellent sword fighter. He was light on his feet, didn't waste his lunges and seemed to be able to read his opponents' moves easily. They were well matched. Will had always excelled at swordsmanship. He and his brother had been given wooden swords by their father at a very young age and they had loved playing at knights and villains. He'd had lessons, of course, like all young men of his social class, but Will had always preferred learning on his own, picking up new techniques and experimenting on what worked for him.

Del Torres fought effortlessly. Will could see why this man had become the Captain of *The Flaming Dragon* at such a young age.

Sword clashed with sword and Will jumped back

as Del Torres quickly ducked and sliced Will's arm on the recovery. The wound was not deep, but his shirtsleeve quickly turned a deep crimson colour and the wound throbbed.

Will was running on adrenaline now, throwing himself into the attack. Out of the corner of his eye he saw his side was still winning. Most of Del Torres's crew had been subdued and were either lying injured on the floor or surrounded by Little's men, brandishing swords. Small pockets of pirates remained, viciously striking out like wounded animals, knowing the end was close.

Will lunged and caught Del Torres in the abdomen. He felt his blade slice through flesh, but knew it was just a superficial wound. The young pirate had been quick enough to jump back and consequently had avoided a more serious outcome.

Del Torres growled and threw himself into the fight, hacking blows at Will and forcing him backwards. Will retreated, parrying every blow, but knowing he had to end this soon or his energy would be spent. Already the muscles in his arms screamed from the exertion.

He felt his back hit the rail beside him and suddenly there was nowhere else to retreat. With a primal roar he flung himself forward, catching Del

Torres on the cheek. Blood dripped down his opponent's face, but Del Torres hardly seemed to notice.

Will pushed forward, taking advantage of Del Torres's momentary distraction. He was just about to strike when Mia rushed between them.

Both men froze. She faced her brother, but Will had seen the tears streaming down her face and the anguish in her eyes as she'd inserted herself between them.

'Stop,' she whispered. 'Please stop.'

Chapter Twenty-Two

'Stop,' Mia repeated, unsure who she should be addressing.

Both men just stared at her in shock.

'Mia?' Del Torres said with astonishment.

'I'm so sorry, Jorge,' Mia said.

'You helped them?'

She nodded and felt her heart contract in agony as the disbelief flooded over her brother's face.

'Why?'

'Jorge,' Mia said taking a step towards him. She raised a hand and stroked his cheek gently. The skin was rough and salty from the sea air.

'Why, Mia?'

'I love you, Jorge. Or at least I loved the little boy you once were.' She could still see the mischievous ruffian in the notorious pirate who stood before her and it made it all that much harder to do what she had to do. 'But the things you've done…'

For a moment she thought he looked a little sheepish, but then his new persona took over and he smiled a winning smile.

'Just doing what a pirate is expected to do,' he said.

'You killed people, Jorge.'

He shrugged. 'I don't place as much value on human life as you do.'

He snatched her wrist and drew her closer to him. Behind her Mia could sense Will tense and hoped he wasn't about to do something rash.

'What about you, little sister, where was your family loyalty when they asked you to hunt me?'

Mia felt the tears stinging her eyes.

'Family loyalty.' Will barked a harsh laugh behind her. 'You speak of family loyalty, but where were you all those years your sister struggled on her own? Cast out by society, hunted by the authorities purely for the fact that she's your sister.'

Jorge had the decency to look a little ashamed, but only for a second.

'They hunted you?' he asked gently.

She nodded, not knowing what else to do. This wasn't going at all how she'd imagined.

'Did he hunt you?' Jorge pointed over her shoulder, seeming to want a focus for his rage.

'Of course not,' Mia said, rolling her eyes at her brother. 'He has protected me.'

'He's used you,' Jorge said, 'to find me.'

'Mia helped me,' Will said, 'but she did it because she's ashamed of what you've done.'

'You let him poison you against me.'

Mia shook her head sadly, 'He didn't need to poison me, Jorge. I know what is right and what is wrong. Just like you do deep down. Mama brought us up with good values.'

Jorge seemed to sag a little at the mention of their mother.

'I never meant to leave you on your own,' he said quietly.

She didn't know what to say. There was no doubt he was a ruthless killer, but underneath it all he was still her brother and he still cared for her.

Suddenly he changed; he straightened and pointed an accusing finger at Will.

'If you've harmed a hair on my sister's head, I'll kill you.'

It seemed a strange declaration for a defeated man to make. Will doubted Del Torres would get anywhere near him without one of Captain Little's men putting a bullet through his heart.

'Oh, stop it, Jorge,' Mia said, finding it ridiculous

that that was what he would focus on at a time like this. 'He hasn't harmed me at all.' She dropped her voice. 'Quite the opposite.'

Del Torres looked at her incredulously. 'You care for this English aristocrat?'

'I love this English aristocrat.'

She saw Will grin out of the corner of her eye.

Her brother took a step forward and dropped his voice, giving it a menacing quality.

'You better not be toying with my sister's heart,' he said. 'Tell me that you love her.'

Mia could see Will's eyes widen at the peculiar demand.

'I love her,' he said.

Mia spun round in shock. She knew he was probably just saying it to appease Jorge, but she needed to be sure.

'I love you,' he said again, this time directing his words directly to her. 'This wasn't how I planned to tell you, but I love you, Mia Del Torres.'

Mia didn't know what to say. She thought her heart might burst with happiness.

'You truly love me?' she asked, just wanting him to say it one more time.

'I truly love you.'

She wanted nothing more than to bound into his

arms and kiss him for evermore, but Mia was very conscious of her brother standing behind her and Captain Little's crew watching their every move.

'I'm glad,' her brother said and Mia turned to face him. 'Truly I am. I'm glad you will be happy.'

She felt the tears spring to her eyes and she stretched up to her tiptoes to plant a kiss on his cheek.

'I don't want you to blame yourself, Mia,' he said softly. 'You did the right thing.'

She looked at him, puzzled. He was regarding his ship, now in the hands of Captain Little's crew, and his comrades who were either lying dead or wounded on the decks or under guard, having surrendered. He looked deflated and lost.

'I've committed terrible deeds these past few years and you were right. I needed to be stopped.'

Mia peered at him, confused. This sounded very much like a farewell to her.

'You're a good girl, Mia, and I don't want you to feel any of this was your fault.'

'Jorge…' she said, trailing off as he caught her around the neck and pulled her towards him.

Del Torres turned her round so she was facing Will and she saw the fear in his eyes.

'Will, don't,' she pleaded. 'He won't hurt me.'

'I will,' Jorge said. 'I'll squeeze her neck until she can't breathe any more.'

Will lifted his pistol and took aim. Mia met his eyes for an instant and silently implored him not to shoot her brother. She saw him hesitate, then lower the pistol.

'You won't hurt her,' Will said.

Jorge gently kissed her head and Mia felt the tears start to stream down her cheeks. He edged back towards the rail of the ship, pulling her along with him.

'I never meant things to get this far,' he whispered in her ear.

Mia suddenly felt herself being propelled forward. She stumbled and instantly Will was in front of her, holding her up. Before Mia could recover and turn to face her brother a shot rang out, followed two seconds later by a splash.

'Jorge...' Mia whispered.

The next instant she was swept up into Will's arms and carried away before she could catch a glimpse of her brother sinking into the Caribbean sea.

'It's okay,' Will murmured. 'Nothing's going to hurt you now.' He nimbly traversed one of the planks of wood and took her away from *The Flaming Dragon*.

Mia sobbed, her whole body heaving. She'd just lost the last member of her family. Now she was truly alone.

'I can't believe he's gone.'

'I'm sorry, Mia.'

Mia looked up into Will's eyes and saw the sympathy in his expression.

'He was sorry,' she whispered quietly. 'In the end he was sorry.'

Will nodded, 'I think you're right, and maybe it's better this way.'

Mia thought he was probably right. It would have been worse to see her brother paraded through the streets, bombarded with hatred from onlookers, then climbing the scaffold and dropping to his death with everyone cheering. At least this way it was quick and relatively private.

Will sat down on an upturned barrel but didn't set Mia back on her feet. She felt safe and secure in his arms and was pleased to have just a few minutes longer of security.

'I meant it, Mia,' Will said as he hugged her closer to him. 'I love you.'

She searched his face, barely able to believe it. This was everything she had wanted.

'I love you and I want to spend the rest of my life with you.'

Her mouth fell open into a little O of shock.

'Say something,' he murmured. 'Or I'll think you've changed your mind about me.'

'Never.'

She stretched upwards and kissed him, closing her eyes and just feeling the softness of his lips against hers.

'I don't care how we're together,' Will said. 'We can marry and live in England or we can live in sin and travel the world.'

Mia felt as if her heart were about to explode. He was her dream, her fantasy, and now he wanted to be her perfect reality, as well.

'As long as I've got you I'll be happy,' Mia said. 'We can work out the details later.'

'Typical,' Ed Redding said hustling over. 'We do all the bloody hard work and the Navy show up afterwards.'

'The Navy are here?' Will asked.

Redding pointed into the distance and Will stood up, still holding Mia in his arms.

'How did they know?'

Redding shrugged. 'Glass must have got a message to them some time yesterday. They've probably been following at a distance ever since.'

'I need to sort a few things out,' Will said to Mia. 'Will you be all right for a few minutes?'

'Of course.'

She would be glad of a few minutes alone if she was honest; she wanted some privacy to mourn her brother.

He set her down on her feet, kissed her gently on the cheek, then clapped Redding on the back.

'Those men of yours are seasoned fighters,' he said. 'I've never seen such a brave crew.'

Redding nodded proudly. 'That's why the Governor asked us to accompany you on this mission. He knew you'd need a strong fighting force if you did manage to catch up with Del Torres.'

'How many casualties do we have?'

Mia looked at the dead and injured sailors being carried from *The Flaming Dragon* and felt the tragedy of the loss of so many young lives.

'Eight dead, many more wounded.'

Will nodded solemnly.

'They fought bravely. I'll make sure their families know that.'

Will and Redding walked off and Mia watched

them go. She couldn't quite fully grasp the events of the past few hours. Whenever she tried to think about any of it she couldn't focus. Instead Will's unexpected declaration kept popping back into her mind.

He loved her. She hugged herself. He actually loved her. And they were going to have a future together. Like him, she didn't really care where they were in the world, or how they lived, as long as they were together.

Mia knew the happiness that flooded over her would last for ever, so for a moment she turned her mind to the more distressing topic that was struggling for attention.

Jorge was dead. Her big brother had welcomed a swift end when he knew all was lost. She knew he'd partly done it for her, to save her the agony of watching his long, drawn-out death. And he had looked truly happy for her when Will had said he loved her.

She allowed herself a few minutes to remember their childhood, when they had been more innocent and carefree. That was the way she was going to remember Jorge, as the brother who had looked after her as a little girl.

She was startled from her memories by a large

ship pulling up alongside theirs, its masts blocking out the sun. Mia shivered involuntarily. It was the Navy, coming to share in the glory after the fight, no doubt.

She watched as men poured from the big ship, most of them boarding *The Flaming Dragon* but a small group making their way onto Captain Little's vessel. Two officers approached the Captain, who was supervising the moving of the wounded.

Now the injured men were back on the ship Mia decided she would go and see what she could do to help. She didn't have any professional training but she was sure she could help dress wounds or bandage limbs.

Mia had just taken a step forward to help when two other Naval men approached her.

'Mia Del Torres?' one of them asked.

There was no point in denying it; she rather suspected she was the only woman in a twenty-mile radius.

'Yes.'

'Come with us, please.'

She stood her ground, instinctively knowing it would not be sensible to go with the Navy men.

'Why?'

'You're a prisoner of the Governor of Barbados.

Now this mission has been brought to a satisfactory conclusion we have orders to deliver you back into the Governor's custody.'

Mia looked around frantically for Will. He'd be able to sort this mess out. She had forgotten in the past few hours that she was still a prisoner, and she had honestly thought her help in catching her brother and *The Flaming Dragon* would have been enough to secure her liberty.

The Navy men took her firmly by each arm and led her forward. Mia wasn't strong enough to resist. They passed Ed Redding as she was propelled forward and she called out to him, 'Get Will.'

He looked at her in alarm, seemingly puzzled as to why the Navy were taking her away. As she craned her neck he gave a quick nod and was immediately on his feet.

Mia felt herself being lifted across the gap between the two ships and her heart started pounding as she realised she was no longer a guest on Captain Little's ship but a prisoner of the Navy.

Chapter Twenty-Three

'You need to come with me—now,' Redding shouted at Will, who was leaning down to close the eyes of one of his fallen comrades.

He straightened immediately, hearing the urgency in Redding's voice.

'What's happened?'

'They've got Miss Del Torres.'

He panicked. He looked around him in confusion. All the pirates had been subdued and now the Navy had arrived they would start to transport the prisoners to their custom-built cells for the voyage back to Barbados.

'The Navy,' Redding panted, trying to catch his breath. 'The Navy have taken her.'

Will moved quickly, wondering what on earth the Navy wanted with Mia. He was sure it must be some misunderstanding, but he couldn't help imagining how scared Mia would be feeling.

'Permission to come aboard?' Will asked as they came alongside the big Naval ship.

'Identify yourself,' demanded the man standing guard.

'I'm the man who's just saved you from your most embarrassing failure by catching Del Torres.'

The man reddened a little at Will's tone but he didn't have time to feel regret. Somewhere on this ship they had the woman he loved. It was his duty to look after her, to keep her safe from anyone who wished her harm, and at the moment he was failing terribly.

Will stepped aboard the Navy ship and looked around him, scanning the deck for any signs of Mia.

'Can I help you, gentlemen?' asked the clipped, cultured tones of a man in an officer's uniform.

'Will Greenacre,' Will said, thrusting his hand forward. 'Lord Sedlescombe. You've just taken my future wife.'

The officer looked stunned at this statement. He shook Will's hand and introduced himself.

'Lieutenant Flame,' he said, 'I have to admit, sir, I have no idea what you're talking about.'

Will felt a feral growl building in his throat.

'I wish to speak to your Captain,' he said, 'Immediately.'

'I don't think that's going to be possible, sir,' Flame said politely. 'The Commodore is very busy overseeing the securing of the survivors from *The Flaming Dragon* and organising a crew to sail the pirate ship back to Bridgetown.'

'He'll speak to me,' Will said.

Lieutenant Flame hesitated, still maintaining his cool reserve.

'As I said, sir, he is very busy. Perhaps I could be of some assistance?'

'He's too busy to speak to the man who did what the entire Navy couldn't?'

Flame looked as if he was about to give some other excuse.

'Mr Greenacre,' a voice boomed behind him. 'Or should I be calling you Lord Sedlescombe now?'

'Greenacre will do just fine,' Will said, turning to face Commodore Wilkins.

'You have our heartfelt thanks,' Wilkins said, shaking his hand. 'The seas will be a much safer place without Del Torres and his band of reprobates.'

'Quite,' Will said. He didn't have time to make small-talk; he needed to get to Mia. 'We can congratulate each other later,' he said. 'Right now I want my fiancée back, and I understand your men have taken her.'

Fiancée was a little bit of an exaggeration—Mia hadn't exactly agreed to marry him—but he hoped the Commodore would see the folly of taking the future wife of a lord prisoner more clearly than the bedfellow of a lord.

Commodore Wilkins frowned. 'You're speaking of Miss Del Torres?'

'Yes.'

'Come with me. We need to talk in private.'

Will followed the dignified man as he walked briskly walked across the deck and down into the Captain's cabin. The Commodore motioned for Will to sit on one side of a small table. He lifted a whisky decanter from a shelf and selected two glasses. Silently he poured two generous measures.

Will took a gulp of the burning liquid and looked Wilkins directly in the eye.

'Tell me,' he said.

'I am under orders to bring Miss Del Torres back to Barbados in custody,' the Commodore said. 'She is to face trial on her return for aiding and abetting pirates.'

Will felt his whole world fall out from under him.

'No,' he whispered. 'She hasn't done anything wrong.

The Commodore grimaced. 'It may all be a misunderstanding,' he offered. 'And I am confident you will be able to argue her case in front of the Governor on your return.'

Will felt his heart squeeze. He didn't want to be apart from Mia for a single second, let alone have to endure an entire voyage not knowing if she was to be released at the end of it.

'Without her we would never have tracked down *The Flaming Dragon*,' Will said, feeling stunned.

The Commodore nodded. 'I understood as much.'

'There's nothing I can do?'

'Unfortunately I'm under orders. There isn't anything anyone can do until we reach Barbados.'

Will felt useless. Mia was his woman—his to love and cherish and protect. He was failing on the last point quite spectacularly.

'Can I see her?' he asked.

The Commodore nodded. 'I had her put in one of the smaller cabins. With a guard outside, of course.'

'Thank you,' Will said, and meant it. It would have been much easier for the Commodore to have thrown Mia in the brig. He doubted she would have lasted the voyage with Del Torres's crew when they realised who she was and how she'd aided in their capture.

With a sinking heart Will followed Commodore Wilkins through the maze of the large ship. Men were hustling everywhere and Will supposed this was what they were good at: the clean-up after a big fight.

'Good morning, Darcey.' Wilkins greeted a young man standing to attention outside a plain wooden door.

Darcey saluted.

'Any problems?'

'No, sir, the prisoner is settled.'

Will felt his heart lurch as he realised they were talking about Mia.

'This gentleman is Mr Greenacre. We have him to thank for the defeat and capture of Del Torres and his crew.'

The young man's eyes widened and Will would bet anything he was wondering what Will was doing outside a prisoner's door.

'Mr Greenacre has requested a few minutes with Miss Del Torres, and after all he has done for us this is the least we can do.'

Darcey nodded uncertainly.

'We can give you ten minutes, Mr Greenacre,'

the Commodore said turning to him. 'And then we will be making ready to leave.'

Will nodded in acknowledgement and waited as Darcey opened the door for him. He stepped forward but paused before he walked over the threshold, steeling himself to be strong for Mia.

'Will?' Mia asked from her position on the bed. She looked dishevelled and he could tell she had been crying.

He crossed the room in two quick strides and scooped her into his arms. Somewhere behind him he heard the door close and lock.

'Have they hurt you?' he asked, scanning her body from top to toe for any sign of injury.

Mia shook her head. 'I thought…' She trailed off as her voice caught in her throat.

'It's all right,' Will reassured her. 'I'm sure it's just a misunderstanding. We'll get this all sorted out when we get back to Barbados.'

'I love you,' Mia whispered into his neck, where she had buried her face.

He lifted her chin gently and looked into her eyes. 'I love you, too, Mia Del Torres. And I promise I won't let anything happen to you.'

'I know you won't.'

Her blind faith in him made Will feel a tremor of

panic. She trusted him so completely, didn't doubt he would be able to sort everything out. He never wanted to let her down. He always wanted to be the man she turned to with those beautiful, dark, trusting eyes.

'I have something to ask you, Mia.'

Gently he set her down on the bed. The time felt right. Whatever trials and tribulations they had in store, Will knew they had to face them together. They were a pair now, a team, and if Mia was in trouble it meant part of *him* was in trouble.

He kneeled down in front of her and took both of her hands in his own.

'I love you, Mia Del Torres,' he said, looking deep into her eyes. 'I want to love you and cherish you for the rest of my life. I can't imagine a life without you in it, by my side. I want to dedicate my life to making you happy. Every morning I want to wake up and see your beautiful face on the pillow next to me and every night I want to fall asleep with you in my arms.'

Mia smiled at his declaration and leaned forward and kissed him quickly on the corner of his mouth.

'Sorry,' she said. 'I couldn't help it.'

'Mia Del Torres, will you do me the honour of becoming my wife?'

She almost fell off the bed with shock.

'Do you mean it?' she asked, all the blood draining from her face.

'Of course I mean it. I love you.'

'But…'

For a horrible instant Will thought she might refuse, and he got an awful glimpse of how terrible life without her would be.

'No one would accept us,' Mia said. 'You'd lose your place in society.'

He breathed a sigh of relief. She was worried for him. She was worried about what he would lose by tying himself to her.

'I don't care if I lose my estate, my place in society. As long as we're together I don't care where we are or how we live.'

Mia's eyes welled up with tears.

'Yes,' she said. 'Yes, yes, yes. A thousand times yes.'

Will slipped the signet ring with his family's crest from his little finger.

'I'll get you something prettier when this whole mess is sorted out,' he promised. 'But for now I want you to have this.'

He slipped the ring on to her finger and watched her face light up as she admired it.

'I love it,' she said. 'I feel like part of your family.'

'You *are* my family.'

He kissed her then, taking her face gently between his hands and pulling her towards him ever so gently. It was unhurried, the kiss of a man who knew he'd got a whole lifetime to enjoy kissing his wife.

A sharp knock on the door interrupted their intimacy and Will reluctantly pulled away. A couple of seconds later Darcey pushed the door open.

'It's time to go, sir,' he said. 'We are getting ready to sail.'

Will knew it was pointless arguing. He turned back to Mia.

'Be strong, my love,' he said. 'I will sort out this misunderstanding with the Governor as soon as we are back in Barbados.'

'I'll miss you.'

She gave him one last kiss.

As Will exited the cabin he glanced back over his shoulder at the woman he loved and felt elation washing over him. She was a prisoner at the moment, but he was confident he could remedy that as soon as they returned to Bridgetown and then they would be married. They had a lifetime to enjoy each other.

Chapter Twenty-Four

The voyage had only taken three days, but they were the worst three days of Mia's life. Her emotions had swung from elation at Will asking her to marry him to despair about her current predicament, then to shock over everything that had happened over the past few days.

When the ship docked in Barbados Mia was hugely relieved. Any more days of uncertainty and she might have gone mad. At least now Will could plead with the Governor and hopefully negotiate her release so they could get on with their lives.

It took a couple of agonisingly long hours between the ship docking and Mia hearing any activity outside her cabin door. Eventually the key turned in the lock and she waited to be escorted off. She wondered if she was to be released immediately. Probably not, she decided. It would undoubtedly be a few hours before Will could argue her case.

'Hold out your hands,' a middle-aged officer said, entering her cabin.

Mia looked aghast at the iron shackles he held in one hand, ready to restrain her.

Mutely Mia realised there was no point in arguing. She held out her wrists and felt the coolness of the metal against her skin. The officer fastened them together, testing once he'd finished to make sure she couldn't wriggle out of them.

The chains were heavy around her wrists and once more Mia felt a bubble of fear. She quashed it immediately. Will would save her. He would reason with the Governor and she would be released.

'Come with me.'

Mia followed the officer out of the cabin and was horrified to see two other Navy men waiting out in the corridor. They both held rifles and were standing to attention. As Mia and the officer passed them they fell into step behind her. They were treating her as if she was a dangerous criminal.

Silently the sombre procession made its way through the ship and out on to the deck. It was the first time in three days Mia had been outside and she found her eyes took a while to adjust to the brightness. As the ache behind her eyelids subsided she revelled in the warmth of the sun on her skin. If she and Will went to live in England when this was all over she would miss the Caribbean sun.

The officer led her to the gangplank and their strange party began its descent. Mia was surprised to see quite so many people assembled at the docks. There was a crowd of at least a few hundred people, jostling and shouting. She supposed they had gathered to see the men who had terrorised the Caribbean finally brought to justice.

'Pirate whore!' someone shouted.

Mia looked around and realised the comment was meant for her.

'Scum!' a woman near the front of the crowd yelled, spitting a large yellow gob of saliva which landed near Mia's feet.

'Murdering lowlife!'

'Evil witch!'

'Scourge of the seas!'

Mia took a deep breath and held her head up high. She was none of those things. She was Mia Del Torres and she would *not* let these people break her spirit.

All the same, deep down she wanted to cry. It

was overwhelming to have such collective hate fo-
cussed on her. To have hundreds of people jeering
and hollering, wanting her to suffer for something
she hadn't done.

'Keep walking,' the officer said, picking up his
pace a little.

Mia saw the uneasiness in his face and realised
they were in real danger. The mob only had to
swell and push forward and they would probably
all be trampled.

She hurried forward and was glad to make it into
the safety of the prison yard. Even though she recognised this would be her prison for at least a little
while, the solid stone walls would serve to protect
her from the hatred of the crowd outside.

The officer led her across the open courtyard and
through a door she remembered from her last stay
in the cells just over a week ago. Mia had changed
so much in that time, and so many things had happened she would never have imagined, but she felt
the same trepidation as she was led from the sunlight into the gloomy cells.

Mia looked from side to side as she walked. During her previous stay the cells had been mostly
empty, with just one or two petty criminals
sprawled out on the straw. Now they were full to

bursting, with men packed into each little cell until they were so crowded they jostled for space. She glanced at the faces of the prisoners and realised most were the captured pirates from *The Flaming Dragon*, awaiting their sentencing and inevitable execution.

She could see the men recognised her from her interception in the stand-off between her brother and Will, but no one made a sound. Instead they looked at her in stony silence. She realised they were broken; they had lost their liberty and lost their will to live. They knew they would be executed in the next few days and there was nothing they could do about it. These were truly dead men walking.

Mia was led through another locked wooden door into a different part of the cell block. Here the tiny barred cells were less overcrowded and she wondered if she might at least get one to herself.

The officer paused outside one cell and indicated for the man on guard duty to open it. He obliged and held open the door.

Mia walked inside and turned to see the door to the cell closing behind her. The key turned in the lock and she felt her freedom slipping away from her.

'So you're the one they've all been talking about.'

Mia nearly expired on the spot; she'd assumed she was the only one in the dimly lit cell. She peered into the gloom and saw a bundle of rags in the corner. The bundle shifted slightly and Mia pressed her back against the bars.

'I heard the commotion from in here.'

'There's been a mistake,' Mia said.

'There always has, dear.'

The bundle shifted again and a woman stood up. Mia could make out soft features in a grimy face. The woman could be anywhere between forty and sixty. She had wrinkles around her eyes and mouth, but that could just be from years of hard living.

'Essie,' she said. 'Your cell mate. At least until they hang you.'

'They won't hang me,' Mia said, trying to sound brave.

Essie barked a laugh which turned into a long, drawn-out coughing fit. Mia really didn't want to get too close; it sounded like something nasty.

'You're the pirate's sister, aren't you?' the older woman asked when she'd caught her breath.

Mia nodded.

'Then they'll hang you.'

'I haven't done anything wrong,' Mia protested.

She knew it was probably pointless, arguing with this crone, but she refused to stand by and let her say things like that unchallenged.

'That doesn't really matter.'

'Of course it matters.'

At least she hoped it did. Doubt tried to push its way into Mia's mind. Guilt should matter, but it hadn't for all those months she'd been hunted by the authorities. And it hadn't mattered when they'd thrown her into a cell just over a week ago. No one had seemed to care then that she hadn't actually broken any law or done anything wrong.

Essie moved closer and looked her up and down. 'The crowd will go wild to see such a pretty young thing swing.'

'Shut up.'

Mia unconsciously raised a hand to her throat and massaged her neck where a noose would sit. Will wouldn't let them execute her. He would save her.

'They'll hang you in your brother's place and there's not anything anyone can do to stop them.'

Mia felt defiance flare in her eyes. She pushed past Essie and flopped on to the mouldy hay. She felt something scuttling beneath her but refused to show weakness by jumping up or whimpering.

'You think someone's going to save you, don't you?' Essie pressed. 'I can see it in your eyes.'

Mia refused to look at her cell mate and instead hugged her arms around herself and inspected the far wall.

'Is it some man who's promised to keep you safe?'

Mia involuntarily glanced at Will's signet ring on her finger.

Essie let out a long cackle and crouched down next to Mia.

'And you believe him?'

Of course she believed him. He was Will Green-acre—the man she loved. The only man capable of tracking down the most notorious pirate in the Caribbean. He would rescue her and take her away from this horrible place.

'Did he tell you he loved you?' Essie asked, gloating a little. 'They all say that. My husband let me take the blame for his crime, said I would be punished less harshly being a woman. Has he bothered to try and contact me whilst I've been festering in this dump?'

By the tone of her voice Mia guessed not.

'Yours will be the same. He might say he loves

you. He might promise to protect you. But in the end he'll let you swing.'

'Shut up,' Mia said quietly. She wanted space to think.

'Maybe he'll even shed a tear or two, or at least raise a toast to your memory in the tavern, but in a few weeks' time he'll have his hands up another woman's skirts and you'll be a distant memory.'

The idea of Will with another woman was enough to make Mia feel sick. He was hers—all hers. She never wanted him to think of another woman again, let alone touch one.

'Shut up,' she said more forcefully. 'Will is a good man and he will save me. Now, if you say another word I will smash every tooth from your head.'

Essie looked as if she was going to say something.

'You think I didn't learn a trick or two from my brother?' Mia asked.

That shut the woman up.

Relieved, Mia sat back and closed her eyes. She was pleased Essie had taken the threat seriously. She wouldn't have the first idea how to smash the teeth from someone's head, and somehow she didn't think she'd come out of the fight the victor.

Despite her protestations Mia despaired. She knew Will would fight with every weapon in his arsenal to get her released, but what if it wasn't enough? She had just found happiness. It would be so cruel to have it all taken away from her now.

Chapter Twenty-Five

Will burst into the dining room unannounced. It had taken him much longer than he would have liked to get back to Barbados. When the ship carrying Mia had departed he had begged Captain Little to follow in hot pursuit. The Captain had agreed, but only after they had paid their respects to their fallen comrades and buried them at sea.

Will could hardly protest. Those men had fought valiantly beside him and given their lives to rid the Caribbean of some of the most vicious pirates in living memory. So they'd had the memorial.

Then he'd been informed Lieutenant Glass was no longer in the brig. Frantically the whole ship was scoured until a young sailor admitted he had seen the Lieutenant being taken away by two Naval Officers. The search had added at least another hour, and Will's temper had not improved with the thought of Glass being spirited away into the protective arms of the Navy.

By the time they'd set off after Commodore Wilkins and his ship they had already been four hours behind, and despite Captain Little's considerable skill there had been no way they could make up the distance between them when the Navy had the bigger, faster vessel.

When they had eventually landed in Bridgetown Will had sprinted off the ship and run straight to the Governor's residence.

'What is the meaning…?' the Governor blustered as his lunch was interrupted. 'Mr Greenacre.' He clearly recognised Will. 'Please sit down.'

Will declined the seat and stood over the Governor.

'I must offer my heartfelt thanks,' Governor Hall said, peering at Will as if trying to work out exactly why he was acting so strangely.

'Greenacre!' Edward Thatcher boomed as he hustled into the room. 'Knew you'd bring in the result.'

'I need you to release Mia Del Torres from your custody,' Will said, getting straight to the point.

The Governor cleared his throat and looked uncomfortably at Thatcher.

'Sit down, Greenacre, have something to drink. Celebrate your success.'

The last thing Will wanted to do right now was celebrate his success.

'Mia Del Torres,' he pushed again.

'The pirate's sister?'

'The pirate's *estranged* sister,' Will corrected him.

Thatcher pulled out a chair and gently pushed Will towards it. 'Sit down, old chap,' he said.

'I've no idea what crime you think she's committed,' Will persevered, 'but she hasn't broken the law in a single way.'

'I'm sure that's not right,' Governor Hall said, looking quite distressed.

'Release her.'

'It's a little more complicated than that, Greenacre,' Thatcher said, pouring two glasses of wine.

'How is it more complicated? The woman's innocent and you're holding her in the cells you use for criminals.'

'She's not really innocent, though, is she?' Hall asked.

Thatcher shot him a warning look and the Governor clamped his lips together firmly.

'If anyone has harmed a hair on that woman's

head, I will kill them,' Will warned. 'She is to be my wife, the future Lady Sedlescombe.'

Both men stared at him, mouths agape.

'You jest, Greenacre,' Thatcher said eventually.

'There's no joke. I have asked Mia Del Torres to marry me.'

'Are you mad?' the Governor asked indelicately. 'She's a criminal, a commoner.'

'Please watch your tongue. You're speaking of my fiancée.'

Will felt as though they were going round in circles. He just wanted them to release her—how hard could it be?

'Greenacre,' Thatcher said, his voice friendly but with strain underneath, 'surely you can see you've made a mistake?'

Will pushed his chair away from the table with such force it went clattering across the floor behind him. He leaned over Thatcher and grabbed the man by his lapels. He pulled gently—not enough to lift Thatcher from his seat but firmly enough to let him know he could if he wanted to.

'There's no mistake,' Will said quietly. 'Mia is a wonderful, kind, caring woman and the only reason she has been persecuted is because her mother gave birth to a boy a few years before she gave birth to her.'

'Calm down, Greenacre,' Thatcher said as Will released him. 'I just meant are you sure you're going to marry her?'

'I'm going to marry her. Just as soon as you release her.'

The Governor cleared his throat and Will spun to face him.

'There might be a problem there, old chap,' Governor Hall said. 'She's been sentenced.'

Will felt his blood run cold. They'd sentenced her? That seemed to imply she'd been found guilty of some crime.

'You've sentenced her?' he asked. 'You've had a trial?'

Both men looked a little uncomfortable.

'She's only been in Barbados for a few hours. How have you had a trial already?'

'We had it this morning,' Thatcher admitted.

'What did you charge her with?' he asked incredulously.

'Piracy.'

Will laughed. It was preposterous. They wouldn't have had any evidence or any witnesses. They wouldn't have any because Mia had never been involved in piracy in her life.

'And?' he asked.

'She was found guilty.'

'On what evidence?'

The Governor and Thatcher both shifted in their chairs. He was making them very uncomfortable. Will was glad. He wanted them to be more than uncomfortable. He wanted them to be in agony.

'There was a witness statement,' Thatcher said.

Will couldn't believe it. He wondered where they had dragged this liar up from.

'What did this witness claim?'

'He stated he had seen Miss Del Torres aiding and abetting her brother on multiple occasions and presented letters of correspondence between the siblings outlining how she was instrumental in giving Del Torres information which allowed him to evade the authorities for so long.'

Will couldn't believe any of it was true. He knew Mia, and he knew she hadn't had anything to do with Del Torres for years.

'Who was this person?' he asked.

'A man of impeccable character and profession.'

Suddenly Will had a sinking feeling in the pit of his stomach.

'Lieutenant Glass?' he growled.

'You must agree he is a trustworthy chap,' the Governor said.

'Trustworthy?' Will asked, his voice dangerously low. 'The man who attacked Mia in her cabin and tried to force himself on her?'

'You must be mistaken,' Governor Hall said.

'I pulled him off her myself.'

'Maybe…' Hall trailed off as he saw the dangerous look in Will's eyes.

'If you dare to suggest she asked for it or in some way deserved it I will strangle you where you sit.'

'The Governor didn't mean that,' Thatcher said, trying to placate him.

'Lieutenant Glass was seen to attack Mia by Captain Little, First Mate Redding and many other members of the crew. That's if the word of a peer of the realm isn't good enough for you.'

Governor Hall was turning a deep beetroot colour.

'You held her trial this morning before I could return—was that on Glass's suggestion, as well?'

He caught the glance between the two men and knew the truth of the matter.

Glass had well and truly got his revenge. Will ran a hand through his tousled hair in agitation.

The Lieutenant must have persuaded the Navy he'd been held under false pretences and then worked on his accusations against Mia.

'And will the Lieutenant be charged with attempted rape?' Will asked coldly.

'That's a matter for the Navy,' Governor Hall said primly.

'So you've condemned Mia in some sham of a trial? Were there any other witnesses? Did anyone speak on her behalf?'

He could just imagine Mia, standing on her own, listening to the cruel allegations against her and wondering why he wasn't there defending her.

'No,' Thatcher said. 'We held the trial this morning. No one else was present. Just the Governor, Lieutenant Glass and myself.'

'And Mia?'

Thatcher and the Governor exchanged yet another sideways glance.

'That's not even legal,' Will said softly. 'She has to be allowed to stand to defend herself.'

'I'm His Majesty's Governor of Barbados. I am the law on this island. If I say something is legal then it's legal.' Governor Hall was getting more and more flustered.

'And what sentence did you give her in this sham trial?'

Neither man spoke.

'What sentence?' Will repeated.

'Death.'

Will collapsed back into a chair and held his head in his hands. He felt as if he couldn't breathe. All through his life he had been in control. He'd sorted things, been the one to organise people and make decisions. Now he just felt helpless.

'Death?' he repeated, his voice sticking in his throat and the word coming out as a croaky whisper.

'She will hang with the rest of the pirates tomorrow morning.' The Governor sounded cold and detached.

Will turned to his old friend and looked at him beseechingly.

'Thatcher, surely you can see this is wrong.'

Thatcher was man enough to hold his eye.

'If we'd known the full circumstances...'

'I'm telling you now,' Will said desperately. 'She's innocent. She's never committed an act of piracy in her life. If you allow her to hang you will be guilty of murder.'

'Nonsense,' the Governor said.

Will ignored him and continued to try and plead with Thatcher.

'Lieutenant Glass has taken his revenge for Mia refusing him and me locking him up. Everything he's told you is a lie.'

Thatcher looked extremely uncomfortable and Will had a tiny spark of hope that he might be getting through to his old friend.

'She hasn't done anything wrong.'

'Even if the letters are forged, she's the sister of a pirate. She deserves to hang,' the Governor said firmly.

'We are not responsible for the actions of our relatives.' Will turned back to Thatcher. 'All I'm asking for is a retrial—a proper trial. Where Glass is exposed as a liar and a rapist and Mia has the chance of a defence.'

'I wish we could, Greenacre,' Thatcher said, and the regret in his eyes made Will believe him. 'I really wish we could.'

'Then do it.'

'Impossible,' Governor Hall said abruptly. 'The executions have been announced.'

'You're refusing to hold a retrial and stop an innocent woman from hanging because you don't want to lose face?' Will couldn't believe this man was allowed to be Governor.

'There will be a riot,' Thatcher said. 'The people have been terrorised by Del Torres for years. Many of them have lost loved ones when he's attacked ships or towns. They can't go and watch Del Torres hang because he's dead, but they can see his sister—and for them that's the next best thing.'

'His innocent sister,' Will reminded them. 'The sister who was instrumental in finding Del Torres and putting a stop to his terrorising ways once and for all.'

'They won't ever believe that,' Governor Hall said. 'We've announced the execution and that's final. I will say no more on the subject.'

Will leapt up and lunged towards Governor Hall. Before he could strike him Thatcher had grabbed his arms and was wrestling him away.

'Don't make me have you arrested, Greenacre. I'm very grateful for what you've done but I will throw you in a cell if you threaten me again.'

'Let's go and cool down,' Thatcher said, tugging him none too gently by the arm.

Will resisted for a second, then sagged. He wasn't going to get anywhere trying to reason with the incompetent fool, or by beating him to a pulp, no matter how good it might make him feel. He allowed Thatcher to drag him from the room and slam the door closed behind them.

'What the hell, Thatcher?' he asked, rounding on the man he'd thought was his friend.

'Keep your voice down.'

Thatcher led him through the spacious corridors and out into a small courtyard. After he'd finally closed the door behind him he sank onto a rough stone wall.

'I'm so sorry, Greenacre,' he said. 'I tried everything I could.'

Will looked at him, astonished. A few minutes earlier he'd been practically defending the Governor.

'Sometimes there's just no reasoning with the man,' Thatcher said. 'I begged him to wait for your return, to hear your side of the story, but he got caught up in the idea of publicly executing Del Torres's sister. He knew the crowds would go crazy for it.'

'So he's doing it for popularity?' Will asked, unable to believe he might lose the woman he loved for the ridiculous goal of increasing the Governor's status with the people.

Thatcher nodded. 'When he heard you had captured *The Flaming Dragon* he announced to the world that he would be the one to hang Del Torres.'

'He didn't know I'd killed him?'

'When Commodore Wilkins told him they had only a few dozen lowly pirates in their cells he was furious. He was sure he was going to look like a fool. So instead of Del Torres he announced he would hang his sister in his place.'

'There must be something we can do.'

Thatcher shook his head. 'The Governor was right when he said he is the law in Barbados. What he says goes.'

'I can't lose her, Thatcher,' Will said, allowing the other man to see him weak and vulnerable. 'I love her.'

Chapter Twenty-Six

'You—out.'

Mia watched as the guard opened the door to the cell and motioned for her to step forward. She didn't know what was happening, but she knew she wasn't being released.

All morning she'd heard chanting outside the walls of the fort. People were screaming her name with added profanities. A few hours ago she'd heard the crowd grow quiet as they listened to an announcement. Mia hadn't been able to make out what had been said, but the loud cheer had rattled her bones and chilled her blood.

She stepped forward cautiously, holding her manacled hands in front of her so the guard could see she wasn't about to attack him. Not that she would have much chance. The beefy man must've weighed at least double her weight, and towered over her by a good foot.

'Get in here.'

He shoved her forward into another cell; this one was a small room with just a wooden door with a small grille in it. It was certainly more private, but she was unsure why she was being given this luxury. Not that she would complain. A whole morning of Essie's taunts was enough to make a murderer out of the most saintly of people.

Mia stumbled into the cell and turned to face the guard, ready to ask him what was happening. She was too slow. The door was already closing and she was left alone.

Looking around her, Mia realised privacy was the only advantage of this cell over her previous one. There was a similar mound of mouldy straw in one corner and she could hear squeaks and rustles from inside it that made her reluctant to sit down. There was a tiny window set high up in the wall which let in a ray of sunlight, but it was too high for Mia even to contemplate trying to see out.

She leaned back against the wall, no longer caring that her dress would get damp and dirty. She doubted she was going to go anywhere that required presentable clothing. Just lately she was doubting whether she would go anywhere ever again.

Mia closed her eyes and tried to picture Will's face. His smile, his laugh—those were the things that were giving her the strength to push on. He would be brave and endure, therefore so must she.

Her eyes jerked open as she heard the cell door opening again. Immediately she felt scared; had they moved her somewhere more private so the guards could take their pleasure from her?

When Will walked into the cell Mia almost cried with relief. The heavy door slammed closed behind him but Mia hardly noticed. She flung herself into his arms and hugged him so tightly she wondered he was still able to breathe.

'I was so scared,' she whispered. 'I thought you might have forgotten me.'

'Never.' His voice was husky and low. 'I'll never forget you.'

She pulled away slightly, just enough so she could see his face.

'What's happening, Will? Why are they holding me here?'

She saw all the pain and anguish etched on his features and she knew whatever was going on was bad.

'They've charged you with piracy,' he said.

Mia felt herself sag. Will caught her and gently

lowered her to the floor, propping her up against the wall.

'Piracy?' she asked as he sat down beside her.

He nodded glumly.

'But I've never been involved in any piracy.'

'There's more…'

She couldn't imagine what more there could be. This was the worst news imaginable.

'They've already held your trial.'

'They can't have,' Mia said. 'I haven't left the cell block.'

'It seems they held it in your absence. And mine.'

'They can't do that.'

'Apparently they can. The Governor just told me he could do anything he liked.'

'And?' Mia asked, knowing she didn't really want to know the answer. 'What was the verdict?'

'Guilty.' He couldn't meet her eyes as he said it.

Mia let out a sob and started gasping for air. It felt as though she were suffocating.

Will reached out and took her hand, trying to comfort her in some way. She started crying, the tears running down her cheeks, making rivulets in the dust on her face.

He gently grasped her round her waist and pulled her into his lap so she was sitting at right angles to him. Mia buried her head in his shoulder and began to cry in earnest.

Silently Will stroked her hair and her back, making soothing noises as she cried.

'And the sentence?' she asked through sobs.

Will shook his head, unable to say it, but Mia understood.

'I don't want to die,' she said into his shoulder, 'not now I've found you.'

They sat in silence for a while, Mia digesting the awful news, trying to process it. It was impossible. She could hardly believe it was true. A few days ago she'd been so happy, and now that was all going to be taken away from her. She was to be hanged for a crime she hadn't committed.

'I won't let them do it to you,' Will whispered into her ear.

She lifted her face from where it had been nuzzled into his shoulder and looked into his clear blue eyes.

'I won't let them take you away from me. I'd rather die myself.'

Mia didn't know what to say. She knew her death was inevitable and that no matter how hard Will wished it she would not escape from her fate.

'Will you promise me something?' Mia asked.

He nodded his head. 'Anything.'

'When I'm gone—when they've done this horrible thing to me—I want you to go. I want you
to return to England and to your estate and get on
with your life.'

'I can't, Mia.'

'I want you to forget about me and live your life
in happiness. Maybe in a few years take a wife
and have lots of beautiful children.' She was crying again, the tears streaming down her cheeks as
she thought of all the things she would never share
with Will.

'Mia, no.'

'I want you to be happy, Will.'

'I'll never be happy without you.'

She looked up at his face and realised his eyes
were moist with tears, as well.

'You'll have to live for both of us.'

He crushed her tightly to him and held her silently, his chest heaving as he sucked air into his
lungs.

'I'm not going to let them take you from me,' he
whispered into her ear. 'No matter what it takes.'

'There's nothing we can do,' Mia said, wishing
she was wrong.

Will tilted her chin up so he could look into her

eyes. 'I promise you, Mia, I won't let them do this to you.'

She wanted to believe him, and a small part of her did. At least she believed he would do everything in his power to stop them from hanging her. But Mia knew it wouldn't be enough. One man couldn't single-handedly outfight and outmanoeuvre the entire British Garrison of Barbados. It just wasn't possible. Even if that man was as resourceful and fearless as Will Greenacre.

'I love you, Will,' she said.

'I promise you,' he repeated, 'we will be together again.'

Mia lifted her head and kissed him. It was gentle and passionate at the same time. Their lips melted together as if they were one. Mia felt all the tension leave her body as for a few seconds she was transported away from the dingy cell in Barbados and was instead soaring above the Caribbean Sea in Will's arms.

His lips moved down her neck, making her shudder as he nipped at her sensitive skin.

'I promise,' he murmured into her neck, 'we shall be together as man and wife.'

She arched her neck, giving him access to every inch of skin, encouraging him to go lower.

He drew his tongue along her collarbone and Mia felt wickedly aroused. She wanted to possess him one last time, to feel him deep inside her. He paused at the hollow at the base of her throat and blew gently. Mia immediately felt her nipples begin to harden beneath her dress.

'I promise we will spend every night of the rest of our lives in each other's arms,' Will whispered.

Mia let out a small moan as his lips reconnected with her skin. Slowly, teasingly, he worked his way down her chest, peppering kisses along the swell of her breasts.

'I love you, Mia, and you will be mine for ever.'

She gasped as he pushed the front of her dress down, exposing her breasts to the air. She could see him taking every moment in, trying to remember every detail about her. Mia wanted the same. She wanted a memory that would sustain her over the next few hours, a picture she could imagine as they fastened the noose around her neck so she wouldn't be quite so scared.

Delicately she started to tug at his shirt, baring the skin of his abdomen. Without stopping his attentions Will allowed Mia to pull the cotton shirt over his head.

She raked her fingers gently over his chest and

felt him shiver in delight. Will became more and more desperate in his attentions, his kisses becoming more frantic. He pushed her tenderly away from him so he could watch her face as he cupped her breasts. She felt her teeth sink gently into her lower lip as pleasure coursed through her. He smiled as she thrust her chest forward, silently begging him for more.

Will's breathing grew ragged as he became more and more aroused and Mia could feel his hardness beneath her. She rocked her hips gently as he grazed a finger over one of her nipples.

'I love you, Mia, and I promise I'll love you for evermore.'

Mia knew she wanted him. She wanted to make love to him one last time, to have one last memory of him to cherish. She didn't care they were in a dingy cell, she didn't care the floor was hard and unforgiving. All she knew was she had to feel Will inside her one final time. Then she would go to her death, not happily, but at least knowing she had lived her last day to the full.

She slipped off his lap and lay back on the floor. He followed immediately, only pausing to pick up his discarded shirt, lift her slightly, and place it under her to protect her back from the stony surface.

'I love you,' Mia said, 'and I want you.'

Her words seemed to set him on fire. He lunged on top of her, gently parting her legs with his own. He grabbed handfuls of her skirt and pushed them up to around her waist, exposing her to his eyes only.

Mia watched as he unfastened his trousers and pushed them down, allowing his hardness to spring free. She tried to remember every sight, every touch, every sensation, knowing this would be what kept her strong as she faced her destiny.

He paused before entering her. He was holding himself up with one arm, the other ready to guide himself inside her. Mia looked deep into his eyes and saw the love and desire burning there, love and desire all for her. She knew she'd been lucky, she'd found the one man she loved and who had loved her back and she knew, given the choice, she wouldn't give the last few days up for a long but lonely life.

Will pushed into her, filling her completely. Mia's hips rose to meet his and they thrust together in perfect synchronisation. Mia felt the heat spreading through her body and the energy thrumming just beneath the surface. The sensation built as he plunged into her again and again and again until Mia knew one last thrust would push her over the edge.

Mia looked up into Will's eyes as she climaxed, enjoying the look of pure pleasure on his face as he exploded inside her.

He collapsed down on top of her, holding enough of his weight on his arms to ensure she wasn't crushed, but allowing his body to press against hers.

'Thank you,' she whispered in his ear.

Chapter Twenty-Seven

William looked down at the woman beneath him and made a silent vow: he wasn't going to let her die. He didn't care what he had to do or what he lost in the process. They could hang him if it meant Mia going free.

He knew she'd wanted him to make love to her to give her one last fond memory before she took her trip to the scaffold and Will had been happy to oblige. But there was no way this was going to be their last moment together.

Will pulled himself off her, knowing time was short. Thatcher had agreed to help him see Mia one last time—in the circumstances it was the least he could do. As much as Will wanted to hold Mia in his arms through the long night that was to follow he had things to do, plans to make.

'I need you to be strong, my love,' he said as he

refastened his trousers and pulled his shirt back over his head.

'I will be.' There was a tremor in her voice that pierced through Will's heart.

'And I need you to believe in me.'

She looked at him questioningly.

'I won't let you die,' he promised her. 'I vow on everything I hold sacred, I vow on the love I have for you, I won't let you die.'

He could see Mia wanted to believe him, but the despair was still in her eyes.

'I won't let you die,' he repeated one final time.

He pulled her to her feet and started to right her dress. The last thing he wanted was the guards to get a glimpse of her honey-coloured flesh and decide they wanted to sample her delights for themselves.

When she was as presentable as possible Will grasped her by both shoulders and bent his head ever so slightly so they were on the same level.

'I need you to listen carefully, Mia,' he said, his voice low and serious. 'Look out for me tomorrow. And be ready.'

She looked confused. 'Be ready for what?'

Will shook his head and motioned to the door. He didn't think anyone was listening, he'd paid the guard handsomely to take himself away to the other end of the cell block, but he couldn't be sure.

'Just be ready,' he repeated cryptically, 'and remember I'll come for you.'

He bent down to give her one last lingering kiss. He never wanted it to end, he wanted to stay locked to her lips for ever, but he knew that just wasn't possible.

With a clenched fist he banged loudly on the door and listened as the guard made his way from the other end of the cell block, inserted the key in the lock, and opened the door.

'Farewell, my love,' he said.

The look of loneliness and desperation on Mia's face as the cell door closed behind him was enough to spur him into action.

His first act was to take out a silver coin from his pocket and hand it to the guard.

'See she isn't put back with any other prisoners and isn't bothered by anyone,' he said, handing the coin over. 'There'll be another one tomorrow if she's well cared for.'

The guard took the coin readily and within an instant it had disappeared somewhere on his person.

'I need some information, too,' he said, producing a second coin.

The guard looked at it greedily. Two silver coins were probably worth more than four months' salary. Will held it back for a second, waiting to hand it over until the guard had answered his question.

'The execution tomorrow—Miss Del Torres is to be last, is that correct?'

The guard nodded, his eyes only leaving the coin for a second.

'And the other pirates will be hanged before her?'

Again he nodded mutely.

'In any particular order?'

'There's twenty to be executed tomorrow, not including her in there,' the guard said, finally speaking. 'They'll go in the order I chain them.'

This was exactly what Will wanted to hear.

'And if I was to ask you to chain a certain man in the middle, would that be possible?'

'For a price, sir.'

'Of course.'

'Which one do you want in the middle?'

Will was glad the guard didn't seem to want to know his motivations for such a request.

'Why don't you take me to them and I can point one out.'

The guard walked back through the cell block with Will following behind. He opened the door at the end and motioned for Will to step through into area with the more crowded cells.

'These will all be hanged tomorrow,' the guard said, indicating the silent men squeezed into the two communal cells.

Will scrutinised them. They were a sorry-looking bunch, once-feared pirates reduced to scared little men by the prospect of inevitable death.

He motioned to a small man in his twenties with a livid scar across one cheek.

'You got any family?' he asked, leaning in and speaking softly so no one else could hear.

At first Will thought the man might not answer. There wasn't much motivation for him to do so.

'Mum and two sisters. They'll probably starve now.'

Perfect. This was just the sort of man Will had been looking for.

'What if I was to promise to take care of them, seek them out and give them a gift of gold?'

The man looked at him suspiciously, but Will was pleased to see some of the life returning to his previously dead eyes.

'Why would you do that?'

'I want you to do something for me in return.'

'You're the man who killed the Captain,' the man said.

Will nodded, hoping this revelation wasn't going to spoil his chance.

'What do you want me to do?'

Will bent forward and spoke quietly so only the man could hear. From the corner of his eye he could see the other pirates edging closer, curious.

When he'd finished explaining, the other man nodded.

'If you can prove my family is going to be taken care of, I'll do it.'

'Deal.'

Will pushed his hand through the bars and grasped the pirate's. They shook firmly.

'Where can I find your family?' he asked.

'Brooker Street. Becky Watts is my mam.'

'That one,' Will said, turning back to the guard. 'And I want him in a separate cell tonight so he doesn't come to any harm. And I don't want you asking any questions.'

Will held out a whole purse full of silver coins.

'Fine by me,' the guard said.

Will watched as he moved the young pirate out from the communal cell and across into the quieter cell block.

'I'll be back later with that man's family.'

'Yes, sir.'

Will felt his plan slowly coming together. It wouldn't be easy—in fact, it would probably be the most difficult thing he'd ever done—but if he managed to pull it off it would most definitely be worth it.

He thought of Mia alone and afraid in her cell and forced himself to resist the urge to go back to her. She would have one night of misery, but if he managed to save her he would make it up to her with a lifetime of love.

Will strode out of the cell block and spied Thatcher leaning against a wall. His old friend looked haggard and haunted and Will wondered if he could trust him.

Taking the risk, he walked over to Thatcher and leaned against the wall next to him.

'How is she?' Thatcher asked gloomily.

'Awful. She's given up hope.'

'I spoke to the Governor again. He's not budging.'

'Thanks for trying.'

'I feel terrible, Greenacre. I only wish there was something I could do.'

Will regarded him for a few seconds, trying to work out how serious he was.

'There is something,' he said slowly, 'but it isn't exactly legal.'

He watched as Thatcher considered his statement.

'How illegal are we talking?'

'It's more turning a blind eye,' Will hedged.

Thatcher thought some more.

'I suppose hanging Miss Del Torres isn't really legal in itself,' he said. 'Let's see if two wrongs can make a right.'

'I need you to arrange the men standing guard at the execution tomorrow in a particular way.'

'The Commodore oversees the Navy men,' Thatcher said.

'But I'm sure if you highlighted a particular security concern and a way to remedy that the Commodore would listen. He strikes me as a reasonable man.'

'He is a reasonable man. We happen to play chess together.'

Will grinned. Maybe, just maybe, he had a chance.

'What do you want me to persuade him to do?' Thatcher asked.

'It's probably best if I show you.'

They walked silently away from the cell block

and out into the square beyond. Already the soldiers from the garrison were setting up the scaffold, readying it for the executions in the morning.

'Point out to me the likely points the Commodore will station his men,' Will requested.

'He'll have a long line in front of the scaffold so the crowd can't surge forward,' Thatcher began explaining. 'Then he'll have men every few feet or so around the perimeter. A couple with each line of prisoners and a couple more to take them to the scaffold. And then he'll station a few up on the walls above to keep an eye out for troublemakers.'

'And how about behind the scaffold?' Will asked.

Thatcher looked over to the half-built platform and assessed it carefully.

'Maybe one or two, not more than that. That alleyway there—' he pointed to the narrow opening that came out just to one side of the scaffold '—you wouldn't get a good view from there so the locals won't be pushing their way through that way.'

'Perfect,' Will said, his plan taking shape. 'Now I need you to persuade Commodore Wilkins to take the man he might have positioned in front of that alleyway and instead get him to guard the prisoners as they wait to be executed.'

Thatcher looked at him assessingly.

'You can say they look to be a rowdy bunch and you think they'll need an extra man there, not wasted on this alleyway.'

Thatcher nodded. 'I don't want to know what you have planned, Greenacre, but I wish you the best of luck.'

'Thank you.'

'If anyone can pull this off, it's you.'

Chapter Twenty-Eight

It had been the longest night of Mia's life. She hadn't slept a wink. Instead, she'd closed her eyes and pictured Will's face, trying to keep herself from going mad with fear.

He'd promised her he would save her. She knew he'd meant it, or at least the intention, but she also knew it was impossible. She would be in chains in front of thousands of people, guarded by dozens of guards. One man on his own couldn't win against odds like that, even if that one man was Will Greenacre.

Mia pushed the plate of stale bread away from her. She didn't want to eat a thing. Better her stomach be empty for what was to come so she couldn't spend her last minutes on earth vomiting from fear.

She held her breath as the keys jangled in the door and watched as it slowly opened.

A tiny part of her expected to see Will's smiling face on the other side of the door, laughing and telling her everything was sorted out, she wasn't going to be hanged. When the guard entered she felt herself deflate.

'Ready, miss?' he asked.

After Will's visit the afternoon before, the guard had been most courteous to her, enquiring every hour or so if she required anything. She wondered how much Will had paid him.

Mia stepped out into the corridor and felt her legs wobble. She was nervous already and they hadn't even made it outside. The guard saw her hesitate and took her gently by the arm, supporting her as they shuffled through the cell block.

Mia glanced at the cell she had shared with Essie the day before and saw the older woman looking at her pityingly. She didn't utter a word, just inclined her head, the small movement conveying the sympathy of one prisoner to another.

They emerged into the morning sunlight and Mia had to scrunch her eyes up it was so bright compared to the gloominess of the cells. The morning was not yet hot, but the cloudless Caribbean sky promised another perfect day. The first day of many Mia would not get to enjoy.

She saw the condemned pirates lined up in front of her, twenty men shackled at the wrists and ankles. A few were openly sobbing, but most just looked dazed, as if they couldn't believe what was about to happen.

The Governor stood before them, his forehead glistening with perspiration under his thick wig.

'You have all been sentenced to hang for crimes of piracy,' the Governor said loudly so they could all hear him. 'You will be hanged by the neck until you are dead. This will be done in full view of your fellow man so they may learn what happens when you break the law.'

Mia rather thought the old man was enjoying himself. He seemed excited, as if he were about to show off his life's work to a bevy of appreciative onlookers.

'We will tolerate no violence or attempts to escape your fate. You will stand quietly in a line until you are called forward.'

Mia didn't see what motivation they had to obey, they were already being given the harshest punishment. Not that the trancelike state of the pirates made her think any of them would try to cause a fuss.

The prisoners were ushered forward into three

carts. The twenty pirates filled up the first two carts and Mia was left on her own staring at the third. The Governor obviously meant for her to be pulled through the streets by herself, so people would have the opportunity to torment her individually as she passed.

The guard gently pushed her forward and Mia stepped up into the wooden cart. Obligingly she held out her hands as a rope was looped above her shackles, securing her to a wooden post at the front of the cart. The back of the cart was secured and Mia was on full display to the world, unable to move or dodge any missiles that flew her way.

The Governor had disappeared, no doubt to settle into his position far above the crowds, ready to watch the procession of pirates. The first cart started rolling out of the courtyard, closely followed by the second. As Mia's cart began to move she heard the roar of the crowd as they laid eyes on the first set of prisoners.

Mia's legs nearly buckled from underneath her as her cart left the protective walls of the prison yard. She tried to focus directly in front of her and ignore the faces filled with hatred as they shouted insults. The first piece of debris that struck her was some sort of mouldy fruit. It hit her on her outstretched arm and didn't hurt, but the shock almost made her shout out. Other stale or mouldy foodstuffs followed, as well as a few small rocks and pebbles. Mia was struck on the cheek by something sharp. It stung and she felt the telltale warm trickle of blood running down her face.

She made the mistake of looking at the crowd and silently swallowed a sob. It wouldn't do to show weakness—they would pounce and destroy her if she did. Nevertheless she found it hard to keep the pure terror from showing itself on her face.

The mob was terrifying—she had never seen so much hate and anger in one place. She knew they were whipping each other up into a frenzy, but somehow the thought that these were normally quiet, respectable people made it all that much worse. She tried not to react as she spotted a woman who had worked in the shipbuilder's kitchens with her. The woman's face was contorted with rage and Mia wondered how people could be so easily swayed by the lies of their Governor.

The cart jerked to a stop and too soon the journey was over. Mia would have endured one hundred cart rides with everyone shouting and spitting their hatred rather than have it come to an end. They had rolled to a stop in the big square. Just in front of them was the scaffold, guarded from the heaving crowd by ten soldiers in their pristine red uniforms. Mia scanned the crowd, wondering if Will was out there watching. Part of her wanted to see his face just one last time, the other part hoped he was somewhere far from here so he wouldn't have to watch as she mounted the platform and had the noose looped around her neck.

A man dressed all in black stepped up on to the scaffold and held up his hands for silence. Gradually the shouts and hollers of the crowd gave way to quiet murmurs.

'Today is a great day for justice,' the man shouted from his position above the assembled hoard. 'We are here to witness the executions of twenty pirates from the notorious *Flaming Dragon* as well as the hanging of Del Torres's devilish sister.'

The crowd jeered and surged forward a little. Mia felt herself cowering back, pulling at the rope that secured her to the pole of the cart. Death by hanging would be bad enough, but having the life beaten out of her would be so much worse.

'So many of you have been affected by the criminal activities of these pirates. Together we shall watch as they are condemned to an eternity of fiery hell.'

The man stepped from the scaffold and Mia watched the executioner take his place. The hangman was huge, with meaty arms and a thick chest. He went through the motions of checking the lever for the trapdoor was working and pulling on the beam that would support the noose. Then he motioned for the first pirate to be brought up to him.

Two soldiers grabbed the selected man under each arm and dragged him forward. He didn't put up much of a fight, his body hanging limply between them as if he were already dead. Expertly the executioner looped the noose around his neck. There was no black sack over his head to spare him the jeering faces of the crowd. The last thing this condemned man would see was the bloodthirsty mob braying for his blood. Mia could see his lips moving and she wondered if he was offering up a last prayer to the God he had forsaken for all the years he had chosen a life of piracy.

Within seconds the trapdoor was opened and the man fell. The drop wasn't far enough to break his neck so for a long thirty seconds he jerked on the end of the rope. No one in the crowd dared to push through the line of guards in front of the scaffold to pull on his legs and shorten his suffering. Mia doubted there was anyone there who cared enough to do so.

After a full minute he was cut down, his body tossed unceremoniously to one side. The next man up was screaming by the time the two guards had hold of him. Mia saw the unmistakable stain of urine down the front of his trousers and tried not to hear the pure terror in his shouts. He begged the guards to let him go, begged the executioner to have mercy and begged the crowds to save him. No one obliged.

Mia closed her eyes as the noose was tightened around his neck; she didn't want to see any more, but she couldn't block out the sound of the man being strangled to death.

Three more executions followed in much the same way. Mia felt numb. She knew this was going to be her in a few more minutes and she tried to steel herself for it. She wasn't going to let her last moments on earth be filled with screams or humiliation. She would stand tall and be brave.

She summoned a picture of Will in her mind, kissing her and looking at her as though she was the only woman that existed. She remembered his smile and the way his hair fell across his forehead. She remembered how his skin felt to her touch and she remembered the moment of pure happiness when he'd told her that he loved her. Mia smiled at the memory and knew at least she would be going to her death having been well and truly loved.

Chapter Twenty-Nine

She was smiling. Will nearly rubbed his eyes to check he was seeing things straight. Yes, she was definitely smiling. He couldn't imagine the strain she was under, watching man after man step on to the scaffold and have his life whipped away as if it were worth nothing, all the time knowing it would be her turn all too soon.

He waited. There was no point in acting prematurely, that would ruin everything. In the past twelve hours he had gone over the plan time and time again in his head until he would be able to carry it out with his eyes shut and one hand tied behind his back. Well, maybe not the hand-behind-the-back bit—he rather thought he might need both hands to fight half of Barbados's garrison.

The young man he'd approached the day before was nearly at the front of the line now. Will saw his family standing off to one side. They'd appreciated the chance to say goodbye the evening before and the pirate had been satisfied his mum and sisters were to be well provided for. Now Will hoped the pirate would fulfil his side of the bargain.

Will tapped his foot impatiently, well aware he was full of nervous energy. Another pirate dropped to his death and suddenly the moment was here. The young man stumbled forward, dragging the two prisoners he was shackled to with him. He thrashed out to the right and the left, making a good show of escaping.

The soldiers were on him immediately, the three who were guarding the prisoners surging forward to subdue the dissident. The young pirate fought valiantly. He lashed out with his shackled wrists, his feet, even his teeth if anyone got close enough. Will was pleased to see the other men he was chained to joining in. They fought viciously, all three having more to fight for than the assembled soldiers. Will waited as the fight developed.

Two more soldiers joined in, stepping away from the second line of prisoners. That only left the one standing next to Mia's cart. Will hesitated, knowing he could take the man out, but also that any struggle would draw attention to him and possibly put an end to his mission. Instead he waited, watching as the final soldier glanced from Mia to the fighting men and decided they were more of a threat than the docile young woman standing next to him.

Will strode forward, confident he wouldn't be noticed as all eyes were on the fracas he'd engineered. The pirates were still going strong despite the soldiers battering them with their rifle butts.

He slipped round the back of the fight and sidled up to Mia's cart. Swiftly he took a knife to the rope binding her to the pole and sliced through it. Mia's eyes flew open and Will could see she was speechless with shock. He wanted to take her into his arms and kiss her, but he knew any such romantic delay would cost them both their lives.

Instead he grabbed her by the waist and swung her over the side of the cart. Will clutched her hand and pulled her towards the alleyway behind the scaffold.

'Hey,' someone shouted, 'stop.'

Suddenly all eyes were on them. Will knew they only had a few seconds before the soldiers positioned on the walls readjusted their aim and fired at them. He shoved his free hand into his pocket and grabbed a handful of gold coins, coins he'd claimed from the Governor earlier that morning as his reward for catching *The Flaming Dragon.*

Will flung the coins into the crowd, allowing some to scatter across the scaffold. He grabbed a second handful and threw them by the entrance to the alley.

'Gold,' he shouted, just in case anyone in the crowd had missed it. As he'd hoped the assembled throng surged forward, their sheer numbers over-powering the soldiers. People were everywhere, grappling for coins on the ground, climbing on to the scaffold and, most importantly, surging forward to the entrance of the alley Will had just pulled Mia into. The soldiers would have a hard time getting through the crowd and beginning their pursuit.

'Run,' he urged.

Together they ran, sprinting through the streets, every few seconds looking over their shoulders for the chasing soldiers. Will whipped Mia around cor-ners and down narrow alleyways on a pre-mapped route he'd walked dozens of times the evening be-fore.

Just holding her hand was exhilarating. For a few brief moments when he'd been with Gover-nor Hall the day before Will had thought every-thing was lost. He'd thought he'd found the woman he loved only to lose her again for ever. Now they were dashing through the streets of Bridgetown, with a fair chance of escape.

Mia stumbled, her foot tripping over a bump in the road. Will felt her lose her balance and quickly swept her up into his arms, not missing a step. With Mia pressed against his chest Will felt his pace quicken despite the extra weight. Holding her was enough to spur him on; he felt her heart thumping against his chest and knew he would do anything to succeed.

They rounded the corner and burst out on to the docks. Will could hear the shouts of their pursuers behind them and felt his lungs burn as they reached the final stretch.

'Go,' he shouted at the top of his voice, unsure whether he was too far away to be heard.

The dock seemed to stretch out in front of him, their destination never getting any closer. He dodged surprised sailors and the few people out and about who had decided not to watch the executions up in the square. He barely heard the shouted curses as he barged past two soldiers standing guard in front of Commodore Wilkins's ship. With a quick glance back over his shoulder he saw them staring after him, but not pursuing. So far they hadn't grasped the significance of Will fleeing with Mia in his arms.

With a final push Will sprinted to the very end of the dock and up the gangplank of the waiting ship. Captain Little shouted an order and immediately the ship's crew sprang to life. The gangplank was pulled on to the deck and the ropes holding them steady hurriedly thrown clear. Will watched as slowly the ship started pulling away from the dock and he hoped it would be just fast enough. He could see half the garrison of soldiers in pursuit, now making their way down the dock towards them. The two soldiers he had pushed past were staring at the approaching force with mouths wide open and perplexed expressions.

'Everyone stay low,' Will shouted, pushing Mia to the deck and throwing himself on top of her.

Five seconds later the first of the bullets whizzed across the deck and embedded itself in one of the masts. A volley followed, then a brief gap whilst the soldiers reloaded. A second round of bullets flew through the air and thudded into the wood of the ship, followed by another pause. Cautiously Will poked his head over the rail and with relief saw they were finally pulling away from Bridgetown.

Out of range of the soldiers Will picked Mia up

from the floor and held her tightly against him. They were both panting with exertion and Will gratefully sucked the salty sea air into his lungs. Captain Little came up beside him and handed him a telescope.

'Have a look,' he prompted, a big grin on his face.

Will looked through the eyepiece, not knowing what he would see.

The sight on the dock made him want to punch the air with elation. Governor Hall had arrived, with Thatcher in tow. The Governor was gesticulating angrily towards Captain Little's ship and then pointing to the large Naval vessel still docked. Will watched as Thatcher shook his head and shrugged his shoulders.

'The Navy don't have enough men still aboard to pursue us,' Ed Redding said, coming to stand beside them. 'I had a chat with the Commodore earlier today and he said he'd had to release many of his men to supervise the execution in the square.' The First Mate chuckled. 'It'll take them at least an hour to get the ship fully manned and ready to depart.'

Bridgetown was getting further and further away and for the first time Will allowed himself to relax.

An hour's head start wasn't bad. The Navy's ship might be bigger and faster than theirs, but with some clever navigation and a little bit of luck they might have a chance. After all, Del Torres and his crew on *The Flaming Dragon* had managed to evade the Navy in the waters of the Caribbean for nearly two years. Will wasn't asking for that long, just long enough to get clear of the Caribbean islands and head for new shores.

'You did it,' Mia said, her eyes wide with shock. 'You saved me.'

'I promised, didn't I?'

'But I never thought you would be able to pull it off.'

'I will never break a promise to you, Mia.'

'I thought I was going to die.'

Will caught her as her knees buckled and lowered her back to the deck. He knelt down and cradled her in his arms. Mia looked up at him with wonder in her eyes.

'I thought I would never see you again.'

'Now you're condemned to a lifetime of looking upon this face,' Will said, brushing her hair from her forehead and tucking it behind her ear.

'How awful for me,' Mia murmured.

Chapter Thirty

Mia stared out into the distance, still not completely at ease. It had been a whole day and night since they'd escaped Barbados but every second she feared being captured. She had no doubt the entire British Navy in the Caribbean would have sprung into action and were now looking for them.

'Spot anything, Miss Del Torres?' Captain Little asked, coming up beside her.

She smiled at him and shook her head.

'They won't find us,' he said, 'I promise you that.'

'How can you be so sure?'

'I know how the Navy thinks—I used to be a Lieutenant before I decided the regimented lifestyle wasn't for me. They won't be expecting us to be heading this way. They'll figure I'm a man of the Caribbean therefore I won't want to leave the area, I'll want to stick to the waters I know the best. Either that or we're headed for England.'

'You've given up a lot for us, haven't you.' It was a statement rather than a question.

The Captain shrugged.

'Your crew have, too.'

They were sailing with a skeleton crew, heading straight across the Atlantic Ocean. Their destination was Cape Town in South Africa.

'I gave the men a choice,' the Captain said, 'and any with families I left behind in Barbados. The rest are eager for the adventure.'

'Thank you,' Mia said. 'Why did you do it? Why did you help us?'

'It was the right thing to do and I was in love once, too,' Captain Little said, 'when I was a very young man.'

Mia waited for him to elaborate.

'Suffice it to say I wish someone had given us a chance.' With that Captain Little gave a quick bow and hurried off.

Mia smiled sadly and realised the older man was a true romantic, obviously still mourning for his lost love so many years later.

'You still looking out for the Navy?' Will asked, coming up behind her.

Mia nodded.

'We won't be looking over our shoulders all our lives,' he promised.

Mia took his hand in hers and squeezed gently.

'I don't care if I have to sleep with one eye open as long as I'm with you.'

'What were you talking to the Captain about?' Will asked.

'I was thanking him. He's given up his whole life just for us.'

'He's a good man. All the crew are. I'm hoping we can set up a trading company when we reach South Africa, have the Captain at its helm.'

'Or maybe we could patrol the waters off the Cape, hunting for pirates,' Mia said with a wicked gleam in her eyes.

'I've got enough pirate right here in front of me to keep me occupied for eternity.'

'That sounds like a promise.'

Mia stretched up and found his lips with her own. Her kiss was languid and passionate. It was the kiss of a woman who knew she had all the time in the world to enjoy her lover.

'I have a surprise for you,' Will said.

Mia's face lit up. 'I do like surprises.'

'I hope you like this one,' he said, grinning, 'otherwise I might have to throw you overboard.'

He grabbed her hand and pulled her away from the rail and up to the prow of the boat. Mia was amazed to see the entire ship's crew assembled, with the Captain standing at the front facing them.

'Friends,' the Captain boomed, 'thank you for assembling. We are gathered to celebrate the joining together of Will Greenacre and Mia Del Torres.'

Mia nearly swooned. And she'd never swooned before in her life.

'We're getting married?' she whispered to Will.

He nodded, smiling like a naughty schoolboy.

'Is it legal?'

He shrugged. 'I'm not really too sure.'

Mia grabbed him round the neck and kissed him firmly on the lips. She didn't really care if it was legal or not, either.

'Not yet!' the Captain boomed. 'We haven't got to the kissing part yet.'

Reluctantly Mia pulled away from Will.

Ed Redding came up beside her and offered her his arm, shooing Will off to the prow of the boat to stand with the Captain.

To the shouts and hollers of the crew Mia walked through the assembled crowd on Ed Redding's arm. When they got to the front Redding took her hand, raised it to his lips, then passed her over to Will.

'Marriage is a sacred bond between two people,' the Captain said. 'Marriage brings mutual comfort and companionship in times of prosperity and adversity.'

'Hopefully not too much more adversity,' Will whispered in her ear.

'William Greenacre, do you take this woman to be your wife? To love and to comfort her, to honour her and keep her in sickness and in health? And forsaking all others to keep to only her as long as you both shall live?'

'I do.'

Mia felt her heart soar and knew she couldn't be any happier than in this moment. It might not be a legal wedding, but it was Will's promise to her that they would be together always.

'Mia Del Torres...' The Captain paused as he glanced at his handwritten notes. 'We'll skip the bit about obeying and serving as we all know that's not going to happen.' This got a laugh from the crowd. 'Will you love, honour and keep this man, in sickness and in health? And forsaking all others to keep to only him as long as you both shall live?'

'I will.'

The Captain read the vows for them to recite after him. Line by line they repeated in unison, 'To have and to hold, from this day forward, for better or for worse, for richer, for poorer, in sickness and in health, to love and to cherish and to rescue from the gallows until death do us part.'

As soon as he had finished Will swooped Mia up into his arms and kissed her fully, passionately in front of the entire crew. Mia could hear their whoops of delight, but she only had eyes for Will. Her husband.

'I love you, Mrs Greenacre,' he murmured so only she could hear.

'I love you, too, Mr Greenacre.'

Epilogue

Lord and Lady Sedlescombe
Redwood House
Cape Town

6th August 1752

Dear Lord Sedlescombe,
I have considered all the evidence pertaining to the accusations and sentencing of your wife in the British Colony of Barbados in the year 1749. After careful consideration I agree Lady Sedlescombe was falsely accused and did not stand a fair trial. I therefore overturn her conviction for Piracy.

Please accept this Official Royal Pardon and be assured all those involved in the matter have been brought to justice.

Yours sincerely,
The office of King George II

William stared open-mouthed at the letter. In the past two years he had often daydreamed about going home to his estate but never thought it would actually be possible. He'd petitioned the King to look over the evidence almost eighteen months before and when he hadn't heard anything for months he had given up. Instead they'd built their lives in the very cosmopolitan, no-questions-asked Cape Town.

'What are you smiling about, darling?' Mia asked as she struggled in through the door.

Will took a second to just look at his wonderful, heavily pregnant wife.

'I've received a letter,' he said solemnly.

Mia reached out her hand to read it.

'You probably want to sit down. I wouldn't want young Master Greenacre to be born here on the kitchen floor.'

Mia's eyebrows furrowed, 'It must be interesting.'

'The King of England has taken an interest in me,' Will said, 'or more specifically in my pirate wife.'

Mia's eyes widened and she grabbed the letter from him. She read it, her mouth dropping open with shock.

'This is real?' she asked.

'It's real.'

'They've actually pardoned me?'

'They've pardoned you.'

Mia pushed herself up from her chair and looped her arms around his neck. 'So this means we can go anywhere in the world we like?' she murmured.

'Anywhere at all.'

'Where would you like to go first?' she asked.

Will shrugged. Right here with Mia seemed just about perfect right now.

'Maybe back to a very special beach on Tortola,' she suggested.

That did sound like a good idea.

'Or you could take me home to meet all those cows and crops you're always talking about.'

The thought of Mia wandering through his ancestral home made him smile. She would be a fantastic Lady of the Manor.

'Or maybe there's another part of the world you'd like to see,' she suggested, nipping at his ears and distracting him completely.

'Maybe.'

Will gently positioned her so she perched on the edge of the table, taking some of the weight off her feet. He kissed her, leaning over the child that was growing inside her, and felt a moment of complete happiness.

'I want to go everywhere with you,' he said, 'but right now I'm exactly where I want to be.'

* * * * *